DEADLY VENGEANCE

A DETECTIVE JANE PHILLIPS NOVEL

OMJ RYAN

INKUBATOR
BOOKS

1

OCTOBER 31ST – HALLOWEEN

HOLLIE HAWKINS CLIMBED INTO THE BACK SEAT OF THE LARGE Range Rover parked outside the family home in Altrincham, taking extra care not to scuff her brand new, gleaming white Adidas trainers. She had bought them just that morning on a solo shopping trip into Manchester, along with the rest of the evening's outfit: skinny jeans and a cute little T-shirt from Topshop, plus a funky black bomber jacket from Harvey Nichols. All courtesy of a credit card, of course.

From the front passenger seat, her mother turned to inspect her. She shook her head and let out a loud sigh of disapproval. 'I do wish you'd get into the spirit a little more, Hollie. We are going to a Halloween party, after all.'

Hollie scoffed. 'Just because you want to dress-up like Paddington Bear doesn't mean I have to.'

'I think you'll find I'm a werewolf.'

'Whatever,' said Hollie, and turned her head away.

At that moment, the drivers' door opened and a version of Count Dracula – Sir Richard Hawkins, the man who called himself her father – pulled himself up and behind the wheel. As normal, he was talking in a loud voice into his phone. 'You tell them to get their bloody arses in gear and sort it out. If they don't, then I'll come over there personally, and they can explain to me why they're so far behind schedule. These delays are costing me a fucking fortune.'

Hollie huffed, loud enough for him to hear. What kind of a man speaks like that in front of a fifteen-year-old daughter? He's such an arsehole, she thought.

Hawkins soon pulled the car away towards their destination, continuing his discussion on his phone. In a vain attempt to drown him out, Hollie connected the tiny Bluetooth headphone pods that sat in her ears and turned up the volume. As music played, she folded her arms and stared out of the window, wishing she was somewhere else. Anywhere was better than being stuck in this fossil-fuel-guzzling monstrosity, driving to a lame Halloween party at her parents' posh country club.

God. Hollie hated her life.

Fifteen minutes later, Hawkins turned the large SUV away from the main drag and onto the long private road leading to Marstons Golf and Leisure Club. Hollie stared out at the array of orange pumpkin lanterns and fake cobwebs that lined the road. The phone call came to an end as they entered the car park, and the car came to a stop. Her mum turned and waited for Hollie to remove her headphones.

With great reluctance, Hollie obliged. 'What now?'

'Do you need some money for food?'

'There won't be anything vegan in this dump,' spat Hollie.

Hawkins let out a sardonic chuckle and locked eyes with Hollie in his rear view mirror. 'At fifteen grand a year for membership fees, it's hardly a dump.'

Hollie held his gaze.

'Ok,' her mum continued. 'Well, how about some money for a diet coke or an orange juice?'

Hollie continued staring at Hawkins in the mirror as she said, 'Twenty quid should do it.'

'Twenty quid for bloody orange juice? What are you, diabetic or something?' moaned Hawkins.

Her mum let out a deep sigh. 'Stop teasing her and just give her the money, will you?'

Hawkins shook his head as he reached into his pocket and pulled out his wallet, then handed a crisp twenty-pound note over his shoulder to Hollie. She snatched the cash away and yanked open the back door of the car. A split second later, she dropped down onto the gravel drive.

Her mother continued to talk from the front seat. 'Now Hollie, remember—'

Hollie slammed the door to cut her off. She had no intention of listening to anything else her mother had to say. Instead, she ran towards the front door of the club.

Inside, the club was decorated in the same style as outside: pumpkin lanterns, fake cobwebs and an assortment of spiders adorned every available surface. The lights were deliberately low to further enhance the ghoulish atmosphere, and it seemed everyone – except her – had chosen to wear fancy dress for the evening. For a split second she felt out of place and uncomfortable, but soon steeled herself, reasoning that they were sheep following the herd – something she would never be.

Keen to get as far away from her mother and Hawkins as possible, she knew she had to stay away from their favourite place, the bar. So she moved through the large ground floor and made her way to the outdoor tennis courts, which had been turned into a funfair for the evening. A mix of rides and amusements, ranging from bumper cars and a waltzer to 'hook a duck' challenges and candy floss machines, adorned the space. It all seemed pretty lame to her.

She let out a frustrated breath, which billowed like smoke in front of her face thanks to the cold autumn night, as she scanned the courts, looking for anyone she knew. She had always made a point of avoiding coming to the club whenever possible, so had yet to make any good friends. However, after a few minutes wandering through the space, she spotted a girl she had chatted to from time to time, and headed in her direction. The girl's name was Charlotte, but everyone called her Lottie. Lottie was leaning against a wall on the edge of the tennis courts, staring down at the phone she held in her hands. Like Hollie, she too had decided to forego a fancy-dress costume.

'Hey?' said Hollie, feeling a little nervous.

Lottie looked up from the screen. 'Hey,' she said, appearing nonplussed.

Hollie had never felt confident in social settings, and small talk wasn't one of her strengths. 'What you looking at?'

Lottie shrugged her shoulders. 'Insta.'

The social media platform, Instagram. Hollie had an account, but rarely updated it. 'Pretty lame party, huh?' she said, hoping to make a connection.

Lottie glanced around and nodded. 'Yeah. My parents make me come here all the time, and I fucking hate it.'

Hollie's heart leapt. 'Me too.'

Lottie looked Hollie up and down. 'You didn't fancy dressing up either?'

Hollie scoffed. 'No way. It's for kids and sad adults trying to recapture their adolescence.'

Lottie nodded. 'Too right.'

Hollie tucked her hands in her pocket and swivelled on her heels, hoping to think of something else to talk about. As she turned back to speak, Lottie's phone began to vibrate and the screen came to life. She answered it, and her demeanour changed in an instant as she stood tall, brimming with excitement. 'Hey, girlfriend. Whatchya doin'?' she said in a fake American accent. She turned away from Hollie, now totally engrossed with her phone call.

Hollie stood and watched Lottie for a moment, wishing she had someone to call too. But she was a bit of a loner at school, and didn't know any of the local kids where she lived.

Standing alone for a few minutes, watching the 'forced fun' taking place around her, a pang of loneliness gripped her abdomen. Try as she might, she didn't seem to fit in anywhere.

'Are you ok, love?' a soft voice behind her said.

Hollie turned, and jumped as she came face to face with a figure, she suspected a woman, in a black mask and a long coat. 'Jesus! You scared me.'

'Oh, yeah. The *Army of Two* mask. It can have that effect sometimes,' said the woman. She offered an outstretched hand. 'I'm Blackie.'

Hollie shook it without conviction, confused. 'Army of two?'

Blackie pointed at her mask. 'You know, the computer game? It's who I've come to the party as.'

Hollie chuckled. 'Sorry. I don't really know much about them, to be honest. Computer games aren't really my thing.'

Blackie nodded. 'What about a spliff? Is that your thing?'

Hollie was taken aback. 'Say what?'

'A spliff. Do you want one?' Blackie raised a gloved hand in front of Hollie's face. In it was a large cone-shaped joint.

Hollie's eyes widened, and a knowing grin spread across her face. 'Is that cannabis?'

'Sure, is,' said Blackie. 'You ever had it?'

Hollie glanced around to ensure they weren't being watched, then nodded. 'Once, when I stayed at my cousin's house last year. He brought some back from uni and let me have some. It gave me the giggles.'

'It can do that,' said Blackie. 'So. Do you want some now?'

Hollie took another cautionary look around before nodding eagerly.

'In that case, follow me. I know the perfect place, just around the corner. No windows or security cameras, so no one can see us.' Blackie began walking, and beckoned Hollie to follow her.

Hollie was excited now, and chattered as she followed her new friend. 'My parents would go ballistic if they found out.'

As they reached the corner of the building, Blackie stepped left and out of sight for a moment. Hollie giggled, then looked back one last time to see if they were being followed. Satisfied they weren't, she darted left and into the darkness. The sight that greeted her almost stopped her heart. Three people, each wearing *Army of Two* masks and long coats, stood in a triangle formation. The shortest, Blackie, stood in the centre, holding a small automatic weapon in her hands. 'Sorry Hollie. It's nothing personal.'

Hollie opened her mouth to scream, but one of the people was on her in an instant, covering her mouth with a large gloved hand as a second rushed forwards and secured her wrists with cable ties. The hand covering her mouth was replaced with thick duct tape, and a moment later a cloth hood was pulled over her head. In a flash, she was bundled forwards, then pulled left and right through a maze of disorientating turns until they came to a sudden stop.

An engine was running in front of her. She attempted to scream, but no sound penetrated the thick tape. She heard what sounded like a set of van doors being opened just in front of her, and then she was lifted from her feet and laid flat on the floor of the vehicle.

'Go! Go! Go!' shouted a male voice from above her. The doors slammed shut, tyres screeched, and the vehicle moved off at speed.

The next thing she knew, Blackie spoke to her. 'Hollie, this will hurt for a split second, but after that you won't care about anything.'

Hollie felt a sharp scratch and a needle was plunged into her right arm. She cried out in pain, muffled by the duct tape, then her world went black.

~

SANDRA HAWKINS TOOK a sip from her glass of Prosecco, then placed it back on the table as she checked her Cartier watch; it was approaching 10 p.m. True to form, she sat alone in the club lounge while Richard held court with a group of young men at the bar. She recognised two as professional footballers, but couldn't recall which of the Manchester teams they currently played for. She was bored, and frustrated that yet another night out with her husband and daughter had turned into a networking event for him and an opportunity for Hollie to demonstrate how much she detested her parents. She sighed. She had never imagined, ten years ago, that marriage to such a charming man would leave her feeling constantly alone.

She picked up her glass again, and wandered out to see if she could locate Hollie. She had had enough, and wanted to go home. Knowing Hollie, she probably felt the same. After all, Hollie never tired of telling her parents how much she hated these kind of events.

As she stepped out into the cold night air, Sandra didn't recognise the floodlit outdoor tennis courts. Many of the noisy rides were still in operation, even at this late hour, the playful screams of teenagers echoing through the night air as Sandra made her way around, looking for Hollie. After five minutes of searching, there was no sign of her, something told Sandra things weren't right. She was tempted to head back inside and talk with Richard, but he would just chastise her for once again being a 'silly, over-protective mother.' So she continued her search, pacing through the funfair as she checked every corner of the tennis courts. When ten minutes had passed and Hollie was still nowhere to be seen, Sandra started to panic. Where could she be?

Making her way back into the main building, Sandra scoured the various rooms that had been made available to parents and their children for the evening. Hollie wasn't in any of them. Her instincts told her something was very wrong. As much as Hollie could be a brat when she wanted to be, she wasn't a confident teenager and rarely strayed far on nights like these. She usually chose to demonstrate her petulance and apparent irritation from a relatively close distance.

On her return to the bar, she came across a young girl she had seen Hollie speaking to on previous occasions – Lottie, or something similar. Sandra thought her father was a television producer in Media City. Lottie was in an armchair, staring at her phone, as Sandra approached. 'Excuse me, Lottie? Have you seen Hollie?'

Lottie looked up from her phone, a waxy gaze across her face. 'Huh?'

'My daughter, Hollie. Have you seen her?'

Lottie took a moment to think, then nodded. 'Yeah. She was outside by court number three.'

'When was that?'

The girl shrugged. 'Dunno. About eight, I 'spose. Maybe half-eight.'

'What was she doing?'

'Nothing really. Just hanging out.'

'Was she with anyone?' Sandra's voice was laced with panic now.

Lottie shook her head. 'Don't think so.'

'Did she say anything to you?'

Lottie's brow furrowed. 'Not really. Just that she hated fancy dress.'

'That was it? That's all she said?'

Lottie nodded and held up her phone so Sandra could see the screen. 'Beatrice FaceTimed me, so we didn't talk for long.'

'And you're sure you haven't seen her since then?'

Lottie offered Sandra a blank look, then shook her head before turning her attention back to her phone.

Sandra felt certain now that something was seriously wrong. It was time to talk to Richard. He would know what to do. He would be able to find Hollie.

She headed back to the bar.

2

DETECTIVE CHIEF INSPECTOR JANE PHILLIPS PULLED HER unmarked squad car into the car park at the Marstons Golf and Leisure Club and parked up between a large Bentley and a Porsche SUV. Following her well-worn routine when arriving at a new investigation, she reset her dark ponytail, then cleaned her lightweight glasses. After so many years, she wasn't sure whether she now did it out of habit or superstition.

As she stepped out onto the gravel, she pulled up the collar of her grey overcoat against the cold night air. A moment later, her second in command, Detective Sergeant Jones, approached her.

'How the other half live, hey Guv?' he said, smiling, his thick South London drawl in contrast to his wiry frame and gaunt features, which were accentuated by his long beige trench-coat.

Phillips returned his smile and pointed at the Bentley. 'This one would cost about the same as a small family home, Jonesy.'

'Not around here it wouldn't, Guv. A hundred and fifty grand'd get you nothing more than a garden shed in Altrincham.'

Phillips let out a chuckle. 'Yeah. You're probably right.'

Just a few metres away, a couple dressed as an angel and a devil walked out of the main entrance. They giggled, arms locked and bodies huddled against the night.

Jones kept his voice low. 'You said on the phone we're investigating a missing girl. How old is she, and how long's she been gone?'

'From the little information I got from Fox, she's a teenager,' said Phillips as she glanced at her watch. It was approaching midnight. 'And she's been missing about an hour and half, I'd say.'

Jones raised his eyebrows. 'The chief super briefed you? Not quite standard procedure for a missing person, is it?'

Phillips shook her head and looked towards the main entrance. 'I think it's fair to say the missing girl's father is not someone you would deem as "standard", Jonesy.'

Jones's eyes widened with anticipation. 'Really? Who is he?'

'Sir Richard Hawkins.'

Jones paused for a moment. 'Richard Hawkins, the munitions trader?'

'That's the one,' said Phillips. 'And he's just been knighted, so mind your Ps and Qs.'

'Friends in high places then, is it?'

'If you call Downing Street "high places", then yeah.'

'Bloody hell,' said Jones. 'I wondered why MCU was involved in a missing persons case. I mean, it's hardly a major crime, is it?'

'Depends on the missing person, doesn't it?'

Jones nodded. 'Yeah, I guess it does. So how come you and I drew the short straw? Why aren't Bov and Entwistle here?'

'It must be because I like spending time with you, Jonesy,' said Phillips, her tone playful. 'Not to mention the fact Fox wants a show of force on this one, as does the chief constable. So they've got the "dream team" – that's you and me. Plus, at this stage I'm not dragging the whole team out to look for a rich kid who's more than likely just run off for the night. For all we know, she's probably partying somewhere with her mates as we speak.'

At that moment, Sir Richard Hawkins's large frame appeared in the main entrance to the club. He was talking at high volume into his phone. He appeared almost surreal, dressed as he was in his Halloween costume.

Phillips nodded in Hawkins's direction. 'That's our guy there, Count Dracula. Quite appropriate, I'd say. He's probably on the phone to the chief constable, questioning our methods already.'

'Oh, God. He's one of those, is he?'

'Yep, I'm afraid so. Which means we should let him know we're here.'

Phillips walked towards Hawkins, who stood with his back to her, and Jones fell in behind. As she approached the large stone steps up to the club entrance, she pulled her credentials from her coat pocket. 'Sir Richard?' she said in a loud voice.

Hawkins turned, the phone still held against his ear. 'Yes?'

'DCI Phillips from the Major Crimes Unit. This is DS Jones. We're here in connection with your daughter's disappearance.'

'I'll call you back,' said Hawkins into his phone, and ended the call.

'Shall we go inside?' asked Phillips.

Hawkins nodded. 'Follow me,' he said, his tone flat, and turned on his heels and walked briskly into the club.

Phillips turned to Jones briefly and raised her eyebrows. As usual, he knew exactly what she was thinking.

'A real charmer, isn't he?' said Jones, in a low voice.

'Isn't he just?' said Phillips, then headed inside.

Phillips found Hawkins in an empty club lounge, standing next to a woman seated in an armchair. Her hair ragged and dishevelled, Phillips suspected she had recently removed some sort of wig. It was obvious from her puffy red eyes and the streaky face paint on her cheeks that she had been crying. A white handkerchief was clasped in her trembling hands.

As Phillips approached, Hawkins wasted no time on pleasantries. 'My daughter is missing, Inspector, and you'd better find her or there'll be hell to pay.'

Phillips bit her lip and chose to ignore the threat. 'Who first discovered Hollie was missing, Sir Richard?'

Jones removed his notepad and prepared to take notes.

'My wife, Sandra.' Hawkins nodded in the direction of the woman in the chair.

'And when was this?'

'About ten-thirty,' Sandra said in a weak voice, without looking up.

Phillips glanced down at her now. 'And what makes you think she's gone missing as opposed to run off somewhere? I have to say that, in most cases relating to a missing person, we usually tell families to wait for twenty-four hours before getting too concerned. Especially when it comes to teenagers.'

Hawkins spoke before Sandra could answer. 'We are not "most cases", Inspector. I can assure you of that.'

'She would never have run off without telling me,' said Sandra, 'never.'

'My wife is right, Inspector. Because of what I do, there are many people who would like to take a pop at me. Any one of them could have snatched her.'

Phillips was taken aback. 'Are you saying you think she's been kidnapped?'

Jones stopped scribbling and looked up from his pad.

'That's *exactly* what I'm saying,' said Hawkins.

Phillips sensed that now was not the time to suggest any other possible theories regarding Hollie's disappearance. Instead, she changed tack. 'Have you tried calling her phone?'

'Of course we bloody have,' said Hawkins, far louder than was necessary in the empty space.

'It's switched off,' Sandra said.

'And that's just not like her. The bloody thing is never out of her hand,' added Hawkins.

Sandra looked up at Phillips and wiped her nose with her handkerchief. 'Richard is right, Inspector. She lives on that phone. That's why I'm so worried.'

Hawkins patted his wife's shoulder, much like a man would pat a dog's head. It seemed evident he was not someone who possessed a soft touch.

Phillips locked eyes with Sandra and produced a warm smile. 'We'll do everything we can to make sure she's found safe and well, Mrs Hawkins—'

'You'd better!' Hawkins interrupted her.

Phillips once more ignored the jibe. 'Well, we need to have a look round the club and speak to the manager. Can you tell us where his office is located?'

Hawkins gestured with an upwards movement of his head. 'Down there.'

Phillips swivelled to see a long corridor behind her. She turned back to the pair. 'Thank you,' she said, keeping her voice soft. 'Hollie may well turn up at home in the next few hours, so there's no sense in you staying here and worrying. Let us check things out here, and if she still hasn't turned up by morning, we'll head over to your house first thing. Ok?'

Sandra looked to her husband, who nodded. 'You'll update *me* the moment you hear anything, Inspector?' he said.

'Of course,' said Phillips, with a reassuring smile to Sandra.

'Very well,' said Hawkins. He helped his wife from her seat and headed off in the direction of the car park.

Once she was sure they were both out of earshot, Phillips puffed out a loud sigh of relief. 'Well, that was fun.'

'Like being stabbed in the scrotum with a rusty nail,' said

Jones, his tone laced with sarcasm. 'What they say about Richard Hawkins being an arsehole clearly isn't true. I mean, he's actually quite pleasant once you get to know him.'

'Come on, Jonesy,' said Phillips with a grin. 'Let's go and see the manager. He's a Mr Green, so I'm told.'

3

JUST AS PHILLIPS WAS ABOUT TO KNOCK ON THE DOOR TO GREEN'S office, it opened. The tall, thick-set, suited man on the other side jumped with shock as he came face to face with Phillips, and Jones stood at her side.

'Mr Green?' asked Phillips.

Green's brow wrinkled, accentuating his large pale forehead, as he maintained his grip on the door handle. 'Yes?'

Once more Phillips produced her credentials, and Jones did the same. 'DCI Phillips and DS Jones from the Major Crimes Unit. Can we talk to you about the disappearance of Hollie Hawkins?'

Green's eyes narrowed for a moment as he studied their IDs. When satisfied they were who they said they were, his face softened. 'Of course, of course. Come in.' He moved to one side to allow them access to his office. 'Please, take a seat,' he said, pointing to two chairs set in front of the large beech desk.

Phillips and Jones sat as Green walked to the other side of the desk and took a seat in the plush leather chair. 'How can I be of help?'

Jones prepared to take notes.

'What can you tell us about what happened here tonight?' said Phillips.

Green's face was blank. 'I really don't know, Chief Inspector. Our annual Halloween party went off as planned, and was a huge hit, *as always*. We had a full house of members and their families, with fairground rides, toffee apples, candy floss, etcetera, and everyone seemed to be having a wonderful time. Then, at around ten-thirty, Mr and Mrs Hawkins came to my office and said they couldn't find their daughter, Hollie. Mrs Hawkins was in quite a state of panic and very upset.'

'And how did Mr Hawkins appear?' asked Phillips.

Green shrugged. 'How he always appears: austere, to the point.'

'So, what happened then?'

'I followed them into the clubhouse to see if we could find her. Together with my head of security, John Robbins, we checked every room in the building, as well as the outdoor tennis courts, but there was no sign of her.'

'I'm assuming you have CCTV, Mr Green?' asked Phillips.

'Naturally. We have one of the most sophisticated security systems on the market,' said Green. 'This is a very exclusive club, Chief Inspector. Our members include Premier League footballers, politicians, lawyers, TV stars, etcetera. They demand the utmost privacy, so only the very best will do at Marstons. Plus, our security team is top-notch, hand-picked by me, with many of them coming to us direct from the military. John Robbins is a retired Royal Marine himself.'

'Can we see the video footage from this evening?' said Phillips.

Green nodded with vigour. 'Certainly. John is looking at the tapes as we speak. Please come with me.'

Green stood and walked round the large desk. Phillips and Jones stood as Green opened the office door, then ushered them back into the corridor. 'John's office is just next door.'

A moment later, Phillips and Jones followed Green into John Robbins's office. Robbins was intent on a series of large CCTV monitors fixed to the wall in front of him.

'John, this is Chief Inspector Phillips and Detective Sergeant Jones. They'd like to take a look at our CCTV,' said Green.

Robbins turned and stood. A well-built man with a barrel chest and broad shoulders, he was not especially tall – probably five foot ten, Phillips guessed – and, despite wearing a shirt and tie, it was evident he still looked after himself physically. His closely cropped hair was a nod to his military background.

Stepping forwards, Robbins offered Jones his outstretched hand. 'Chief Inspector. John Robbins, head of security.'

Jones flinched and glanced at Phillips before shaking Robbins's hand. 'I'm *Detective Sergeant* Jones.'

Green did his best to rectify Robbins's obvious assumption. 'Er, John, *this* is Detective Chief Inspector Phillips,' he said, gesturing to Phillips.

Robbins flushed and offered his hand to Phillips. 'My apologies, Chief Inspector, it's just I—'

'Can we see the videos, Mr Robbins?' said Phillips. She had little interest in his apology.

Robbins cleared his throat. 'Of course.' He retook his seat in front of the monitors. Phillips and Jones moved to stand behind him.

'I've spent the last half hour going through tonight's footage. I started by checking the car park camera's number plate recognition data against Mr Hawkins's registration plate.' Robbins showed them the footage as he spoke. 'I was able to identify his time of arrival, which was just after 19.30. I then looked at the main entrance cameras. A moment later, we see Hollie making her way into the club. I've followed her through the clubhouse and outside onto the tennis courts, where the funfair was set up for this evening's event. As I switch between cameras, you can see she walks round the entire space before finally stopping to talk to a girl of a similar age.' Robbins tapped the screen with the index finger of his left hand, revealing a heavily tattooed wrist.

'Can you zoom in on them?' asked Phillips.

Robbins followed her instructions.

'Do you recognise the other girl?' said Jones.

'Her name is Charlotte Jenkins,' Green said. 'Her father works in television.'

'Has anyone spoken to her?' said Phillips.

It was again Green who answered. 'Yes. Mrs Hawkins spoke to her when she first went looking for Hollie. Miss Jenkins said she and Hollie had spoken earlier in the evening, but that nothing much had been said. Apparently their conversation had ended when Miss Jenkins took a call from a friend, and I'm afraid she couldn't recall seeing Hollie after that and—.'

'The footage backs up her story,' Robbins interjected, rolling the tape forwards. 'As we can see here, Charlotte takes a call and walks away.' He paused the tape.

Phillips studied the screen in front of her for a moment. 'What happens next?'

'I don't know. This is where I'd got up to when you arrived.'

'Ok,' said Phillips. 'Let's play the tape and see.'

On the monitor, Hollie watched Lottie as she walked away, talking directly at her phone screen. Hollie took a moment to scan her surroundings before folding her arms tightly across her chest and leaning against the wall of the tennis court – the unmistakable slouch of a teenager trying to hide the fact she was upset. Hollie stood for a few minutes on her own before she was approached by someone in full costume.

'So who's this then, I wonder?' said Phillips.

They watched as the person, wearing what appeared to be a

black head-mask and a long coat, tapped Hollie on the shoulder and began a conversation.

'How far does the zoom go in on this?' asked Phillips.

'It's at the optimum level for pixilation just now. I can go further in, but the picture quality will suffer.'

'Ok,' said Phillips.

The conversation continued until the person in the mask produced something in her hand and showed it to Hollie.

'Pause it there. Zoom in on whatever is in their hand,' said Phillips.

Robbins obliged, but as he had warned, the image blurred.

'Is that a joint?' said Jones.

'Hard to tell for sure, but it looks like it to me,' replied Phillips.

'It can't be. We have a zero-tolerance drugs policy,' spat Green.

Phillips ignored him. 'Ok, zoom out again and let's see what happens next.'

As the tape played, Hollie followed the masked individual into a darkened corner of the tennis courts, at the side of the clubhouse building, before disappearing out of sight around the corner.

'What's around that corner?' asked Phillips.

'Air conditioning units,' said Robbins.

'Do you have cameras there?'

'No, I'm afraid not. There's no real need. No windows or access into the building. There is a gate, but it only allows access to the air conditioning units. If anyone decided to make their way round onto the courts from there, this camera would pick them up,' said Robbins. 'Having said that, there is one on the other side of the fence, just a bit farther along at the side of the building. It points at the pro-shop for the golf course, where we keep the golf-carts. That one might be of use.'

'Ok. We may need to check it in a moment. For now, let's see if they come back round onto this camera.'

Robbins played the footage in realtime for the next couple of minutes, but nothing significant happened. So he fast-forwarded it at six times normal speed for a little while longer. The timestamp on screen showed that in the ensuing thirty minutes, Hollie still did not return.

Phillips was starting to lose patience. 'Check the golf shop camera.'

Robbins pulled up the footage and located the time when they had last seen Hollie on the tennis court. This camera was secured to the wall at least twenty metres away from the air-conditioning units, and the lighting was poor. Robbins pressed play and they watched in realtime.

For a few minutes nothing happened aside from a fox trotting out of a hedge onto the concrete driveway before heading back into the bushes. Then, a moment later, the gate to the air-conditioning units opened tentatively, and a masked head peeped out before retreating back inside. Another minute passed, and a van approached. Its lights were switched off and it stopped just in front of the gates. A masked man jumped from the driver's seat, moved round to the back of the van and opened the rear doors. He then opened the gate and signalled to someone on the other side. Two more masked men appeared, guiding someone wearing a hood over their head and with their hands tied in front of them to the back of the van.

'Stop it there,' said Phillips. 'Zoom in on the person in the hood.'

She scrutinised the grainy image for a moment. 'Flick back to the tennis court camera.'

Robbins pulled up the previous footage.

'Can we see them side-by-side to compare?'

'Sure,' said Robbins.

Staring at the two images, Phillips was sure the person under the hood was Hollie Hawkins. From what she could see, the height, build and clothes were identical.

'So, that looks like Hollie. Play the rest of the golf shop footage.'

Robbins obliged, and they watched as Hollie was lifted inside the van. Bringing up the rear, a final masked man shut the gate, then jumped into the van and closed the doors. A split second later, the vehicle roared off down the path towards the main entrance to the country club.

'Jesus,' said Phillips, 'it looks like Hawkins was right. She *was* kidnapped.'

'Oh my God,' said Green – with an unnecessary amount of drama, Phillips felt. 'This can't be happening. Not a kidnapping. *Not at Marstons.*'

Phillips ignored him and turned to Jones, who was already nodding. 'Jonesy, get Bov and Entwistle down here. And call in forensics.'

'On it,' said Jones, his phone already in his hand.

'Mr Green, Mr Robbins. I need that area cordoned off immediately. Nobody is to go anywhere near it without my express permission. I'm also going to need copies of all your CCTV footage from the last twenty-four hours.'

'I'll start downloading the files immediately,' said Robbins.

'Thank you. Also, what you've just witnessed must remain totally confidential. You cannot say anything about this to anyone. Until I've spoken to Hollie's parents, this has to remain between us. Ok?'

Both men nodded.

'You can count on us Chief Inspector,' said Green, regaining his composure.

PHILLIPS AND JONES surveyed the area where Hollie had been taken under torchlight. The forensic team would bring flood-lights, but Phillips wanted to see if there was any immediate and obvious evidence. Sadly, there wasn't, but she noted that the padlock was hanging on the gate, unlocked. That clearly didn't match Green's boast about the Marstons's level of security, so she took a number of photos with her phone for future reference.

Her attention was soon drawn to the sound of voices drawing closer from the direction of the tennis courts, and a moment later, Senior CSI Andy Evans appeared from around the corner, followed by a number of his team.

'We really must stop meeting like this,' he quipped.

'Andy,' said Phillips.

Jones nodded his acknowledgement.

'Can we have the space, Ma'am?' said Evans.

Phillips nodded. 'Sure. We'll head back inside. Can you let me know if you find anything significant?'

'Will do.'

Phillips and Jones made their way back through the tennis courts towards the main building. She was keen to speak to Robbins without Green and his drama getting in the way. As they reached the clubhouse, they were met by the other two members of Phillips's core team from MCU, DCs Bovalino and Entwistle. At over six foot four and a former cage-fighter, Bovalino was a big man, and looked even bigger in his thick winter coat with the fur-lined hood bunched up behind his head. Entwistle, on the other hand, was slimmer and more athletic than his fellow DC, and dressed like an Armani model. His chiselled, mixed-race features were accentuated by the crisp collar of his overcoat, pulled up as much to look good as to protect him from the cold.

'Here they are, "Bert and Ernie,"' joked Jones. 'Good of you to join us.'

Bovalino shot Jones a playful V-sign in response. Entwistle ignored the jibe.

'Right, guys. Looks like we've got the kidnapping of a minor on our hands. Let's get inside and we'll bring you up to speed.

In the deserted bar, Phillips wasted no time in briefing Bovalino and Entwistle on the events of the evening so far. Given Sir Richard Hawkins's relationship with the Greater Manchester Police top-brass, she warned them that the pressure to get a result would be immense.

'Entwistle, I need you to speak to the manager, Mr Green. You'll find him in his office down there,' she said, pointing to the corridor that led off the bar. 'Get the names of every guest who attended the event tonight, then see if any of them have criminal records or questionable backgrounds.'

'Sure thing, Guv.'

'Bov, I want you to suit-up and get out there with Evans and the team. See if you can find any signs of who took Hollie.'

Bov nodded with a heavy sigh. 'I see. So the peasant Italian has to do the donkey work out in the cold whilst golden-balls here gets a nice warm office.' He landed a playful punch on Entwistle's shoulder.

'What you complaining for?' teased Jones, tapping Bovalino's thick midriff. 'You've got plenty of meat on you to keep you warm.'

'Piss off!' joked Bovalino, swatting Jones's hand away.

Phillips allowed herself a smile before refocusing the team. 'Right. Jonesy and I need to talk to the head of security. I want to know why that gate wasn't locked. Everyone clear on what they're doing?'

'Yes, Guv!' the team replied in unison, and got busy.

～

JOHN ROBBINS WAS BACK in front of the monitors, checking the CCTV footage, when Phillips and Jones walked into his office, this time without knocking. He spun round to face them.

'Found anything else of interest?' asked Phillips.

Robbins's brow furrowed. 'Nothing yet, but I'll keep looking. The footage you wanted will be downloaded within the hour. It's a massive file.'

'Thank you,' said Phillips.

'Happy to help.'

'In the meantime, we have some more questions.'

'Go ahead. What can I tell you?'

'Is the gate where Hollie was taken usually locked?'

'Of course. As Mr Green said, the members are often subject to unwanted media attention, so every exit and entrance is secured.'

Phillips produced her phone and presented Robbins with one of the photos she'd taken earlier. 'Well, this is how we found it when we went over there just now.'

Robbins took the phone and studied the photo for a moment, using his fingers to zoom in.

'As you can see, the lock is open, but remains intact,' Phillips continued. 'It was either left that way or the kidnappers had a key.'

Robbins's mouth fell open. 'But that's impossible. Every lock is checked at the start and end of each shift. No one mentioned any issues with the gates down there to me.'

'Who would have been the last person to check it?'

Robbins thought for a moment. 'Erm, it would be Sam Cartwright. She's been looking after that section of the building tonight.'

'And do you trust her?' asked Jones.

Robbins jerked his head back. 'Sam? Absolutely. She's one of my best. A former medic in the Army. She served in Afghanistan and Iraq.'

'Where is she now?'

'She's still here. She's on until 6 a.m., when the next shift takes over. She'll be doing her rounds.'

'Can we speak to her please?'

'Of course. I'll radio her now.'

A few minutes later, the door to Robbins's office opened and Sam Cartwright stepped inside. Short and stocky, with close-cropped hair, someone not paying attention could easily have mistaken her for a man.

'Sam, this is DCI Phillips and DS Jones from the Major Crimes team. They'd like to talk to you,' said Robbins. 'Please, take a seat.'

Cartwright moved across the room, her stooped posture giving her an apologetic air. She smiled weakly as she sat down, revealing heavily stained teeth. Like Robbins, she wore a shirt and tie, but the collar could not fully hide a tattoo running up the left side of her neck to just under her jawline.

Phillips wasted no time getting to the point. 'Sam, where were you at 8 p.m. this evening?'

Cartwright repeated the question. 'Where was I at eight o'clock?'

'Yes.'

Cartwright's eyes narrowed. 'Er. I'm sorry, I don't understand.'

'What don't you understand?' shot Phillips. 'It's a simple enough question.'

'Well, I was here, wasn't I?' Cartwright said, and glanced at Robbins, half smiling.

'Yes, we know that,' said Phillips, 'but where specifically were you within the club at that time?'

Phillips watched Cartwright closely as she gazed up at the ceiling. 'Er, well, I don't remember exactly, but I think I would have been out on the tennis courts.'

'Did you see Hollie Hawkins at all?'

Cartwright shook her head. 'No. I'm afraid not. I mean, to be honest, with all the guests wearing costumes, it was hard to tell who anyone was this evening.'

Phillips turned to Robbins. 'Could you bring up the footage of Hollie talking to the masked man, please?'

Robbins obliged, and the image filled the middle screen on the wall.

'Did you see this man anywhere tonight?'

Cartwright spun the ring on the middle finger of her right hand with her thumb as she scrutinised the image. She shook her head. 'No, I can't recall seeing him.'

Phillips said nothing for a moment, allowing the silence to linger as she watched Cartwright's face.

Cartwright shifted in her seat.

'Do you recognise this?' Phillips presented her with the image of the padlock they'd witnessed on the external gates.

Again, Cartwright scrutinised the image for a long moment before shaking her head. 'No, sorry.'

'This is the lock that secures the gates to the air-conditioning units. That area was under your watch tonight, wasn't it?'

'Yes, it was.'

'And Mr Robbins tells me they should remain locked at all times?'

'Absolutely,' Cartwright affirmed.

'Yet tonight they were left *unlocked*, which allowed four men to abduct a person we believe to be Hollie Hawkins.'

Cartwright's eyes widened. 'You don't think *I* had anything to do with that, do you?'

Phillips stared at Cartwright for a long moment. '*Did* you?'

'Oh my God, no. This job is my life. I would never do anything to jeopardise it.'

'So how do you explain the open lock, then?'

Cartwright's mouth fell open, but she said nothing, her eyes

darting to Robbins before staring back at Phillips. She
continued to spin the ring on her middle finger at a pace. 'I
honestly don't know. I checked all the locks tonight at the start
of my shift, as per usual. They were all secure then. Every single
one of them.'

'Sam is one of my best operatives, Chief Inspector, with a
decorated military record,' Robbins cut in. 'If she says they
were secure, I believe her.'

Phillips locked eyes with Robbins now. 'Of course, Mr
Robbins,' she said, without feeling, 'I'm sure you understand
the seriousness of the situation, though. We have to check
everybody involved, including *you*.'

Robbins eyes bulged, and he leaned back in his chair. 'I can
assure you, I have nothing to hide.'

Phillips offered a polite smile. 'Of course, Mr Robbins. I'm
merely stating that, in order to eliminate people from our
enquiries, we have to check *every* avenue – and *every* person.'

This seemed to placate Robbins somewhat, and his shoulders and face softened. 'Yes, yes. I understand.'

Phillips knew there was nothing more to be gained from
pressing either Robbins or Cartwright further at this exact
moment. Plus, she was keen to hear what forensics had found,
if anything. 'How's that download, going?'

Robbins moved back to the PC positioned in front of the
CCTV and reactivated the screen. 'All done,' he said a moment
later, and ejected the USB stick and handed it to Phillips.

'Thank you. Much appreciated.' Phillips forced a thin smile.
'We'll get this back to the tech guys and see if they spot
anything we've missed.'

She pushed back her chair with her legs and stood. Jones
followed. 'Will you be here much longer, Mr Robbins?'

He nodded. 'You tell me. I can't leave until your forensic
team are finished.'

'In that case, based on experience, I'm afraid you may be in for a long night.'

Robbins remained stoic. 'It won't be the first time I've gone without sleep, Chief Inspector.'

'Quite,' said Phillips. 'Well, thank you for your time. You've been most helpful.'

'Like I said, anything I can do to help.'

Phillips and Jones made their way back towards the tennis courts and the forensic team. On the way there, at a safe distance from the offices, they stopped to debrief.

'What do you make of them, Guv?' asked Jones.

'I haven't made my mind up, Jonesy. Robbins seems pretty straight, and his arsy reaction to my suggestion that he might be involved seemed genuine enough. But Cartwright? There's something going on with her. I'm not sure what just yet, but I'm keen to find out more about her.'

'She did seem a bit edgy, didn't she?'

'*Anxious* is the word, Jonesy,' said Phillips. 'Believe me, once you've suffered with anxiety, you can spot it a mile off in others, and she was as jumpy as a frog. Did you see how she was spinning that ring on her middle finger?'

'You noticed that too?'

'Impossible not to. I thought she might pull it off at one point. Anyway, let's see what Evans and the team have found, then head back to Ashton House. I want a full background check on Robbins and Cartwright, and first thing in the morning we need to update the Hawkinses on what happened to Hollie.'

Jones's face fell. 'Oh God. I'd forgotten about them.'

Phillips bit her lip. 'Yeah. I'm really *not* looking forward to that, I can tell you.'

4

THE CONVERSATION WITH THE HAWKINSES WAS AS UNPLEASANT AS Phillips had expected, especially given the fact that the forensic team had found no evidence that could help trace Hollie. They had, however, found her mobile phone, which had been discarded near the exit to the main road. It was a long shot, but Phillips had sent it to the digital forensics team in the hope Hollie may have inadvertently taken photos or videos of her kidnappers before she was abducted.

Rather than pull resources away from the office, she had made the trip alone. It was never easy to tell a parent their child had been hurt – or may be in danger – and her job was made harder by Richard Hawkins's clear mistrust of Phillips and her team. At one point he had been at pains to remind her of his connections in Whitehall who, he suggested, would have a significant bearing on how the case was to be managed. When she pushed him on what he meant, he said it would become clear soon enough, then refused to expand any further.

Sir Richard Hawkins was the kind of man whose words and actions made it very difficult to like him. Phillips had to remind herself of the fear and anguish he must be feeling, not knowing where his only daughter had been taken – or by whom. She resisted the temptation to defend herself and her team against his constant criticism and chose a more pragmatic approach. So, after assuring Sir Richard and his wife, Sandra, that she and her team were doing everything they could – and would utilise every available resource – to find Hollie, she had taken her leave and set off back to Headquarters.

As she left the suburb of Altrincham behind, Sir Richard's threats rang in her ears. What did he mean when he said his connections in Whitehall would have a bearing on the case? There was one person in Ashton House who never missed a trick, so she decided to call Chief Superintendent Fox to update her.

A moment later, Fox's assistant, Ms Blair, put her through, and the chief super's voice boomed through the car's speakers.

'DCI Phillips. *How was your meeting with Sir Richard?*'

'Not the easiest, Ma'am, I must say.'

'*Yes,*' said Fox. '*Knowing his reputation, I can believe that.*'

'He seems very unhappy with the pace of the investigation, which feels a little premature considering it's less than fourteen hours since Hollie was snatched.'

'*That sounds like Sir Richard.*'

Phillips paused for a moment as she searched for the right words. 'Ma'am, is there something I need to know about his connections in Whitehall in relation to this investigation?'

Fox didn't miss a beat. '*Why do you ask?*'

'Well. It's just that he said Whitehall would have a significant bearing on how the case would be handled, but when I pressed him on what that actually meant, he wouldn't say.'

'*He's probably just venting,*' said Fox.

'No. It was more than that, Ma'am. It sounded like a threat.'

'*Well, whatever he meant, I'm afraid I don't have the time to try*' *and second-guess his motives.'* Fox appeared keen to change the subject now. *'So, where are we up to on finding the girl?'*

'Well, we know Hollie spoke to an individual shortly before she was snatched, someone wearing identical mask and clothing to three other people.'

'Sounds like it was well organised, in that case,' said Fox.

'Yes, Ma'am. And I'm beginning to think they may have had help from someone connected to Marstons.'

'What makes you say that?'

'The lock on the gate through which Hollie was taken was left unlocked,' said Phillips.

'And do you have anyone you like for it within the club?'

'Nothing concrete yet, but the security guard in charge of that section of the club seemed very edgy when we spoke to her last night.'

'Do you have any background on him yet?'

'No Ma'am,' said Phillips. 'I'm hoping for an update when I get back to the station. Oh, and *he's a she.'*

'Ok. Do you have anything else?'

'No, Ma'am. Not at this stage.'

'Well, in that case, you'd better do yourself a favour and get on with finding Sir Richard's daughter pronto, hadn't you?' said Fox, and ended the call.

Phillips drove for the next few minutes in silence, replaying the two conversations in her head. She was convinced Sir Richard's comments were threatening, but couldn't figure out how. Something was in play, she was certain. As she drew nearer to Ashton House Police Headquarters, her heart rate began to climb. 'How come I get all the shitty cases?' she whispered to herself as she turned into the car park.

She parked the car and killed the engine. To calm her racing heart, she closed her eyes and breathed deeply, in through her nose and out through her mouth, for exactly one minute. Her nerves steadied, she stepped out of the car.

A few minutes later, she strode into the incident room hoping for positive news. Given the importance of the case, MCU's wider support team had almost doubled, and every available desk was taken by both plain-clothes and uniformed officers. The noise level in the room had ratcheted up significantly since the previous afternoon.

She spotted Jones staring at his screen, eyes narrow, a thick frown on his face. Her interest piqued, she approached his desk, nodding to Bov and Entwistle as they looked up from their own screens. Jones still hadn't noticed her as she stood next to his desk.

'Everything all right, Jonesy?' she asked.

Jones jerked his head up. 'Huh?'

'You look like you're in pain,' said Phillips.

'He's constipated, Guv,' joked Bovalino, eliciting a chuckle from Entwistle.

'Shut it, you bell-end!' was Jones's indignant reply.

Phillips grinned. 'Seriously, though. What's up?'

Jones sat back and pointed at his computer screen. 'It's this CCTV footage from the club.'

'What about it?' asked Phillips.

'I've been watching it over and over, and there's something about the gang that's bothering me.'

'Go on,' urged Phillips.

Jones folded his arms across his stomach. 'It's the way they move when the van arrives. I'm not sure how best to describe it, but it's...it's...er...how can I put it?'

'Just spit it out, man,' teased Bovalino.

'Ok. Well, this is going to sound weird, but it's almost *hypnotic*.'

Bovalino guffawed. 'You've been awake too long, Jonesy. You're bloody hallucinating.'

Jones shot Bovalino an agitated look. 'I'm serious, Bov. I've never seen anything like it. It's as if they move as one. Like each of them knows what the other is going to do next. See, look here.' Jones beckoned them to watch.

Bovalino and Entwistle stood and moved to join Phillips. Jones pressed play, and they watched the footage of Hollie being placed into the van as it unfolded on the screen.

'Do you see what I mean?' asked Jones. 'They're in and out in a matter of seconds, each of them knows their job, and there's not a movement, or second, wasted.'

'Play it again,' said Phillips.

Jones obliged, and for the next few minutes the team watched the footage on repeat.

'I can kind of see what you mean,' said Phillips.

'And look at this,' said Jones, touching his pen against the screen, 'When the driver opens the gate, watch his fist.'

'He shakes it,' said Bovalino. 'What's odd about that?'

'It's the *way* he shakes it, Bov. It looks so deliberate. Then, a split second later, the rest of the gang appears with Hollie.'

'So they used hand signals. It's not uncommon. Saves being heard,' said Phillips.

Jones ran his hand through his thinning hair. 'I know, but this just seems different.'

Entwistle moved back to his PC. 'I've seen something like that before.' He began typing. A moment later, he shouted, 'Got it!'

'Got what?' asked Phillips.

Entwistle began reading aloud from the screen. '"All military recruits from all forces are taught basic silent commands... a shake of the fist is used as the command – *to run*."'

'They're ex-military,' whispered Phillips.

Jones clapped his hands. 'I knew there was something special about these boys. See, I told you, Bov!'

Bovalino patted his heavy hand on Jones's shoulder. 'Well done, mate. You're not as daft as you look after all.'

Phillips nodded. 'Indeed you're not, Jonesy. And who do we know at the club who are both ex-military?'

Jones's eyes widened, and a grin spread across his face. 'Robbins and Cartwright!'

'Robbins and Cartwright,' repeated Phillips. 'I think it's time we made another trip to Marstons, don't you?'

5

As Phillips and Jones entered the clubhouse, it felt like a totally different building. The Halloween decorations had been removed, and the atmosphere was tranquil. After signing in at reception, they made their way towards Robbins's office, but were intercepted by Mr Green. Like his clubhouse, he too appeared different: more in control, less panicked.

'Chief Inspector. To what do we owe the privilege of another visit?' he said, offering an outstretched hand, which Phillips and Jones shook in turn.

'Just a few more questions for your security team.'

Green raised his eyebrows. 'My, they are popular today. One of your team is already in with Mr Robbins.'

Phillips recoiled. 'One of *my* team? I think you must be mistaken.'

Green's chest puffed. 'No mistake. He showed me his credentials when he arrived.'

Phillips glanced at Jones, who was frowning, before turning back to Green. 'Would you excuse us?' she said. Without waiting for his reply, she headed for Robbins's office with Jones at her heel.

Knocking once, Phillips opened the door and walked inside. Robbins, who was behind his desk facing a man Phillips did not know, shot her a look of surprise. 'Chief Inspector Phillips? I wasn't expecting you.'

Phillips ignored him and turned her attention to the stranger. 'Would you mind telling me who you are, sir?'

The man stood, straightened his blazer, and held his hands together behind his back to amplify his tall, slim frame. 'The name's Harry Saxby,' he said in a confident public-school accent.

Phillips forced a thin smile. 'And can I ask why the club manager seems to think you're part of my team?'

Saxby chuckled, exposing crooked, nicotine-stained teeth. 'Oh, I'm certainly not part of *your* team. Far from it, Inspector.'

'Well, who the fuck are you with, then? The press?'

'Hardly,' Saxby sneered. He reached inside an overcoat pocket to retrieve his official ID. 'Chief Inspector Harry Saxby, kidnapping and negotiation expert with the Metropolitan Police. I'm here to advise you on how to handle the kidnapping of Hollie Hawkins. Don't you read memos in the north?' His tone was sarcastic.

Phillips pursed her lips as Jones shot her a furtive look she had seen many times before. His wide eyes urged her to keep her cool. 'I must have missed that one,' she said, just about holding her temper.

Saxby smiled, appearing pleased with himself. 'Well, it seems Mr Hawkins has friends in *very* high places in Whitehall who are super-keen to see his daughter returned to him, unharmed, and as soon as possible. So they asked for me.'

Hawkins's words now made total sense. Saxby was the 'big bearing on the case' he had threatened. Phillips was in no doubt Chief Superintendent Fox had been fully aware of his involvement at the time of her phone call. No wonder she had been so keen to end it. In true Fox style, she had taken the easy option of letting Phillips find out for herself.

Phillips needed time to process. 'I need to verify this with Chief Superintendent Fox.'

Saxby pulled his phone from his pocket. 'Would you like to use my phone to call her?' he said, half smiling.

'That won't be necessary. I'll speak to her when I get back to Ashton House.'

'Well, if it's ok with you, Chief Inspector, I'll just finish up here with Mr Robbins.'

'No, it's not all right with me,' said Phillips. 'This is my investigation and I don't care who sent you – or how well connected you are. Until I verify your involvement with Chief Superintendent Fox, you have no business speaking to anyone involved in this investigation. Do I make myself clear?'

Saxby shrugged his shoulders and sucked air through his teeth. 'Very well, Inspector, if that's how you want to play it. But I can assure you, delaying my involvement won't change anything. I've been instructed to insert myself into the middle of this investigation – whether you like it or not.'

'I think you'll find it's *Chief* Inspector, and I don't give a flying fuck what you've been instructed to do. I'm the SIO on this case and you have no place in this investigation. Now, if you don't mind, DS Jones and I would like to speak with Mr Robbins, in private.'

Saxby released a heavy sigh. 'As you wish, but you're simply delaying the inevitable, *Chief* Inspector.' He turned to face Robbins and smiled. 'Thank you for your time, Mr Robbins. You've been most helpful.' And with that, he left the room.

SHORTLY AFTER SAXBY'S EXIT, Phillips excused herself and made her way to the ladies' to try and recalibrate her head. As she stared at her reflection in the mirror, anger burned in the pit of her stomach. Based on Hawkins's threats, plus Fox's furtive responses, she had no doubt that major politics was now in play. Saxby was here to stay, and there was likely very little she could do to keep him out of her investigation. Outside involvement was the last thing she needed. With the pressure to get a result mounting by the minute, some arrogant arsehole from London constantly second-guessing her every move would only make matters ten times worse.

Splashing her face with water, she took a deep breath and steadied herself. She pulled her hair back and reset her ponytail before replacing her spectacles. Regardless of whatever was going on, she still had a missing girl to find, and that had to be her priority. Everything else could wait.

When she returned to Robbins's office, a large tray carrying filter coffee and fresh cakes had arrived.

'Well, this is a little nicer than we're used to,' she said, attempting to lighten the mood as Robbins poured the steaming hot liquid into three cups.

Jones, as ever, was ready, notepad and pen in hand.

Phillips waited until they each had a drink. 'Mr Robbins—'

'Please, call me John.'

Phillips nodded. 'Ok. John. Can you tell us a bit more about your background before you began working here?'

Robbins's brow furrowed. 'What do you want to know?'

'You were in the military. Is that correct?'

'I was. Twenty years in the Royal Marines.'

'And did you see active combat?'

'Three tours of Afghanistan and two of Iraq.'

'That must have been pretty hairy at times,' said Phillips.

Robbins took a drink of his coffee before cradling the cup in both hands, his heavily tattooed wrist once more on show. 'It was. I lost a lot of good friends out there.'

'Are you still in touch with anyone from your regiment?'

'Through Facebook and social media, but not much else. A lot of the guys stayed down near the base in Plymouth, but I decided to move back north. I'm from Leeds and my wife's a Manc. She missed her family, and after dragging her around the world for so many years, I thought it was only fair we lived where she wanted to, for a change.'

'You're still married?'

'Yes, to Liz, and we have two grown-up kids too – Sally and Mark.'

'And how old are they?'

'Sally's seventeen. She's just started at college. Mark is nineteen, and followed his old man into the Marines. He's doing his commando training at the moment.' Robbins's wide grin oozed pride.

Jones scribbled in his pad as Phillips took a sip of coffee. 'So when did you leave the military?' she asked.

'March 2015.'

'What rank were you at that point?'

'Warrant Officer, Class 1,' said Robbins.

Phillips nodded. 'Pretty senior, then?'

'Yeah, and I was sorry to leave. I'd have stayed if they'd let me, but I'd done my time.'

'So I'm assuming you receive a decent military pension, then, on top of your salary here?'

'I do ok, yeah.' Robbins placed his cup on the desk and leaned forwards. 'Look, I don't mean to be rude, but what do my family and finances have to do with all this?'

Phillips flashed a smile. 'Just standard background stuff, John.'

'Ok. In that case, why is the GMP interested in *my* background?'

'Well. We have reason to believe that the men who took Hollie had military training—'

'What? And you think *I* was involved?'

'That's not what I'm saying—'

'No, but it's what you're *thinking,* isn't it?'

Phillips paused for a moment as Robbins's face reddened.

'I'm a decorated war veteran with kids of my own. I could never do anything to endanger a child.'

Robbins seemed genuine enough, but Phillips had been in this game long enough to reserve judgement at this stage of an investigation. 'Look, John, we're not saying you were involved in Hollie's kidnapping, but as I mentioned the other night, we have to check every angle in order to eliminate people from our enquiries.'

Robbins nodded, but appeared unconvinced.

Phillips changed tack. 'What can you tell us about Sam Cartwright?'

'What do you want to know?'

'When we spoke on the night Hollie was taken, you told us she was an ex-combat medic.'

'That's right.'

'Did you know her before she came to work at Marstons?'

Robbins shook his head. 'No. I'd never met her until she came for the interview.'

'Have you ever had any issues with her work?'

'None whatsoever. She's a first-rate operative.'

'I see,' said Phillips. 'Do you know if she stayed in touch with anyone from her regiment?'

'I don't. To be honest, I've never asked her. Keeps herself to herself. She comes to work, does her shift and goes home. Aside from a quick "Hello" when she comes in to pick up her radio and keys, I rarely speak to her.'

'Have you noticed anything different in her behaviour since the night Hollie was taken?'

'Nothing,' said Robbins.

'We'll need to talk to her, of course. When is she next on shift?'

'She's in now.'

Phillips raised her eyebrows. 'I thought she worked nights?'

'It varies. We move them around the rota. Stops them getting complacent, and means we can get a better quality of operative. Security people who only work nights tend to be a little less qualified, shall we say.'

'Can we speak to her?' asked Phillips.

Robbins nodded, and radioed Cartwright.

CARTWRIGHT APPEARED ANXIOUS, and agitated, as she took her seat opposite Phillips and Jones. Robbins had left to give them privacy.

Phillips got straight to the point. 'Do you keep in touch with your ex-military mates?'

Cartwright jerked her head back a little, clearly not expecting the question. 'Er...sometimes. We have the odd night out when I'm not working here.'

'What regiment were you in?'

'The Yorkshire Regiment. Used to be the Duke of Wellington's.'

'And you were a combat medic, weren't you?'

'That's right. I served in Afghanistan and Iraq.'

'And when did you leave the military?'

'June 2010.'

'Why did you leave?'

Cartwright shifted in her seat and swallowed hard. 'I was diagnosed with PTSD.' She stared at the floor.

'Do you mind me asking what caused it?'

Cartwright looked Phillips dead in the eye now. 'I watched a good mate get blown to pieces in front of me. He stepped on an IED.'

Phillips's tone softened. 'I'm sorry to hear that.'

Cartwright nodded.

'What happened after you left the military?'

'I did a few jobs and eventually ended up here.'

'Those jobs, were they all in security?'

'Pretty much, yeah. I had a couple of driving gigs on and off for a while, but I didn't fancy the long journeys. I'm not a fan of having too much time with my own thoughts. If you know what I mean?'

Phillips could indeed sympathise, having fought her own mental health battles over the last few years. It was usually when she was alone that her thoughts were at their darkest.

'Sam, have any of your ex-military mates been in touch unexpectedly in the last few months?'

'Not that I can think of...just the usual crew.'

'We'll need their names and contact details, if that's ok?'

Cartwright shrugged her shoulders. 'Sure, but what for?'

Phillips smiled. 'Oh, just standard procedure. Nothing to worry about.'

As Cartwright dictated the list of her ex-colleagues, Jones scribbled the names down in his pad whilst Phillips drained her remaining coffee. 'Well, thank you for your time, Sam. I think that's all we need for now. We'll be in touch if we require anything else.'

Cartwright nodded silently as Phillips and Jones stood.

'We'll see ourselves out,' said Phillips, and they headed for the door.

6

NOVEMBER 2ND

THE NEXT MORNING, AS EVER, JONES, BOVALINO AND ENTWISTLE were in early. Phillips gathered them in her office to debrief on the visit to Marstons. Bovalino had made the short trip to the canteen on the ground floor, returning with hot bacon rolls and tea for each of the team. As he handed them out, Phillips took a couple of minutes to bring them up to date on the previous afternoon's events.

'So we're no further forward then, Guv?' Bovalino asked as he took a seat opposite Phillips, followed by a large bite of his own roll.

'No, but I'd like a full background check on both Robbins and Cartwright. It's just too much of a coincidence that they both have military backgrounds.'

'And you don't believe in coincidences do you, Guv?' Entwistle quipped with a knowing smile.

Phillips feigned surprise. 'Have I said that before, then?'

'Once or twice,' said Jones.

Entwistle made a note in his pad. 'I'll look into them both this morning.'

'There's something else you guys need to be aware of.' Phillips tapped the desk with her finger.

Bovalino stopped chewing and raised his eyebrows. 'Oh?'

'It looks like Hawkins has followed up on his threat to involve Whitehall. They've sent us a special advisor from the Met.'

'A special advisor? That's all we bloody need,' moaned Bovalino.

'I know, Bov. I know,' said Phillips.

'What does he look like, Guv, this special advisor?' asked Entwistle.

Phillips brow furrowed. 'Tall, thin, official looking. Why do you ask?'

'Sounds like the guy who was in here yesterday, asking where he could find Fox,' said Entwistle.

'And what did you tell him?' asked Phillips.

'Well, er...I took him up to her office. I was going that way anyway, and—'

'Jesus, Entwistle!' Bovalino moaned. 'Talk about letting the cat amongst the pigeons.'

Entwistle glared at Bovalino. 'I didn't know who he was, did I? And what was I supposed to do? Ignore him?'

Phillips raised her hands. 'Look, it's no use blaming anybody and fighting amongst ourselves. This is not of our making. This is down to Hawkins and his cronies in Whitehall. I called Fox last night, and she confirmed we're stuck with Harry Saxby for the foreseeable future.'

'So she admitted she knew about it, then?' asked Jones.

'Not quite,' Phillips scoffed. 'Let's just say she made it clear resistance was futile.'

Bovalino swallowed his last mouthful of the bacon roll. 'So what's he like, this Saxby fella?'

Jones sneered. 'Typical Met Police – a patronising prick. Thinks we're all farmers and yokels this far north,'

Phillips chuckled. 'That about sums him up. So I think *you're* gonna love him, Bov.'

'Well, he can't be as bad as Brown was,' said Bovalino.

'I wouldn't bank on it, Bov.' Phillips nodded in the direction of the main office. 'Anyway, you'll find out soon enough. He's just walked in.'

All three men turned as the door to Phillips's office opened.

'DCI Saxby,' she said, forcing herself to be polite. 'Let me introduce you to the team,'

Saxby ignored the faces staring at him. 'No time for that. Sir Richard Hawkins has just received a ransom demand from the kidnappers. Fox wants us over there immediately.'

Phillips's mouth fell open. Why was Fox talking to Saxby *before* her own DCI?

'Come on, Phillips. There's no time to waste,' added Saxby, before turning and walking out of the office.

'Jones, you're coming with me,' Phillips snarled in a low voice.

Jones nodded and began gathering his things.

'Entwistle, get me everything there is to know on Robbins and Cartwright.'

'No problem, Guv.'

'And Bovalino...'

'Yes boss?' said the big Italian.

'Find out exactly who Harry-fucking-Saxby is. I want to know just how well-connected this guy is – or *isn't*, for that matter.'

'Bovalino smiled. 'It'll be my pleasure, Guv.'

～

SAXBY INSISTED on taking his own car, so followed Phillips and Jones to the Hawkins's Altrincham home – which was just fine by Phillips. She had no desire to spend any more time than was necessary with the man.

When they arrived, Phillips pressed the buzzer at the gate and presented her ID to the small security camera.

'Come up to the house,' was the reply from the console, and the gates began to open.

The sweeping gravel drive up to the house snaked alongside manicured lawns through rows of mature trees and hedges, leading to a large circular fountain outside the front door, where Hawkins's top-of-the-range silver Range Rover was parked.

As Phillips brought the squad car to a halt, the large oak front door opened and Richard Hawkins came into view. Hands on hips, he looked agitated, which was not surprising given the circumstances.

'Whatever he says in there, Guv, don't let him get to you,' said Jones.

Phillips nodded. Jones did indeed know her better than anyone else on the force. Having worked together for over ten years on many challenging cases, he knew only too well the types of people who pushed Phillips's buttons. Hawkins was one such person. Saxby was another. Rude and arrogant didn't sit well with Phillips's down-to-earth values. 'Trust me, Jonesy, since I started therapy, I'm a new woman.' She flashed a wry smile.

'Yeah? I'll believe it when I see it,' chuckled Jones.

By the time Phillips and Jones stepped out of their car, Saxby had left his vehicle and was en route to the front door, arm outstretched.

'Sir Richard. Detective Chief Inspector Saxby.'

Hawkins shook his hand.

Saxby continued, 'I've been seconded to the GMP from the Metropolitan Police. *I'm* the kidnapping and negotiation expert you requested.'

Hawkins stared at Saxby for a moment in silence, then nodded as Phillips and Jones made their way up the steps. 'Detectives,' he said without feeling, 'you'd better come inside. The ransom video is on my laptop.'

Phillips, Jones and Saxby followed Hawkins through the large reception area of the house and into the kitchen at the rear of the property. Reminiscent of those often featured in celebrity magazines, it was an enormous white and grey space with floor-to-ceiling windows on three sides and overlooking an outdoor swimming pool with its winter covers in place.

Sandra Hawkins sat on one of the tall stools, leaning against the gargantuan kitchen island in the middle of the room. Her eyes and nose were red and swollen, and a handkerchief was locked in her right hand. Richard Hawkins grabbed the open laptop on the bench in front of her, and turned it towards him.

'This was sent to my email at 3 a.m. Sandra, maybe you don't need to see this again?'

Sandra shook her head. 'No, Richard. I want to hear what the officers have to say.'

'Very well.' He punched the keyboard with a finger. A video began to play on the screen.

The footage was dark, and initially the front page of the previous day's edition of the *Manchester Evening News* filled the screen.

'The kidnappers are providing proof of life,' said Saxby, as if he was the only person in the room who understood why the newspaper had been featured.

About fifteen seconds passed, then the newspaper was removed and Hollie Hawkins could be seen in the centre of the shot. Her head was tilted forwards and to the right. Her eyes were barely open, and her matted hair fell over much of her face. After a long moment she spoke, as if reading from a script.

'*My name is Hollie Hawkins. So far, I have not been harmed. That will change if my kidnappers' demands are not met.*' She paused as if trying to maintain control of her emotions, her breathing laboured. *'In order to secure my safe return, my father, Sir Richard Hawkins, must pay four million pounds in unmarked notes. In exactly seven days, you will receive the location of where to deliver the money. There are to be no excuses...'* A tear streaked down her grubby cheek as she took a sharp intake of breath. *'If you fail to pay the four million pounds, I will be killed, my body will be dismembered...'* Hollie stopped and broke down, her shoulders shaking as she began to sob.

From the right of the screen, a handgun clasped in a gloved hand appeared and was placed against Hollie's temple before the hammer was cocked.

'Read the rest,' said a distorted voice in an evil, ghoulish tone.

With what appeared to be a considerable effort, Hollie stopped crying and attempted to read the remainder of the script. *'...and you will never see me again. There will be no body to bury, and you will never know the pain of my final hours.'* She began to sob again, then looked up and screamed into the camera, *'Please, Dad, give them what they want!'*

The footage ended, but Hollie's image remained frozen on the screen in front of them.

Phillips was not surprised to see Sandra Hawkins begin to sob, reminiscent of her daughter on the video.

Hawkins patted his wife on the shoulder in the same awkward manner Phillips had noted at the leisure club on the night Hollie had disappeared.

The poor woman, Phillips thought. Her heart went out to her.

Hawkins turned to face them now. 'So, what do we do?'

'We pay them, Richard!' Sandra shouted through her tears as snot and saliva fell from her nose and mouth.

Hawkins ignored his wife and stared at Saxby. 'You're the expert. What do you think we should do?'

Saxby's chest puffed out like a peacock's. 'I don't mean to be forward, but do you have access to four million pounds, Mr Hawkins?'

'Yes, but it will take time to raise that kind of cash.'

'In that case, I think you should make arrangements to access the funds. Just for the time being,' Saxby said.

Hawkins's face twisted. 'But what if I pay the ransom and they kill her anyway?'

'Don't talk like that, Richard!' screamed Sandra. 'She has to live. She has to!'

Phillips had seen enough of Hawkins's and Saxby's insensitivity, and stepped in. She placed an arm around Sandra's shoulders. 'Please don't upset yourself, Mrs Hawkins,' she said in a gentle voice. 'We're going to do everything we can to get Hollie back, I promise.'

Sandra continued to sob, holding the handkerchief against her mouth as tears streaked down her cheeks.

Hawkins shrugged. 'Look, all I'm asking is, is paying the ransom the only option? Don't you have special forces for this kind of investigation? You know, teams that can track and rescue her?'

Saxby's mouth opened, but he remained silent a moment, as if trying to find the right words. 'Erm, well, Mr Hawkins, it doesn't quite work like that, I'm afraid. Not in a civilian investigation such as this. Those kinds of teams are reserved for military extractions.'

'Well, that's even more reason to use one, then. My business provides weapons for most of the British military! Let's not forget who my friends in Whitehall are.'

Phillips still had no idea who Hawkins's friends were, but was keen to find out. At least then she would know who she was up against. In the meantime, she watched on as Saxby tried to regain control of the situation.

'Let me make some calls to London, Mr Hawkins, see what I

can do.' Saxby raised his arms in placation. 'In the meantime, it would seem prudent for you to source the funds in readiness for the next stage of the negotiations. I can assure you, we have no intention of letting your daughter's kidnappers walk away with your money. Our goal is to get Hollie back and send these evil men to prison for the rest of their lives.'

Hawkins nodded. 'Very well. In that case, I'll pull the money together. But if anything happens to Hollie or my four million pounds—' He pointed to Saxby and Phillips in turn. '— I'll hold you both *personally* responsible.'

'We understand *completely*,' said Saxby.

We? thought Phillips. Whatever story Saxby was peddling, she was in no doubt that if this investigation went sideways, the so-called 'kidnapping and negotiation expert' would disappear down the rabbit hole he had come from, leaving *her* to carry the can.

Phillips and the team had to find Hollie quickly. The consequences of not doing so didn't bear thinking about.

7

THE SOUND OF THE LOCK ON THE HEAVY METAL DOOR BEING
released woke Hollie. She sat upright on the small bed, still
under the blanket in her windowless cell. The small space,
which smelled of damp, was lit by a free-standing lamp in the
corner, alongside a portable gas heater that did very little to
warm the room. The door opened and she braced herself,
pulling her knees up to her chin under the blanket, and wrapping her arms around them.

The first thing she saw of her captor was the mask. Each of
the gang members wore one. The only difference was that each
had a different coloured one-inch horizontal strip where the
wearer's nose would be. This gang member's stripe was white,
which matched his codename – White. Hollie had heard them
refer to each other as White, Red, Blue and Black, but never by
their real names. The gang member who had referred to herself
as Blackie at the Halloween party had called it an *Army of Two*
mask, claiming it was from some kind of computer game.
Hollie had never seen the game, but stared intently at the mask
that covered her captor's face. She noted it was matte black,

reminiscent of a smooth, featureless skull, with large eyeholes covered in a black mesh.

White closed the door behind him before he moved across the room to place a tray of food on the small metal table in the middle of the room. He wore black combat fatigues with matching black gloves and boots. 'Here's your breakfast,' he said, his voice muffled by the mask.

Hollie peered at the plate of bacon and eggs in front of her. 'I can't eat dead animal carcasses. I'm a vegan!'

The cold, soulless mask stared back at her in silence. 'Suit yourself.' White shrugged, turned his back on her and walked towards the door.

'You kidnapped the wrong girl, you know,' Hollie snapped, hoping to get his attention – though quite why, she wasn't entirely sure.

White turned back to face her again. 'What did you say?'

Hollie panicked that he might punish her for her outburst. 'Well, er, I just said...I think you might have kidnapped the wrong girl.'

'And why would you think that?'

'He's not my real dad.'

'Who isn't?' said White.

Hollie had his full attention now, so continued, her confidence growing. 'Richard Hawkins. He's not my real dad. My real dad's *dead*.'

'How sad,' said White, with no emotion at all.

Hollie nodded. 'Richard is my stepdad. He married my mum when I was five, and adopted me when I was ten.'

'Fascinating,' said White, his tone sarcastic.

'He probably won't pay the ransom, you know. He loves his money more than me and my mum. More than *anything*, in fact. I'd be surprised if he'd pay four thousand pounds for me, never mind four million.'

White stared at her for a long moment without saying a word.

Then Hollie's new-found confidence began to evaporate as White crept towards her, stopping just a few inches from her bed. She reeled backwards against the wall as he leaned forwards. His eyes were partially visible through the mesh-covered eyeholes just inches away from her own. 'Well, Princess, you'd better hope "stepdaddy" has a change of heart, then, because if not...you're gonna be pig-feed.' White squealed like a pig, then chuckled.

Hollie swallowed hard but remained stoic, trying her best not to cry.

White stood upright, then turned and walked towards the door. When he reached it, he banged on it three times, waited a few seconds, then opened it a fraction before turning back to face Hollie. 'Now eat your breakfast, you little brat!' he said, before he stepped outside and closed the door behind him with a bang.

'*You're* the bloody pig!' shouted Hollie to the empty room. Her words echoed around her, then faded away into silence.

She stared at the plate of meat and eggs on the table in front of her, then took long, deep breaths as she tried to control her emotions – just as her therapist had taught her to do in times of stress. She was angry, frustrated and very frightened. A moment later, the tears began to flow, and she fell back down onto the mattress to bury her face in the pillow to drown out her sobs.

All she wanted was her mum.

8

AFTER COMPLETING THEIR VISIT TO THE HAWKINS'S HOME, SAXBY made his excuses and set off for an undisclosed appointment. With Jones driving them back to Ashton House, Phillips was impatient to find out who Harry Saxby really was. She called Bovalino's mobile on the hands-free unit.

'Guv. How did it go?'

'As well as it could, given the circumstances. They've given Hawkins a week to find the money, or they said Hollie dies,' said Phillips.

'A week? Why a week? I'd have thought they'd want their money sooner.'

'Yeah, but four million quid? That's a lot of money to raise. Maybe they're giving him time to get it together,' said Phillips.

'Yeah, maybe. And what about that prick, Saxby? How was he?'

'As expected, I'm afraid. He acts as if we work for him, and that he knows more about the case than anyone else.' Phillips looked across at Jonesy and winked. 'What you might call, a typical "London-wanker", Bov.'

'Hey! Not everyone from Laaarndon is a wanker, you know,' Jones protested, exaggerating his own South London accent.

Phillips grinned. 'Anyway, Bov, that's why I'm calling. Did you manage to get any background on Saxby?'

'Indeed I did, Guv. Let me just go somewhere quiet.'

'Use my office,' said Phillips.

Phillips and Jones waited in silence, listening as Bovalino made his way across the incident room to Phillips's office. The door was closed, then Bovalino returned to the call. 'Right, Guv. His full name is Henry Bartholomew Saxby. He's fifty-two and currently a DCI in the Met Police, specialising in kidnapping and negotiation – which he's been doing for the last five years. He joined the Met ten years ago after serving in the Coldstream Guards for twenty-seven years, rising to the rank of Major.'

'Major arsehole, more like,' joked Jones, drawing a chuckle from Phillips.

'Sounds about right,' continued Bovalino. 'He did multiple tours of Iraq and Afghanistan, but only in a diplomatic role. He never actually saw combat. He retired in 2010 and headed straight into the police, where he rose through the ranks like a rocket. He made DCI in just five years.'

'Amazing what you can achieve if your face fits,' said Phillips.

'Yeah, well, funny you should say that. I checked his background prior to joining the military, and it appears he studied Classics at Durham University with Sir Malcolm Lewis – the current Deputy Commissioner of the Met'.'

'Jobs for the boys,' said Jones.

Phillips nodded. 'Anything else, Bov?'

'Just that he's divorced with two grown-up sons. One lives in Melbourne, Australia. Works as a teacher. The other is a web-developer in California.'

'Running away from Daddy, perhaps?' asked Jones.

'I certainly would if he was my dad!' said Phillips. 'So, what about the ex-wife; where is she?'

Bov shuffled some papers, taking a moment to answer. 'Er,

looks like she lives in France. *Runs a boutique guesthouse in Brittany.*'

'Does he have a girlfriend – or maybe a boyfriend, even?' asked Phillips.

'*Not that I can see. Looks like he's a bit of a loner, by all accounts.*'

Phillips took a moment to process the information.

'*That's as much as I've found so far, Guv,*'

'You've done well, Bov,' said Phillips.

'*Do you want me to keep digging?*'

'No, that'll do for now,' said Phillips. 'We've got more important things to worry about, like finding Hollie. How's Entwistle getting on with Robbins's and Cartwright's backgrounds?'

'*I dunno, but he's sat opposite me, looking as gormless as ever.*' Bovalino chortled. '*Do you want me to transfer you?*'

Just then, Phillips's phone began to beep. Checking the screen, she could see Fox was on the other line. 'No, not right now. Fox is calling me. I'd better see what she wants. Tell Entwistle we'll be back in the office in twenty minutes, and I want a full update ready.'

'*Will do, Guv.*'

'Thanks Bov.' She ended the call and answered Fox's. 'Ma'am?'

～

AT ASHTON HOUSE, Phillips followed Jones up the stairs from the car park to the fifth floor.

'You ok, Jonesy?' she asked, noting his slumped posture and heavy legs.

Jones glanced back over his shoulder, but continued upwards. 'Fine, Guv.'

She suspected he wasn't telling the whole truth. 'You're not worried about the meeting with Fox, are you?'

He shook his head softly. 'No, of course not.' His words lacked conviction.

'Like she said on the call, it's just a debrief. Nothing to worry about.'

Jones reached the landing on the fifth floor and turned to face Phillips. 'So why does she want *me* in there? *You* always handle this stuff.'

Phillips joined him on the landing and placed a reassuring hand on his shoulder. 'Maybe she's getting rid of *me* and wants *you* to take over.' She grinned.

Jones's eyes widened. 'Don't even joke about shit like that.'

Phillips chuckled. 'Well, whatever she wants, we'll find out soon enough. Come on.'

A few minutes later, they were ushered into Fox's office by Ms Blair.

Fox, as usual, was in full uniform. Her glasses were perched on the end of her tanned nose, which contrasted with her cheaply dyed blonde hair, and she was perusing a thick file. As was her wont, she took some moments before she acknowledged them, but when she did, her trademark Cheshire Cat smile spread across her face. 'DCI Phillips, and DS Jones. Please, take a seat.'

As they each took a chair opposite Fox, she scribbled something in the margin of the report she'd been reading, and placed it to one side on her large, frosted-glass desk, along with her glasses.

'So, tell me about your visit to the Hawkins's this morning. Where are we at with tracing their daughter?'

Phillips explained the details of the video, and the demands delivered through Hollie's message to her father.

Fox raised an eyebrow when she heard the terms. 'A week to find the money? I see.' She tapped her pen on her veneered teeth. 'Why a week?'

'We have no idea, Ma'am,' said Phillips.

'And what was Saxby's take on it all?'

Phillips shrugged. 'Nothing exceptional. To be honest, he advised Mr Hawkins in exactly the same way I would have done.'

'Which was?'

'Play along, for now, until we have more information.'

'And what do you make of him?' asked Fox.

'Hawkins?' said Phillips.

'No. Saxby.'

Phillips blew her lips gently as she searched for the most diplomatic response. 'Well, he's, erm...well, he's very *Met Police* Ma'am.'

'What do you mean by that?'

'It's just that he thinks he knows better than everyone else.'

'And does he?' pushed Fox.

Phillips shook her head. 'Based on the evidence I've seen so far, I'd have to say no. Seems quite old-school.'

Fox turned her attention to Jones now. 'What about you, DS Jones? What's your take on him?'

Jones, unprepared for the question, shifted in his seat and cleared his throat. 'Er, well, like the Guv said, he's very "Met Police", Ma'am.'

Fox's eyes narrowed. 'Now, DS Jones. I'm quite sure you have more to offer than merely parroting your DCI.'

Jones's mouth fell open as he searched for the right words.

'And be *honest*, Jones,' said Fox, her gaze unflinching. 'You can speak freely in here.'

Phillips's heart went out to Jones as she watched him squirm in his chair. Fox was playing with him like a cat with an injured bird. She loved to put people on the back foot, as she believed it forced them into telling the truth. It was a technique she had used to great effect in the past, back when she herself was a DCI.

'Erm, well, Ma'am. It's just that he's quite superior in his approach, and appears unwilling to listen to any opinions that don't match his own.'

Fox stared at Jones in silence for a long moment before she nodded and turned her attention back to Phillips. 'Right. Well, *whatever* either of you think of Saxby, I've been told, in no uncertain terms, by Chief Constable Morris, that he's here for the duration of the investigation. He's even been given his own office – two doors down from mine.' Fox appeared to snarl a bit as she shared this development. Acquiring an office on the fifth floor was seen as a rite of passage, a privilege reserved for the ranks of Superintendent and above. 'So, it would seem he gets whatever he wants.'

Phillips knew there was little to be gained from arguing against Saxby's involvement, especially if the directive had come down from the chief constable himself. 'We'll do what we can to accommodate him, Ma'am,' she said through gritted teeth.

Fox continued. 'Apparently Sir Richard has connections in Downing Street and personally asked for them to intervene, which puts us in a very difficult situation. Chief Constable Morris is not happy. He sees it as a slight on the Greater Manchester Police that we've been forced to take on outside help, particularly on such an important case. He spent most of this morning's briefing telling me how pissed off he was – the stupid old fool.'

Phillips quashed the grin that flashed to her lips. It was no secret Fox thought Chief Constable Morris should have retired years ago. Everyone in Ashton House knew *she* had designs on his job – including Morris.

'I want this case wrapped up in double time. I don't care how you do it, just find Hollie Hawkins alive, *and quickly*. Ideally before any money is handed over. Do you understand?'

Phillips and Jones nodded in unison. 'Yes, Ma'am.'

'This is a high-profile case. I want to show Morris how it's done. Maybe then he'll finally piss off and retire.'

'Understood, Ma'am,' said Phillips.

'Right. Well, as you've only got seven days to find her, I think it's *time* you two pissed off, don't you?'

'Of course, Ma'am,' said Phillips, without feeling, as she pushed back her chair and stood.

Jones couldn't get out of his chair quick enough, which made Phillips smile to herself as they left.

A few minutes later, they walked along the third-floor corridor towards the Major Crimes Incident Room.

'So the pressure's really ramped up on this one then, Guv?' said Jones.

Phillips stopped walking and exhaled loudly. 'Looks that way, Jonesy.'

'So what's the plan?'

'The plan?' Phillips checked to ensure they were alone before answering, in hushed tones, 'The plan is, we avoid Saxby wherever possible, and we sweat the only leads we have so far – Robbins and Cartwright.'

'Do you really think they were involved?'

'At this stage I couldn't say either way, but the military angle definitely needs further investigation.'

'Agreed.'

'Right. So, first things first. Let's see what Entwistle has managed to dig up on each of them. We can go from there.'

Jones nodded before Phillips turned on her heels and made her way towards the Incident Room.

9

FOLLOWING THE MEETING WITH FOX, PHILLIPS DEBRIEFED THE team, then despatched Jones and Bovalino back to Marstons to have another conversation with Robbins. Entwistle had found nothing untoward in his background, but Phillips was keen to see how he would react when talking to two male officers, particularly one as physically imposing and masculine as Bovalino. Over-sharing due to ego had been the downfall of many a hardened male criminal, and from what she had observed during their interactions so far, Robbins was what she would call a 'man's man'. Maybe, if he felt more comfortable talking to men, he would let something slip.

As for Cartwright, Entwistle had faced a number of challenges in accessing any information regarding her military career. The data he had been able to locate so far only went back as far as 2014. Nothing before that date. That in itself set alarms bells ringing, and Phillips instructed him to keep digging as a matter of urgency.

∾

An hour later, Jones opened the door to Robbins's office – without knocking – and stepped inside with Bovalino just behind him.

Robbins's head shot up from his laptop, which he closed with one rapid movement. His wide eyes traced Bovalino's large frame as he stepped into full view.

'Can I help you officers?' he said.

Jones feigned innocence. 'I'm sorry, Mr Robbins. Did we disturb you?'

Robbins forced a thin smile and shook his head. 'Not at all. How can I help?'

'I should introduce my partner, Detective Constable Bovalino.'

Bovalino offered his large hand, which Robbins shook with vigour.

'Do you have a minute?' asked Jones.

Robbins gestured for them to sit down opposite him. 'Of course. Can I get you gents a tea or coffee? A soft drink, perhaps?'

'No thank you,' said Jones. 'If you don't mind, I'll get straight to the point.'

Robbins's brow furrowed. 'Go on.'

Bovalino pulled out his notepad and pen as Jones continued. 'Can you talk us through your movements on the night Hollie Hawkins was taken?'

'Well, I was here all night.'

'Where, specifically?'

'I was in my office mainly, as well as out and about across the clubhouse and tennis courts.'

'And what about when Hollie was taken?' pushed Jones. 'Can you tell us where you were at that time?'

Robbins thrust his chin out in defiance as he opened his laptop. 'No, but I can *show* you.' He tapped at the keyboard for a moment before turning it to face Jones and Bovalino. CCTV footage played on the small screen.

'Check the timestamp on the video,' said Robbins. 'Eight p.m. As you can see, I was in the restaurant, talking to the maître d' at the time. The restaurant is on the opposite side of the club to the air conditioning units and golf pro shop, where Hollie was taken from.' Robbins then sped up the footage to double time.

Jones and Bovalino watched on as they viewed Robbins's movements through the next fifteen minutes of footage, from the restaurant into the main bar, then along to Green's office before heading back into his office. Robbins paused the video, then leaned back into his large, leather chair and folded his arms. 'I'm visible the *entire* time when Hollie was taken.'

Jones cleared his throat. 'It certainly appears that way.'

Robbins seemed very pleased. 'So, I'm in the clear, right?'

Jones knew better than to take anything at face value, but the footage did seem to eliminate Robbins, for now. He nodded. 'Like I say, it certainly appears that way.'

Robbins clasped his hands together, sat forwards and spun the laptop back to face him. 'In that case, let me show you something else.' Once again, he tapped at the keyboard for a few moments before he turned the laptop back so Jones and Bovalino could see the screen. 'Watch this.'

Jones and Bovalino watched as more CCTV footage unfolded. Jones noted the timestamp: 7.23 p.m.

'This is the corridor that leads to the ladies' and gents' toilets, leading off from the main bar,' Robbins explained. 'Looking here, you can see party guests in fancy dress, heading down the corridor and then turning left, out of sight.' Robbins tapped on the screen with his pen. 'Around that corner is where the toilets are located.'

They watched for another few minutes as the party guests

reappeared and headed back towards the camera, each of them easily recognisable by their Halloween costumes.

'You with me so far?' asked Robbins.

Jones and Bovalino nodded.

'Now watch this,' said Robbins, just as three figures appeared on screen from around the same corner, walking in a V-formation. Each was dressed in identical dark clothing, long coats and gloves, and wearing identical masks.

Robbins hit pause on the video, and a wide grin spread across his face. 'These guys are definitely ex-military. Combat veterans too.'

'How can you tell?' asked Bovalino.

'The way they move. When you've been there, detective, you can spot a combat veteran a mile off.'

Robbins pointed to the figure leading the way. 'I think this one could be female.'

Jones's eyes narrowed as he stared at the still image. 'How can you tell?'

'It's just the way she moves, her gait. It's very, very subtle, but it seems different to the others.'

Jones continued to scrutinise the footage for a long moment before he recoiled. 'Hang on a second. Where did they suddenly come from?'

'Exactly!' Robbins's grin grew even wider. 'We never saw those three go into the toilets from this side. Just coming into the club from that direction.'

'Is there an external exit down there?' asked Jones.

'Yes, a fire door.'

'Alarmed?' said Jones.

'Ordinarily, yes—' Robbins reached into a folder on his desk and pulled out a sheet of paper, which he handed to Jones. '—but I've checked the logs for the night and the alarm was deactivated for that particular door at around 5 p.m. that afternoon.'

Jones reviewed the data in his hand for a moment, then passed it Bovalino.

'So, who was guarding it that afternoon?' said Jones.

Robbins's face fell as he cleared his throat. 'Look, I know what you're going to think, but I'm telling you, it wasn't her.'

'Let me guess. Cartwright? said Jones.

Robbins nodded, and leaned back into his chair again, drumming his fingers on the edge of his desk. 'Trust me, this just isn't Sam's style. It's not in her nature. She's a professional operator, one of my best, in fact—'

'But she's also ex-military and, by your own admission, this crew is most definitely military trained,' Jones interrupted.

Robbins sighed. 'I know that. But I'm telling you, Sam wasn't involved.'

Jones offered a thin smile. 'Well, luckily that's for us to determine. Is she here today?'

'No. It's her day off. She's back in on the late shift tomorrow night.'

'Do you have her address? We'll need to speak with her as soon as possible.'

Robbins went to work on the laptop once more, then scribbled on a Post-it Note and handed it to Jones.

'Thank you, Mr Robbins,' Jones said as he took the note. 'You've been very helpful.'

'My pleasure. Anything I can do to help find Hollie, just let me know.'

Jones and Bovalino took their leave and headed for the door. As Bovalino opened it, Jones turned back to Robbins for a moment. 'Oh, and please. Keep what we've just discussed between us. It's important we limit the flow of information on this one to a very select few.'

This seemed to please Robbins, who pulled his shoulders back, his eyes gleaming. 'Understood, Sergeant, understood.'

10

PAYING A VISIT TO SAXBY'S OFFICE WAS THE LAST THING PHILLIPS wanted to do with such an urgent case on her hands. However, she knew that if she left her colleague from the Met to his own devices, it would most likely cause more grief than if she kept him at close quarters. So she made the pilgrimage to his hastily set up temporary office on the fifth floor. The door was open as she arrived, and he looked surprised to see her when she knocked.

'DCI Phillips. To what do I owe the pleasure this late in the evening?'

'Can I come in?'

'Of course,' Saxby replied, gesturing for her to take the seat opposite.

Phillips sat and surveyed the room. It was normally used as a private meeting space for the top brass but, under orders from the chief constable, the tables had been rearranged so it now looked like an expansive office.

'Looks like you're getting your feet under the table,' she observed. 'You planning on staying awhile?'

Saxby leaned back in his chair as a wide grin spread across

his face. 'As long as it takes.'

Phillips nodded. 'So, what exactly is your role in this investigation? I've yet to figure that out.'

Saxby looked puzzled. 'I thought it was pretty clear. I'm a kidnapping and negotiation expert.'

'I see. So, what exactly does that entail? Because as far as I can see, you've been here for two days now, and so far offered sweet FA in regards to helping us find Hollie.'

'Chief Inspector,' said Saxby with a chortle, 'I'm not here to help you *find* her. I'm here to help you communicate with the kidnappers – as well as to be the direct liaison with Sir Richard and his wife.'

'In that case, what were you doing at Marston's on the day we met?'

'I may not be a foot soldier, but I'm not immune to a short recce every now and again.'

'Hmmn. So, if I'm understanding this correctly, me and my team do the grunt work – you know, get our hands dirty and do everything we can to figure out who took Hollie and where she might be – and whilst we're doing all that, you just sit here and wait for either the kidnappers or Sir Richard to call. At which point you'll jump to it. Is that about right?'

Saxby smiled thinly. 'Chief Inspector. If you have an issue with the division of labour on this case, you need to take it up with your superiors. In the meantime, unless you have anything of value to share with me, I'd be grateful if you could leave me to get on with my work.'

Phillips nodded and started to stand, but dropped back into her chair. 'Actually, there is one thing I could do with your *expert* opinion on.'

Saxby folded his arms across his chest. 'And what might that be?'

'Why seven days?'

'I'm sorry. I'm not following you.'

'The kidnappers. Why be specific and tell Sir Richard he would hear from them in *seven days?*' said Phillips. 'That's unusual, don't you think? I mean, most kidnappers give nothing away. Every message comes without warning, to give themselves the edge.'

Saxby said nothing for a moment as he appeared to process Phillips words. 'In my experience, I'd agree that's true, yes.'

'So why did these guys specifically tell Sir Richard he'd hear from them in seven days? It doesn't make sense, does it?' said Phillips.

Saxby shrugged his shoulders. 'It's certainly not something I've seen before, but I can't say I'm overly concerned by it. I'm sure the reason will present itself in the fullness of time.'

Phillips would have laughed if she wasn't so concerned about how clueless Saxby appeared to be. In her experience, a gang capable of kidnapping a teenage girl from the middle of a crowded party – without leaving a single trace – would leave nothing to chance. The fact they had given him seven days was significant, but Saxby seemed oblivious to it.

'Right. Well, I can't sit around on the fifth floor all day. I'd better be getting back to the team. That grunt work won't do itself.' She stood and headed for the door.

'Oh, Chief Inspector,' Saxby called after her.

Phillips turned back towards him.

'You will keep me in the loop on *everything* now, won't you?'

Phillips did her best to appear earnest. 'Of course. Like the Aerosmith song says, "You won't miss a thing."' She was just about able to keep a straight face before she ducked out the door.

Back in her office sometime later, Phillips stood staring out of the window onto the dimly lit car park below, mulling the case over in her mind.

'You got a minute, Guv?' asked Jones from behind her.

Phillips turned to find Jones and Bovalino standing inside

the door. 'How did you get on?'

Jones appeared excited. He and Bovalino brought Phillips up to speed on the CCTV footage they'd seen, and what it implied for both Robbins and Cartwright.

'So, Cartwright's royally in the frame then?' said Phillips.

'Totally, Guv,' said Jones.

At that moment, Entwistle walked in carrying a large file. 'What was that about Cartwright?'

'Looks like she could be the person who let the kidnappers into the building,' said Phillips.

Entwistle hitched his buttocks onto the low cabinet next to Phillips's desk and handed her the file. 'Well, this lot doesn't look good for her either.'

Phillips opened the folder and began leafing through the pages as Entwistle narrated his findings.

'There was a good reason it was so hard to find anything on her before 2014. She changed her name that year, taking her mother's maiden name – Cartwright. Prior to that, she was Sam Blackwood.' Entwistle pointed to the folder in Phillips's hands. 'As you can see from the files, Blackwood was a combat medic with the Yorkshire Regiment. She served from 1997 to 2010, and completed multiple front-line tours of Iraq and Afghanistan before being medically discharged with PTSD. Since then, she's had a number of convictions for drug use, assault and using threatening behaviour.'

Phillips blew her lips and passed out some of the pages to Jones and Bovalino. 'Bloody hell, Entwistle, this is brilliant.'

Entwistle produced a knowing grin. 'If you look at the last couple of pages in the file, you'll see I also checked with the company she gave to the Marstons Club as a reference. They've never heard of either Sam Blackwood or Sam Cartwright.'

Jones chuckled. 'So, Mr Green's recruitment policy is not quite as meticulous as he made out then, Guv?'

'Clearly not,' said Phillips.

Entwistle continued, 'The final document in there is her current account bank statement. She deposited two grand in cash into it just last week. It's not her salary, as Marstons pays her electronically, and you can see her monthly payments going in on the first of every month. So I checked to see if she'd had any previous or regular transactions to gambling sites or any similar payments, in case she was doing any freelance or cash-in-hand work. I found nothing. The two grand cash is a totally random, one-off payment. Now, obviously, we can't prove where that money came from—'

'No, but it's a good place to start asking questions,' Phillips said. 'Great work, Entwistle. What did we do before you joined the team, hey?'

'Had a lot less conversations about bloody urban music,' joked Bovalino, which drew a collective chuckle from the room.

Phillips was excited now. 'Cartwright *has to be* our insider. It's just too much of a coincidence. And you know how I feel about *them*, don't you, Entwistle?'

Entwistle grinned and nodded his head. 'No such thing, Guv.'

'Exactly. No such thing,' Phillips repeated, playfully slamming her hand down on the desk. 'Right. Jonesy and Bov, first thing in the morning, you head over to Cartwright's and see if she can explain where the cash came from – and why she lied to get the job. See what else she's been lying about.'

Both men nodded.

Phillips continued, 'Entwistle, while they do that, I want you to pull up the CCTV footage of the Marstons Club on the night of the kidnapping. I want to take a closer look at the three masked individuals who came in through that fire door.'

'Consider it done, Guv,' said Entwistle.

Phillips checked her watch. 'Right, it's very late, and we all need to get some rest. Let's regroup in the morning with fresh eyes,' she said, pulling on her coat.

11

NOVEMBER 3RD

As always, Bovalino, an amateur rally driver in his spare time, insisted on driving. Jones had become accustomed to the sound of a car engine working at peak revs when Bovalino drove. He also knew better than to take a hot drink, as the big Italian regularly threw the car around corners with incredible speed and precision. By the time they parked the car on Broadwood Road in Wythenshawe, one of Manchester's southern suburbs and just a few miles from the airport, Jones breathed a silent sigh of relief and thanked God they'd made it in one piece.

Stepping out of the car, Jones surveyed the street. They were surrounded by large, semi-detached red-brick houses built in the 1960s. Aside from the roar of planes coming in to land and taking off at the airport, it was relatively quiet for the early morning. The weather was typical of an autumnal day in Manchester, with grey skies and rain not far away.

'What number is she at, Bov?' Jones asked.

Bov pulled his notepad from his coat pocket and leafed through the pages until he found what he was looking for. 'Thirty-six,' he said, and scanned the doors around them before pointing at a house a few metres away. 'That's the one. With the red door.'

A moment later, Jones led the way up the cracked concrete path to the front door of number thirty-six Broadwood Road. According to Entwistle, Cartwright's property was still council-owned, unlike the majority of her neighbours' homes. It showed, too. Whereas every other house on the street had been personalised and looked well cared for, it was evident that Cartwright's would benefit from a large dose of TLC. The front door needed a new coat of paint, the grass was almost knee-high, and a broken armchair – soaking wet and minus cushions – sat against the front wall of the house, just under the lounge window, which was covered by net curtains.

'I thought these military guys were trained to be tidy?' Bovalino muttered as they stopped at the front step.

Jones nodded. While he understood Bovalino's question, he knew that PTSD could change people in the most dramatic of ways.

In the absence of a working doorbell or knocker, Jones rapped on the weather-beaten front door with his knuckles. They waited a moment. No answer. He tried once more, harder and louder this time. Again, no response.

'Let's try round the back,' said Jones.

Bovalino agreed, and led the way down the path to the left of the house, trudging through the wet autumnal leaves that had fallen from the trees above them. When they reached the rear of the property, Jones banged on the back door. This time he hit it with such force, the frame shook. A few doors away, a dog barked in response, but the house remained unyielding.

'Maybe she's out?' said Bovalino.

'Maybe,' said Jones, and arched his back in an attempt to see into the upstairs windows – without success.

The grass at the rear of the house was knee-high, and a

rusted folding washing line stuck out of the ground, pegs hanging from the horizontal plastic cords.

Whilst Bovalino watched on, Jones stepped forwards, cupped his hands against the side of his head and pressed his face against the wide kitchen window. He waited a moment to allow his vision to adjust to the dark interior. That was when he saw it.

'Oh shit!'

'What is it, Jonesy?'

'We've gotta get this door open right now. Someone is lying flat on the floor in there, behind the kitchen table.'

Bovalino pressed his face to the glass. 'Jesus! I'll get the crowbar from the car.' He rushed back to the street.

He returned a minute later, a large metal bar in his right hand. He slipped on forensic gloves and handed a pair to Jones, then stepped up to the back door and smashed through the pane of glass above the lock and handle.

Once it was clear of all debris, Jones reached inside, released the Yale lock, pushed the door inwards and rushed inside, Bovalino close behind.

Jones immediately recognised Cartwright, her face visible to the side, her eyes black and wide open. Kneeling next to her, he checked her pulse at the neck for a long moment, then shook his head. 'She's dead.'

'Jesus,' said Bovalino. 'How?'

Jones stood and took a few careful steps round to the other side of the body, where he had full sight of her left arm. A large hypodermic needle was sticking out of her wrist. 'Looks like she OD'd,' he said, pointing to the needle.

Bovalino moved next to him. 'Bloody hell. Looks like she's been keeping a lot of things secret from her boss, doesn't it?'

'You're not kidding, Bov,' Jones said as he pulled his phone from his pocket and selected Phillips's number from the favourites. He activated the speaker function.

Phillips answered quickly. *'What you got Jonesy?'*

'Cartwright's dead, Guv.'

'You what?'

'Cartwright, Guv. She's dead. Looks like a heroin overdose.'

'Bollocks!' Phillips went silent for a long moment. *'How long do you think she's been dead?'*

Jones looked down at the body once more. 'Hard to say without Evans and his team.'

'Shit. Fox is gonna go mental on this one. Cartwright was our only lead.'

Phillips went silent once more. Jones knew her well enough to know her brain would be firing at lightning speed, trying to work out their next move.

After a long moment, she returned. *'Jonesy, call Evans and get him down there ASAP. I'm coming too.'*

'And what about Fox, Guv?'

'Leave her out of this for now. Let's see if we can find anything at the scene that might be of use. I'd prefer to break the news that our only lead is dead along with some new evidence rather than nothing.'

'Good point,' said Jones. 'And Saxby? When do we share this with him?'

'Ah shit. I'd forgotten about him,' said Phillips. *'He's the last person we need sniffing around at the moment. Look, he doesn't need to know for now. Let's crack on as normal. I'm leaving the office now, so I'll be with you in about forty-five minutes.'*

Jones ended the call and exhaled loudly. 'It's never bloody straightforward in Major Crimes, is it, Bov?'

'Never, Jonesy. But it'd be boring if it was.' Bovalino produced a half smile.

Jones pulled up Andy Evans's number. It was time to see if SOCO could salvage anything from this mess.

12

By the time Phillips arrived at Cartwright's house, the white SOCO tent had been erected outside number thirty-six. She parked the car in the only available spot – a few doors up the street – and sat for a moment to gather her thoughts. She had never enjoyed this part of the job – seeing a dead person for the first time. It was always in those initial moments of discovery that she could see and sense the loss of life, a fleeting sensation soon replaced by a cold numbness that allowed her to do her job. She tried to remember when that numbness had first set in, but having investigated so many deaths in her near-twenty-year career, she found herself struggling to pinpoint any one particular case. Checking her reflection in the rear view mirror, she straightened her ponytail, then cleaned her glasses. She wasn't sure why, but a deep sense of foreboding gnawed at her gut about the way this case was shaping up.

A few minutes later, Phillips arrived at the SOCO tent and began suiting up.

Jones appeared next to her in his forensic suit. 'Hi, Guv. They're ready for you.'

Phillips zipped up and pulled on her latex gloves. 'Ok. Let's have a look inside then, shall we?'

Jones led the way into the house and down the narrow hallway to the kitchen at the back. A host of scene of crime officers were busy taking photos and discussing various elements about the body. Bovalino's large frame – his white SOCO suit, as ever, bursting at the seams – stood with them. Seeing them walk in, he nodded.

'Looks like a heroin overdose, Guv,' said Jones.

'No signs of forced entry or anyone else here?' asked Phillips.

'I'm afraid not. We had to break down the back door to get in. Everything else was locked down tight.'

Phillips nodded and scanned the room before walking over to the body. Cartwright's face was squashed against the floor, but turned towards her right. Behind her lay an overturned dining room chair.

'From what we can see, so far, we think she took a fatal hit of heroin – or whatever she injected – then fell forwards off the chair and onto the floor. Evans reckons the needle's buckled and embedded in her arm, which would back up that theory.'

At that moment, Senior CSI Andy Evans approached. 'Jane.'

'So, we think it's an overdose then, Andy?'

'Looks that way,' said Evans. 'We've seen a spate of them in the last twelve months, with the introduction of fentanyl into the food chain. Nearly all ODs at the moment are down to it. It's bloody lethal stuff.'

Phillips nodded. 'I've heard a lot about it being cut with standard heroin.'

'It's super potent and indiscriminate, I'm afraid,' said Evans. 'Anyone taking heroin right now is playing Russian roulette.'

'Jones says there's no sign of foul play?'

'None at all. It appears to be an open-and-shut case.'

'And what about the time of death? Any ideas?'

'Based on rigor mortis and body temperature, I'd say between 1 and 3 p.m. yesterday.' Evans moved across the room to speak to one of his colleagues.

That gnawing sensation returned. Something wasn't right.

'What you thinking, Guv?' asked Jones.

Phillips breathed heavily through her nose. 'Our only link to the kidnapping gang accidentally dies hours before we can question her. It's all a bit neat, don't you think?'

'Yeah. I was thinking that too. But the problem is, there's not a single sign of anyone else being here, so if someone did kill her, how did they get in and out without leaving a trace?'

'Good question,' said Phillips.

Bovalino joined them. 'Guv. Jonesy.'

'Are you buying this as an overdose, Bov?' asked Phillips.

'It's pretty neat if it is.'

'That's what we were thinking,' said Phillips. 'Right, as we've established there seems to be nothing in here to contradict the overdose theory, let's try the neighbours. See if any of them saw anything out of the ordinary.'

Jones and Bovalino nodded.

At that moment, Phillips's mobile began to ring in her pocket. Stepping away, she removed her latex gloves and pulled the phone from her pocket. It was Superintendent Fox. *Shit.*

'Ma'am?' said Phillips, trying her best to sound natural as she walked outside onto the front path.

'Phillips, I need an update on the Hawkins case. I'm due to meet with the chief constable first thing in the morning. He'll want to know where we're at with it.'

'Well, naturally we're looking at all avenues, Ma'am.'

Fox scoffed. 'Don't spout PR shit to me, Phillips. I wasn't born yesterday. I want facts.' At that moment, a plane coming in to land thundered above Phillips's head. 'Where exactly are you?'

Phillips took a deep breath. Fox had a way of triggering her anxiety. 'I'm at Sam Cartwright's house.'

'Who?'

'She was one of the security team at the Marstons Club. She was on duty the night Hollie was taken.'

'I see. And how is she important?' said Fox.

'We dug up some interesting background on her and had hoped she was somehow connected to the gang.'

'You said "had hoped". Are you saying that she isn't?'

Phillips took another breath. 'I'm afraid we don't know, Ma'am. She's dead.'

'Dead? How?'

'Evans says it looks like an overdose. Potentially heroin mixed with fentanyl.'

'And do you agree with him?'

'Well, based on the evidence in the room, I'd have to say yes. To all intents and purposes, it does look like an overdose,' said Phillips, unconvinced by her own words.

'I sense a but?'

'Well, Ma'am. It all just feels a bit neat, to me. We get our first solid lead on the gang, and when we arrive to investigate, we find her dead.'

'You said "on the evidence in the room". What do you mean by that?' asked Fox.

'Well, there's no sign of forced entry – or a struggle – and it appears as though Cartwright was alone when she died,' said Phillips.

'Well, if there's no evidence to suggest otherwise – and it sounds as if there isn't – why can't you just accept it was an overdose?'

'I just think there's more at play here, Ma'am.'

'Of course you do.' Fox's tone was sarcastic.

Phillips continued, 'We're about to start canvassing the neighbours to see if they saw anything. Maybe—'

'You'll do no such thing!' interrupted Fox. 'You'll leave the SOCOs to it and get back where you should be – *on the case of finding Hollie Hawkins*. Time is critical in kidnapping cases, and we cannot be wasting it on investigating a bloody overdose.'

'But Ma'am—'

'No buts, Phillips. Round up your guys and leave it alone. I can probably fob off the chief constable in the morning, but I'll need to give him something concrete in the next forty-eight hours. If not, then Whitehall will be breathing down our necks, which will be very career-limiting for all involved. Do you understand what I'm saying, Phillips?'

Phillips bit her bottom lip. 'Yes, Ma'am.'

'Don't let me down. Believe me when I say this, Jane. Letting me down would not be good for *you*, or *your team*.' Fox ended the call.

13

CHIEF PATHOLOGIST DR TANVI CHAKRABORTTY GREETED Phillips in the reception to the mortuary, which was situated in the lower basement of the MRI – Manchester Royal Infirmary – in the heart of the city. As ever, her tall, athletic frame was covered with perfectly pressed blue scrubs. Her long brown hair was tied back against her head to reveal blemish-free brown skin, which carried the slightest hint of make-up.

'Afternoon, Jane,' said Chakrabortty.

'Afternoon, Tan.'

'You ready?'

Phillips nodded her agreement and Chakrabortty led the way through to the examination room.

Once inside, they took up their positions on either side of the examination table, on which Cartwright's naked body was laid out, torso and genitals covered by a green sheet.

For the next twenty minutes, Phillips watched on in silence as Chakrabortty worked her way through the post mortem, carefully dissecting the chest before opening up the large cavity. It was in moments like this that Phillips found herself questioning her choice of career. Surely there were less macabre ways to earn a living?

Chakrabortty worked quickly but with grace, and with the utmost respect for the person the body had once been. Phillips admired her immensely, as well as considered her a friend. Together they had witnessed many strange – and, at times, brutal – things over the years, which had further strengthened their bond.

After ninety minutes, the post mortem was complete. Chakrabortty had confirmed that the cause of Cartwright's death was a straightforward heroin overdose. As Evans had suggested, small traces of fentanyl were found in Cartwright's blood.

'So, there's no sign of anything that would suggest foul play, Tan?' asked Phillips.

'Nothing that I can see. Like I said, the heart condition was almost certainly the reason she arrested, and it's more than likely that the introduction of fentanyl triggered the heart attack. So, unless someone was aware she had the condition and spiked her heroin – which would seem a bit of stretch – it looks to me like a simple overdose.'

This was not what Phillips wanted to hear. 'But what if that *is* what happened?'

'What? Someone spiked her drugs?'

'Yeah. What if someone put the fentanyl in her normal supply and that's what killed her? It could be possible, right?'

Chakrabortty considered the question for a moment, before answering. '*Possible*, yes. But probable? I'm not so sure. This death is identical to twenty or more I've worked on already this year. Fentanyl is lethal, and it's *everywhere* at the moment. It's November now, and I can pretty much guarantee that, before Christmas, I'll see probably five more bodies in this room where the death is connected to heroin mixed with fentanyl.'

Phillips shook her head with dismay. She was back to square one.

'Sorry, Jane. You know I'll always be straight with you. The evidence points to Sam Cartwright having died from massive heart failure, the cause of which was a heroin overdose.' Chakrabortty removed her latex gloves and gestured for them to leave the examination room. Phillips took her leave.

Back in the mortuary reception, Phillips thanked Chakrabortty and said goodbye before heading for the door back into the main hospital.

As she climbed the stairs to the ground floor and the exit to the car park, she considered what to do next. Her thoughts turned to Hollie and the ransom video; a scared and vulnerable teenager, locked away, threatened with a violent death. Her heart went out to the young woman, and she prayed she and the team would make a breakthrough soon. If not, she knew only too well what it could mean for Hollie. Finding her quickly was a matter of life and death.

BACK IN THE CAR, Phillips drove on autopilot, alone with her thoughts; something that, at times, could prove destructive. She was her own worst critic, and her lack of progress was very frustrating. As she guided the car onto Oldham Road, her phone began to ring through the car stereo system, jolting her back to reality. She didn't recognise the number, but answered it anyway.

'Phillips,' she said as she passed the Wing Yip Chinese supermarket on her left.

'There, she is.' The tone was condescending, and she recognised it immediately.

'DCI Saxby,' she said, wishing she hadn't answered the call after all.

'I understand you've been chasing a dead end since we last spoke.'

Phillips felt her hackles rise. 'That's a matter of opinion.'

Saxby chuckled. *'Really? Well in that case, why don't you bring me up to speed with what you've been doing.'*

Phillips took a deep breath and held it for a moment, before releasing it in silence. She then spent the next few minutes debriefing Saxby on Cartwright.

When she was finished, Saxby was quick to deliver his assessment of their efforts, so far. *'So, you're no further forward, then?'*

Phillips was tempted to tell him exactly what his opinion meant to her, in the most colourful language she could muster, but thought better of it. She'd worked with Saxby's type before, and felt confident he wouldn't hesitate to use it against her further down the line. Instead, she threw the onus back on him. 'Well, as the resident expert, have you managed to find any leads?'

Saxby scoffed. *'As I explained last night, I'm not a bloody beat copper, Phillips.'*

Phillips felt a snarl forming on her lips, but kept her cool. 'Silly me. Sorry, I forgot. You're just the "liaison" guy.'

'Exactly,' said Saxby. *'I'm so glad we understand each other. Well, I can't stay on the phone chatting to you all day. I'm on my way to see Sir Richard now. Of course, I'll have to debrief him on how you and your team are progressing with the investigation. And I have to say, based on your lack of progress so far, it's not a conversation I'm relishing.'*

'I'm sure you'll survive,' said Phillips, and ended the call without saying goodbye.

She drove in silence for the remainder of the journey, all the time replaying the conversation in her mind.

As she pulled into her space in the car park of Ashton House, a sick, nervous agitation lay heavy on her stomach. As if this case wasn't difficult enough, now she had to contend with

Saxby roaming around in the shadows, saying God-knew-what to Hawkins. She had felt this way before, and she was damn sure of one thing; the longer MCU went without a breakthrough, the bigger the shit-storm that would be heading her way.

14

PHILLIPS OPENED THE DOOR TO THE MAJOR CRIMES INCIDENT room with a heavy heart. The investigation was going nowhere, and she had no idea how to kickstart it. As she stepped into the room, the noise that greeted her lifted her spirits. Excitement hung in the air alongside the buzz of phone chatter and phones ringing across the room. Phillips stopped in her tracks and stood for a moment, watching with pride. Her team hadn't given up hope. Neither should she.

Jones spotted her and made his way across the room with one of the young uniformed officers in tow, clutching a Manila folder against her chest. 'Guv, PC Lawford has found something you should see.'

'Come into my office,' said Phillips.

Jones and Lawford took a seat each opposite Phillips, and the young constable passed over the file. She couldn't be any older than twenty-five, and appeared bright-eyed and enthusiastic. Her natural red hair was striking against her white and black uniform.

Phillips opened the file. Inside were three one-page profiles of two men and one woman. 'Who are we looking at?'

Lawford's neck had flushed, and she cleared her throat before speaking. 'Well, Ma'am,' she said, clearly a little nervous, 'Sergeant Jones asked me to look into Hawkins and anyone connected to him that has a military background. I've found some people I think are of interest. The first one is Ian Holmes. He's fifty, and Hawkins's current head of security at the Hawkins Industries PLC HQ in Trafford. He's a retired Major from the Royal Signals. Served twenty-two years and left the Army in 2012.'

Phillips scrutinised Holmes's profile. The picture was from his old army ID card.

Lawford continued, 'The next one is Marcus Baker. This guy's forty-nine and used to work for Hawkins, but he left twelve months ago – under a bit of a cloud, according to the person I spoke to. He was head of security before he quit and Holmes took over. A retired Staff Sergeant in the Parachute Regiment—'

'A Para?' asked Phillips, her eyebrows raised.

'Yes Ma'am. Highly decorated after tours in Northern Ireland, Bosnia, Belize, Iraq and Afghanistan. He left the military in 2010 and, since quitting his job with Hawkins, manages the security for a property developer in Manchester.'

Phillips stared at Baker's picture. His steely eyes seemed to stare back at her. 'Ok, and who's the woman?'

'Kerry Matthews, Ma'am. She's currently on the Hawkins payroll as part of the security team at HQ. She reports to Holmes. A retired Lance Corporal and combat medic from the Mercian Regiment. She also saw active combat in Iraq and Afghanistan. She's thirty-nine and left the military in 2016.'

Phillips laid the file on her desk and leaned forwards. 'Any criminal records in their histories?'

'No Ma'am. They're all clean. Not so much as a parking ticket on any of them.'

Phillips glanced at Jones, who produced a knowing grin; the young officer had done well.

'This is great work, Lawford,' said Phillips, tapping the file on the desk, 'and very detailed.'

Lawford blushed and a coy smile flashed across her face. 'Thank you, Ma'am.'

Phillips retrieved Baker's profile and stared at it for a moment before speaking. 'You mentioned Baker had left under a bit of a cloud. That's hardly standard HR chatter. Where did you get that info from?'

Lawford smiled again. 'I have an old friend from university who works at Hawkins's place. I figured she would be able to give me the kind of information I couldn't get from regular sources. So I arranged to meet her for a drink last night. With a few G&T's in her, she filled me in on some of the gossip. It seems Baker and Hawkins had a disagreement that ended in a bit of scuffle. That's not the official line, of course, but everyone reckons it's what happened. Baker left the same day, according to my friend.'

Phillips's eyes widened. 'Did he now? Well, that *is* interesting. Very interesting, in fact. Where did you say he works now?'

Lawford checked her notes. 'Fletcher and Henderson Developments in Spinningfields. Just behind the Magistrates' Courts.'

'Well, I think I owe Mr Baker a visit. I'll head over there first thing tomorrow morning,' said Phillips. 'Jonesy, while I'm doing that, you and Bov head over to Hawkins's Trafford HQ and speak to Holmes and Matthews. Let's see if they can vouch for themselves the night Hollie was taken.'

'No worries,' said Jones. He got up from his chair and headed for the door.

Phillips turned her attention back to Lawford. 'Well done, Constable. This is first rate work.'

Lawford blushed again.

'Have you ever held any ambitions of being a detective?'

Lawford's eyes seemed to double in size, and almost sparkled. 'Oh yes, Ma'am. That's what I'm hoping to do.'

Phillips tapped the file on the desk with her index finger. 'Keep coming up with work like this, and I'm sure it won't be long before you do.'

'Thank you, Ma'am.'

'Right. Get back out there and see what else you can find on these three. Plus anyone else with a military background who might be connected to Hawkins.'

'Yes, Ma'am,' said Lawford as she stood, her chest pushed out with pride. 'Thank you,' she added as she left the room.

Phillips watched the young constable stride away, and smiled. Lawford reminded her of herself at that age. She'd shown real initiative, and a willingness to go above and beyond to get a result. Phillips expected she'd be seeing a lot more from her in the future.

15

NOVEMBER 4TH

THE OFFICES OF FLETCHER AND HENDERSON DEVELOPMENTS were located on the top floor of 3 Hardman Square, an uber trendy office block situated in Spinningfields, in the heart of Manchester city centre. Phillips stepped out of the lift into the double-height office space, which was fully glazed from floor to ceiling and offered magnificent views across the city and beyond. In the distance, to her left, she could see the arched roof of the Etihad Stadium, home to Manchester City Football Club, while to her right stood Manchester United's Old Trafford Stadium. Straight in front of her, a sleek, curved reception desk housed a smart-looking receptionist, who sat behind a huge Apple Mac computer, wearing a phone-headset.

As Phillips approached, the receptionist offered a broad smile. 'Welcome to Fletcher and Henderson Developments. How can I help?'

Phillips returned her smile. 'I'd like to speak to Marcus Baker, if possible.'

The receptionist nodded. 'I'll just see if he's in his office. Can I ask who's calling?'

Phillips looked her dead in the eye. 'Detective Chief Inspector Phillips.'

The receptionist raised her eyebrows. 'I won't be a second,' she said as she keyed into her computer. A moment later her call connected, and she explained who was waiting at the front desk to the person on the other end – Phillips assumed it was Baker. The receptionist finished the call and looked up at Phillips once more. 'Mr Baker is on his way down. Please take a seat. He won't be long.'

Phillips did as requested and sank into one of the lush grey leather sofas set aside for waiting guests. They were positioned alongside a tall smoked-glass refrigerator stocked full of 'designer' water bottles, as well as Prosecco and bottles of Peroni. You wouldn't find anything like that in Ashton House, thought Phillips. Just getting milk for the tea and coffee was a challenge some days.

A few minutes later, Phillips spied a tall, well-built man walking towards her. He wore a navy blue suit that fitted immaculately, and was coupled with a maroon tie.

As he moved to just a few feet away, he made eye contact and offered her a wide smile, as well as his outstretched hand. 'Chief Inspector Phillips?'

Phillips stood and shook his thick hand, which enveloped hers in a tight grip.

'I'm Marcus Baker. Head of security at Fletcher and Henderson. What can I do for you?'

Up close, Phillips realised he was about the same height as Bovalino – around six foot four – but slimmer and more athletic. She noted a thick vertical scar on the left-hand side of his face, running from a point above his left eye, along the length of his cheek and down to his jugular.

'I'd like to talk to you about your time working for Sir Richard Hawkins,' said Phillips.

An awkward smile flashed across Baker's face. 'Hawkins? I'm not sure there's much I can tell you.'

'Oh?'

'Legal reasons, I'm afraid,' Baker added by way of explanation.

'Could we speak somewhere more private?' asked Phillips.

'Of course. We can go to my office. Please, follow me.'

Phillips followed Baker as he led the way through the middle of the large open-plan space, fitted with myriad desks. Each, it seemed, came complete with a young, bright-looking individual, glued to their computer. At the end of the office, they reached a row of private offices with frosted glazing. Baker opened a door emblazoned with his name and title. As she followed him inside, Phillips took a moment to survey the space. It was military neat and simply furnished in some style. Lots of smoked-metal fixtures, and yet more frosted glass on the huge desk next to the window, which again offered more of the views of the city. Baker offered her a chair opposite him and took a seat himself. Sitting forwards, he linked his fingers on the desk. His eyes were wide and expectant.

Phillips wasted no time in getting to the point of her visit. 'I understand you worked for Mr Hawkins as his head of security until about twelve months ago?'

'That's correct,' said Baker.

'Can you tell me why you left the company?'

Baker flashed a wry smile. 'I'm afraid not, Chief Inspector. I signed a gagging order in return for a lump-sum payment.'

Phillips nodded. 'I can assure you that anything you tell me will be treated in the strictest confidence.'

'I understand that, but I really don't think I can share anything with you. I'm sorry.'

Phillips fixed him with a steely glare. 'This is police business, Mr Baker. I don't think gagging orders apply.'

'Look. I promise I'm not trying to be difficult here,' said

Baker. 'It's just, I could get into a lot of trouble if I speak to you about what happened.'

Phillips sat back in her chair and folded her arms across her chest. 'Well. I could always come back with a bunch of paperwork that would compel you to tell me, plus a gang of uniformed coppers, if you'd prefer that option?'

Baker raised his hands in mock defence. 'No. No, that won't be necessary. If you put it like that, then I'll tell you what you need to know.'

Phillips said nothing, but maintained her glare.

'But if *anything* gets back to him, it's on *you*. Ok?'

'Of course,' said Phillips. 'So, what happened?'

Baker sat back in his large office chair, but kept his fingers connected to the desk. 'The truth of the matter is, we had a disagreement and I punched him in the gut.' Baker smiled briefly at the memory. 'He fell to the floor like a sack of potatoes.'

'Must have been some disagreement to end in a fight?'

'It was. And I wouldn't call it a fight. A fight takes two people to actually *throw* punches.'

'So, you hit your boss. Isn't that a bit excessive?'

'Ordinarily, I'd say yes. But if you've ever met Hawkins, you'll know he's a massive arsehole. He'd had it coming for a very long time.'

Phillips found herself half smiling.

Baker obviously noticed. 'So you *have* met him, then?'

Phillips nodded. 'Yes. I have met Richard Hawkins. And off the record, I'd have to say your assessment seems pretty accurate. But then again, *having* met him, it seems odd to me that he would pay anyone off for punching him to the ground.'

Baker chortled. 'Pride, Chief Inspector. The man thinks he's smarter, fitter and stronger than anyone else. News of him hitting the ground like a lead weight, with one punch? Well, that's not the sort of thing he wanted out in the public domain.

He also knew that if I was arrested, I wouldn't have gone quietly. You see, I know all about some of his more private business dealings. So he did what he always does – he threw money at the problem to make it go away. I left that day, and walked away with six months' salary to keep my mouth shut.'

'Can you tell me what the argument was about?' said Phillips.

Baker shook his head. 'I'm afraid not. *That* detail must stay with me. Unless – as you say – you compel me to tell you. That way, Hawkins's Rottweiler lawyer will come after you as opposed to me.'

'When you say, "Hawkins's more private business dealings", what do you mean by that?'

'I'm sorry, Inspector. You'll have to ask him about that. My lips are legally sealed on that, I'm afraid.'

Phillips nodded. As interesting as this information was, it wasn't the real reason she was here. So she changed tack. 'Where were you on the night of the thirty-first of October?'

Baker's brow furrowed. 'Halloween?'

'Yes.'

'Why do you need to know?'

'Just standard procedure,' said Phillips.

'Er, well, I'm pretty sure I was here. Let me check my calendar.' Baker took a moment to type in his computer, and waited a few seconds. He stared intently at the monitor for a long moment, then tapped a finger on the screen. 'October thirty-first, I was here all day and worked into the evening. Ah yes, I remember now. I was behind schedule on a security plan for a new development in Salford. I worked late to catch up.' He clicked the computer mouse. 'According to the security log, I left just after midnight.'

'And is there anyone who can verify that?'

Baker recoiled. 'Verify it? I'm sorry, Chief Inspector. Have I done something wrong?'

Phillips remained stoic. 'I'm looking into something confidentially. At this stage, I just need to know if anyone can vouch for your whereabouts on the night of Halloween.'

'Should I be calling my lawyer about now?'

Phillips stared him straight in the eye. 'I don't know, Mr Baker. Should you?'

Baker flashed an awkward smile. 'I have nothing to hide, I can *assure* you of that. Here, I can prove it to you.' He once again tapped on his keyboard. A moment later, he turned the monitor to face Phillips, then clicked his mouse, which activated the video on the screen. It was CCTV footage taken from the main office. According to the timestamp, it showed Baker entering his office at 7 p.m. He was carrying what looked like cartons of Chinese food. Baker engaged the fast-forward function on the video, and for the next few minutes they watched as time passed and his office door remained closed. At 00.03 a.m., Baker emerged, wearing a long coat and carrying an umbrella. He switched off the light and walked out of the shot.

'I can show you the other cameras, if you like,' said Baker. 'There's a bunch of them that will have tracked me all the way to the car park.'

Phillips did her best to hide her growing frustration. 'Thank you, but that won't be necessary.'

Baker's smile returned, and a glint lit his eyes. 'So, my whereabouts have been verified then?'

'It looks that way, yes,' said Phillips, without feeling.

'So, is there anything else I can help you with?'

'No, thank you. I think I have everything I need.' Phillips stepped up from the chair. 'You've been most helpful,' she said, and moved towards the door.

'Off the record, Chief Inspector,' said Baker, 'what's Hawkins been up to now?'

Phillips turned and forced a thin smile. 'Thank you for your time, Mr Baker. I can see myself out.'

16

JONES AND BOVALINO PRESENTED THEMSELVES, ALONG WITH THEIR credentials, at the reception of Hawkins Industries PLC HQ in Trafford Park, and asked to see Holmes and Matthews. They remained standing whilst they waited.

Holmes was the first to appear, a short, stocky man with a shaven head to hide his receding hairline.

'Detective Sergeant Jones,' said Holmes, his tone clipped, his accent the middle-England drawl of a military officer. 'I understand you would like to speak to me?'

Jones stepped forwards and offered his outstretched hand, which Holmes gripped and shook, with force. 'Yes, Mr Holmes. Could we go somewhere more private?'

'Of course,' said Holmes, eyeing Bovalino.

'Sorry. This is my partner, Detective Constable Bovalino.' The big Italian nodded as Jones continued. 'He's here to speak to Kerry Matthews.'

Holmes's brow furrowed. 'Can I ask what this is about?'

Jones produced a wide grin. 'I'll explain everything once we're out of earshot.' He inclined his head in the direction of the receptionist.

Holmes followed his movement. 'Very well. Come this way please.' He turned on his heels and set off towards the belly of the building.

Jones turned to Bovalino and winked before dropping in behind Holmes.

A few minutes later, Holmes poured two mugs of coffee from the percolator in the corner of his plush office on the eighth floor of the nine-storey building. He presented one to Jones and took a seat in silence. He sipped from his mug.

Jones took the initiative. 'When was the last time you spoke to Sir Richard?'

Holmes took a moment to answer. 'Yesterday at 3 p.m. He called regarding a shipment that's due to be sent to Islamabad in the next few days. Why do you ask?'

Jones dodged the question. 'How did he sound?'

'Like he always does: *to the point.*'

'And are you aware of his personal circumstances at the moment?'

Holmes's eyes narrowed. 'Are you referring to his daughter, Hollie?'

'Yes.'

'I know she's disappeared, and that Sandra is very upset,' said Holmes.

Jones wondered whether Holmes was being coy or whether Hawkins had been economical with the truth. He decided to keep his cards close to his chest and let things play out. 'And what about Sir Richard? Did he sound upset?'

'Upset? No. Irritated? Most definitely. But then Hollie is a highly strung teenage girl – not the type of person Sir Richard has much time for.'

Jones felt his lips purse. 'Are you saying he doesn't get on with his daughter?'

Holmes took another drink of coffee. 'They're not close, that much I know. He's old-school – like me. We believe the father's job is to provide for the family. The cuddles, and what-have-you, is the domain of the mother.'

Jones nodded softly. 'How well do *you* get on with Sir Richard?'

'He's my employer and he pays me well to do a job for him. I get on with him just fine.'

'Is he a good boss?'

Holmes's face remained deadpan. 'He's blunt, and he has very high standards. If you meet those standards, you have no reason to worry. If you don't, he'll let you know – in no uncertain terms. It's not too dissimilar to the military. So it suits me fine.'

'That's right. You were a Major in the Royal Signals, weren't you?'

Holmes's eyes widened. 'I see you've done your homework, Sergeant.'

Jones smiled and wiggled his fingers in the air, as if typing. 'Google. What did we do before it?'

'Can I ask *why* you googled me?'

'Oh. Just standard practice when I'm making enquiries,' said Jones.

Holmes sat forwards now, clasping his hands together on the desk. 'Yes. And you still haven't managed to explain your reasons for being here.'

'Like I said. Just making enquiries,' said Jones. He changed tack. 'Where were you on the evening of Halloween, Mr Holmes?'

Holmes didn't flinch. 'The night Sir Richard's daughter disappeared? I was working.'

'Whereabouts?'

'Here. I was in my office all night, working on the transport routes for the Islamabad shipment. When you're transporting munitions, security is paramount.'

'I see,' said Jones. 'And can anyone verify that?'

'Do they need to? Have I done something wrong, Sergeant?'

Jones shook his head. 'Just checking where you were.'

'Why? Do you think I had something to do with the girl's disappearance?'

'Did you?' said Jones, his eyes locked on Holmes's.

Holmes said nothing for a moment, and instead stared back at Jones. 'No. I was here all night. My second in command, Kerry Matthews, can vouch for me on that one. She was here, working with me until the early hours.'

~

KERRY MATTHEWS ARRIVED a few minutes after Jones and Holmes had left the reception area. She was smartly dressed in a light grey suit with a white shirt. Her hair was tied back in a neat bun on the top of her head, and her thin-framed spectacles reminded Bovalino of Phillips. She was certainly around the same height.

Bovalino introduced himself, and suggested they move to a private room for a quick chat. A few minutes later, they stepped out of the lift onto the fourth floor.

'My office is just down here,' Matthews said as she beckoned for her guest to follow her.

Bovalino made mental notes of the office layout, and couldn't help but sense this was a serious place of work. There was next to no chatter, and the predominant sound was that of fingers typing furiously at keyboards.

Matthews opened the door to a glass office, ushered Bovalino inside, and closed the door firmly behind her.

'I must say, this is a very tidy office, Miss Matthews,' Bovalino said as he glanced around the small, but impeccably clean, space.

Matthews appeared to blush slightly as she sat opposite him. 'Old habits die hard.'

'How long have you been on civvy street?'

'Too long,' said Matthews.

'You miss it, then? Life behind the wire?'

A look of sadness flashed across Matthews's face. 'Yes, I bloody do. I wish I'd never left.'

'And why did you leave?'

'I thought the grass would be greener. But it's not. Look, do you mind if I ask what this is about?'

'At this stage, it's confidential,' said Bovalino.

'I'm guessing it has to be something to do with Hollie Hawkins going missing.'

'You know about that?'

Matthews nodded. 'Everyone does. Sir Richard's not what you might call discreet. When he's on the phone, his voice carries a long way, if you know what I mean?'

'So what's it like working for Hawkins, then?' asked Bovalino.

Matthews blew her lips. 'Could be worse, I suppose.'

'Do you have much to do with Sir Richard?'

Matthews shook her head and chuckled. 'Me? A lowly fourth-floorer? No, he doesn't venture down here where the plebs live. He deals strictly with our head of security, Mr Holmes.'

'And what's he like?'

'Is this confidential?' asked Matthews.

'Strictly,' said Bovalino.

'Well. He's a typical officer. Likes everything to be done formally and to the letter. Insists on being called Mr. Holmes. To be honest, I don't even know his first name. And there's also a clear hierarchy, with Holmes at the top. And trust me, he doesn't *ever* let anyone forget it.'

'Did you work with Marcus Baker, before he left?'

'Yes, I did. That's half the problem,' Matthews said with a

sigh. 'Marcus hired me, so Holmes still thinks I'm "Baker's man". Even though I'm a woman.'

'Why did Baker leave?' said Bovalino.

'You're sure this is confidential?'

'One hundred per cent.'

Matthews grinned. 'Rumour has it he punched the old man out cold.'

Bovalino feigned ignorance. 'The "old man"?'

'Sir Richard. Apparently Baker knocked him clean out during an argument.'

'What was the argument about?'

Matthews shrugged. 'I dunno. Baker never said. Just came into the office and told me he was leaving, there and then. But it didn't take long for the rumours to start doing the rounds. It was the most exciting thing to happen round here for years.' Matthews stared into space, seemingly lost in her own thoughts, for a moment. 'God, I wish I'd seen that.'

'And have you seen Baker since then?'

'No. Not a word. I heard he picked up a new plush gig in the city, but I don't know the details. It's a shame. I liked him. He was a decent bloke. But then again, he wasn't an officer, was he?'

Bovalino changed tack. 'Can you tell me where you were on the 31st October between 7 p.m. and midnight?'

'Halloween?'

'Yes.'

'Well, I was here working with Mr Holmes,' said Matthews. 'I remember it because I was relieved that I wouldn't have to spend the night answering the door to trick-or-treaters.'

'And what were you doing working so late?'

'Planning the transport route for a shipment of munitions. It's due in the next few days, and Sir Richard and Mr Holmes like everything planned in detail – well in advance. Hawkins signs off the routes personally.'

'And you didn't go out at all? For food, perhaps?'

Matthews shook her head. 'No, we ordered in. Dominos.'

'I see,' said Bovalino. He placed his pad and pen back in his jacket pocket. 'Well, I won't take up anymore of your time.'

'I'm not sure I've been much help, detective?' said Matthews, as Bovalino stood up.

'Actually, you've been very helpful. Thank you. I'll see myself out.'

WALKING out onto the streets of Spinningfields, Phillips cursed her luck. On paper, Baker looked like a viable suspect, with his military background and an abject hatred for Hawkins. But with a new successful career and not a single criminal conviction, it seemed unlikely he was involved in the kidnapping. Plus, CCTV made for a compelling alibi in court.

To satisfy her own curiosity, Phillips stepped away from the building and stared up in the direction of Baker's office, hoping to see some means of exit – a balcony, or fire stairs that would have allowed him to leave his office without being seen on the internal cameras. But the building was made of sheer glass with no opening windows.

She pulled her phone from her pocket and called Jones.

'Hi, Guv. I'm in the car with Bov, so you're on speaker. How did you get on with Baker?'

Phillips let out a loud sigh. 'Solid alibi with CCTV evidence. How about you guys? Did you get anywhere with Holmes and Matthews?'

'Holmes and Matthews were working *together* that night,' said Jones.

'Yeah,' added Bovalino, 'with a bunch of witnesses, and CCTV, to back them up, too.'

'So everyone has an alibi?' said Phillips.

Bovalino continued, 'Yep. Pretty convenient that Holmes's and Matthews's alibis are each other, though. They could be lying to cover for each other.'

'It's possible, Bov,' said Phillips. 'But even if they are lying, it'll take time to break those alibis. And time is one thing we don't have right now. Like Fox said to me the other day, the longer this goes on, the less chance we have of finding Hollie alive.'

'So what's our next move, Guv?' said Jones.

Phillips said nothing for a long moment as she considered her options. 'Let's get back to Ashton House and regroup. See if Entwistle, or any of the wider team, have found anything else that might help.'

'No worries. We'll be back there in half an hour,' said Jones.

Phillips checked her watch; it was 11.00 a.m. 'Right. I reckon I'll be there about the same time. I'll see you in my office at 11.30.' She ended the call.

17

HOLLIE LAY HUDDLED UNDER THE BLANKET IN AN ATTEMPT TO fend off the cold. She stared at the cracked ceiling, wondering where in the world she was. She had no idea what day it was, and with no windows in her tiny room, she had lost all sense of time. She was hungry, though, and her stomach growled for food. What was going to happen next? she wondered.

Without warning, she heard the lock in the door being released. She scrambled to sit up, back against the wall, knees bent to her chest and the blanket covering her up to her neck. She had taken to sitting like that whenever one of the gang entered the room. She wasn't so certain it made her any safer, but it was something.

Which of her captors would be visiting this time? The first thing to appear from behind the door was a tray containing a plate of food, followed by a pair of black gloved hands, and finally one of the gang members, wearing an *Army of Two* mask. This mask had a blue stripe fixed across the nose-plate, and the man wearing it was short and thickset. Hollie had not seen him before.

He said nothing as he placed the tray on the table in the middle of the room.

'What is it this time? Roast beef?' she said, her tone sarcastic.

He didn't respond.

Hollie continued. 'Well, whatever it is, you're wasting your time. There's no way I'd *ever* eat anything *you lot* made.'

'Blue' stared at her for a long moment, silent.

Hollie felt a shiver run down her spine. 'You don't say much do you?'

Blue moved a few steps closer and folded his thick arms across his chest. Then he leant forwards so that the mesh that covered his eyes was level with Hollie's eyes. He remained creepily silent as he stared at her.

Hollie swallowed hard as she tried to control the fear that rose in her chest.

Blue continued to stare, and she could hear him breathing heavily through the mask. She wanted desperately to hold his gaze, but it was too uncomfortable and she finally looked away. Then without warning, Blue turned on his heels and moved back to the door. He knocked three times, then opened it without looking back. The heavy door closed behind him with a thud, and a second later, she could hear the lock as it was reinstated.

Hollie let out a loud breath of relief as she attempted to fight back her tears, trying desperately to remain calm. It was no use, and a moment later her tears erupted and her shoulders began to shake.

After a few minutes, she regained some level of control and, as she wiped her face, her eyes fell on the steam rising from the plate of hot food. Intrigued, she threw off the blanket and placed her sock feet on the icy concrete floor, then walked over to the table. She stared down at the plate of food. She wasn't sure exactly what it was, but it appeared to be vegetarian. She looked back towards the door and wondered if someone was watching her from the other side.

She was determined to follow through on her threat not to eat, but as the delicious aromas hit her nose, her mouth watered and her stomach rumbled, begging her to eat. It was no use.

Resistance was futile, and in one rapid movement, she took a seat and began to devour the hot food with haste.

18

Back at Ashton House, Phillips was already in her office when Jones and Bovalino strode through the incident room. She signalled for them to join her, along with Entwistle, for a debrief.

Entwistle was last to share his update. 'I don't know if this is anything, Guv, but I took a look into Hawkins's extended family. I found this.' He passed over a set of papers, stapled together. 'These are the latest accounts for Gerry Donald, Sandra Hawkins's brother – Richard's brother-in-law.'

Phillips began flicking through the pages as the rest of the team looked on.

'Gerry is a former business partner of Hawkins,' Entwistle narrated. 'They invested in some future tech that had come out of Cambridge University.' He passed across a printout of a *Financial Times* newspaper article dated from the previous year. 'At the time of this article, Gerry had bragged they were on the cusp of creating something as game-changing as Facebook, or the iPhone.'

Phillips scanned the article briefly. 'This is Donald in the picture?'

'Yes. That's him.'

'So, why no Hawkins in the article?' asked Phillips.

'I thought that was strange, too. So I checked him out, and found there's almost nothing on him in print – particularly around his business dealings. There's the odd bit about his charity donations and occasional bouts of philanthropy, but nothing else.'

Jones chimed in. 'I've heard that about Hawkins before. He's supposed to be fiercely protective of his privacy.'

'Most arms dealers are,' said Bovalino, sardonically.

'So, what does all this have to do with Hollie's kidnapping?' asked Phillips.

Entwistle continued, 'Well, in the end, the deal went south. Turns out the PhD students from Cambridge, who they claimed came up with the concept, had copied someone else's idea. When Donald talked to the press, it alerted the guy who had created the technology, and he sued Donald and Hawkins for breach of copyright. They eventually settled out of court for an undisclosed sum – rumoured to be in the millions – and Hawkins abandoned the project.'

'Jesus. He wouldn't have liked that, would he?' said Jones.

Phillips found herself smiling again. 'Can you imagine his temper tantrum when he found out the students had lied to him?'

'The things is,' said Entwistle, 'Hawkins had the money to walk away. His net worth is in the region of a hundred million. But Donald? Well, before this deal, he ran his own estate agency. He borrowed heavily – where from, I'm not sure yet. And when it all went pear-shaped, he lost everything. Came out of it with £750,000 of debt, according to his accounts.'

'Which makes for a *very* compelling motive to kidnap Hollie Hawkins,' said Phillips, as she sat forwards and placed the files on her desk, 'and then demand four million quid to give her back!'

'Exactly,' said Entwistle.

'Excellent work. Well done,' said Phillips.

'Bloody teacher's pet,' joked Bovalino under his breath, drawing a smile from Jones and Entwistle.

Phillips picked up the newspaper article from the desk once more and stared at the picture of Donald. 'He looks like an estate agent, doesn't he? Proper smarmy in this picture,' she observed, feeling her face screw up as she turned the article round to show the team. 'Jonesy and Bov, I want you to pay Mr Donald a visit. Let's see where he was on the night of Halloween.'

Bovalino nodded, and Jones smiled. 'It'll be our pleasure, Guv,' he said.

Phillips continued. 'Entwistle, find out who financed the deal for Donald. Did the money come from a bank, or somewhere else? That information could be very important to this case.'

'Consider it done.'

'And see what else you can find on him. Known associates, criminal records, you know the drill. I don't need to tell you, time's ticking, guys. If you find anything of interest, *anything at all*, let me know immediately.'

A chorus of 'Yes Guv' filled the room.

'Right. Let's crack on,' said Phillips. She dismissed them to their duties.

19

IF HE WAS SHORT ON MONEY, GERRY DONALD DIDN'T SHOW IT. His home address was a penthouse apartment in the exclusive NV Building in Salford Quays, overlooking the water, and complete with a concierge to announce visitors.

After explaining who they were and who they wished to speak to, the concierge rang Donald, who gave his approval to let them up to his apartment. The concierge stepped out from behind the desk, ushered them into the elevator and used his security pass to select the correct floor. A moment later, as the doors started to close, he wished them well.

Jones and Bovalino found themselves surrounded by mirrors as the elevator moved upwards at speed. They watched in silence as the digital display above their heads counted up with each floor that passed, until they reached their destination – the penthouse.

The doors opened smoothly, and they stepped out into a small, brightly lit hallway that contained only one door. Jones knocked on it, and they waited. A moment later, the door opened, and they came face to face with the man they had seen in the newspaper article, Gerry Donald.

Jones introduced them as they presented their credentials, which Donald scrutinised for a long moment.

'Officers. Please come in,' said Donald, clearly satisfied, as he stepped aside and held out his arm.

As Jones moved into the apartment, he was struck by the sheer size and opulence of the place. The open-plan design encompassed an enormous lounge area, complete with a flat-screen TV that filled most of the wall, and a designer kitchen built around a large black cooking island. Polished wood covered every inch of the floor and a grand, sweeping staircase at the opposite end of the apartment led up to a mezzanine floor where, Jones assumed, the bedrooms were located. Three of the four double-height walls were made of glass, and one led onto a large balcony that offered almost 360-degree views of Manchester.

A strong aroma of brewing coffee hung in the air, and it smelt expensive.

'This is some place you have here, Mr Donald,' said Jones.

Donald flashed a wide grin. 'I like it.'

'It's a bit bigger than my gaff,' added Bovalino.

Donald's grin remained. 'Can I get you gentlemen a coffee? I'm just about to have one myself. It's fresh.'

Jones and Bovalino nodded, and Donald moved into the kitchen.

Whilst he prepared the coffee, Jones and Bovalino moved to stand next to one of the windows, taking a moment to enjoy the spectacular views in silence. With the autumnal sun shining brightly in the clear blue sky, the water of the Quays sparkled like precious gems. They watched as a plane landed at Manchester Airport to the south. The cities of Salford and Manchester were sprawled out below them, giving way to hills in the distance, leading towards the Peak District beyond. It was quite breath-taking.

Donald returned with their coffees on a tray, which he

placed on the enormous glass and chrome coffee table in the centre of the lounge area. He motioned for them to take a seat on the large designer cream sofa, whilst he chose the matching armchair.

'I'm assuming you're here about my niece?' Donald said as he passed out the steaming mugs, complete with coasters.

'Yes, Mr Donald. I'm afraid so,' said Jones.

'My sister called and told me. She's very upset, as you can imagine,' said Donald.

Bovalino took a polite sip from his coffee mug before replacing it on the coaster on the table. Then he retrieved his notepad and pen.

Jones started in. 'Could you tell us when you last saw Hollie?'

Donald sat back in the armchair, cradling his mug, and his eyes moved up towards the ceiling. He said nothing for a moment. 'I'm guessing it would be about eighteen months ago. Maybe even two years.'

'Really? That seems a long time,' said Jones.

Donald took a drink of coffee. 'Yes, I suppose it does.'

'Is there a reason for the long absence? I mean, living in the same city, I would have thought you might have seen her more regularly.'

Donald produced a thin smile. 'I've never been a kid person, Sergeant. They're just not my thing. Plus, it's no secret my brother-in-law and I don't get on.'

'You're talking about Sir Richard Hawkins?'

'Yes, I am. Wherever possible, I try not to say his name. And I certainly never use his bloody *title*.'

'We understand you were in business together. Can you tell us about that?' said Jones.

Donald shrugged. 'What's to tell you? I asked him to invest in a project that would have made us millions – if not billions – and at the first sign of trouble, he bailed out.'

'And did you lose money on that deal?' asked Jones, feigning ignorance of the man's financial affairs.

Donald drained the remainder of his coffee and set the mug down on the table. 'Yes I did. A *lot* of money.'

'Can you tell us how much?'

Donald fixed Jones with an icy glare. 'A lot, Sergeant. *A lot.*'

'Did Hawkins lose on the deal too?'

'Hardly,' scoffed Donald. 'It was bloody pocket change to him.'

Jones moved forwards to the edge of his seat. 'Is it true you were sued for breach of copyright on the idea?'

'Yes we were. But if *he'd* held his nerve, instead of panicking, they'd have backed down in the end. Even his flash lawyer told him to fight it, and that bitch – Johnson – rarely loses.'

Jones raised an eyebrow and glanced at Bovalino, who had stopped writing. 'Johnson? As in Nicolette Johnson?'

'Oh, you know her?' said Donald.

'You could say we're familiar with her, yes,' said Jones, nodding.

'Well, in that case, you'll know that if Nic Johnson thinks a case is worth fighting, you fight it. But Richard wouldn't. Said he didn't need the publicity and just wanted it to go away. So he paid the guy off, and that was that. No more investment, no more money.'

'I'm guessing that upset you?' said Jones.

'Yes it bloody did! If he'd shown some balls, instead of acting like a total pussy, I'd be a very rich man right now.'

Jones made a point of scanning the apartment around them. 'By the looks of things, you seem to be doing ok, Mr Donald.'

Donald's eyes narrowed. 'I don't want to be "doing ok", Sergeant. I want to be filthy rich! And that prick ruined everything.'

'You sound pretty angry about it all.'

'Well, wouldn't you be? Imagine it, Sergeant. If you were just a few months away from sealing the deal of a lifetime, with enough money at the end of it all to buy an island. And then your partner here, Constable Bovalino, walked away and it collapsed.' He pointed at the big Italian. 'How would you feel about *him*?'

Jones looked at Bovalino, who grinned back at him. 'Well, I guess if you put it like that—'

'Exactly!' said Donald. 'So, in answer to your question, yes, I am angry. Very bloody angry, in fact.'

Jones locked eyes with Donald. 'Angry enough to kidnap your niece?'

Donald guffawed. 'Are you being serious?'

'Very,' said Jones.

'Me? A kidnapper? *Don't be ridiculous.* There's no love lost between me and my brother-in-law – and he still owes me a lot of money – but I wouldn't have the first clue how to kidnap anyone. Nor would I want to. That kind of thing is far too dangerous for me. I'm a businessman, Sergeant. Not a criminal.'

'When you say businessman, do you mean estate agent?' said Jones, deliberately trying to dent his ego in order to provoke a reaction.

Donald was barely able to hide the snarl that appeared on his lips. 'I'm a property developer these days, Sergeant. *There's a difference.*'

Jones glanced at Bovalino, and suppressed the grin that threatened to spread across his face. 'Can you tell us where you were on the night of Halloween?'

'The night Hollie was taken?'

'Yes.'

Donald's brow furrowed. 'You can't *seriously* think I had anything to do with it?'

'We're asking everyone who's close to the family, Mr Donald, for the purpose of elimination. That's all.'

'Well, if you must know, I was here with my girlfriend, Shelley.'

'And she can vouch for you, can she?'

'Of course.'

Jones looked around the apartment once more, noting the overtly masculine decor. 'Does she live with you?'

'Pah! Good God, no. I'm not the settling-down type, Sergeant. She has her own place in the city, but stays here from time to time. Has her own toiletries in the bathroom, but that's about the extent of my commitment.'

'And did Shelley stay over on Halloween?

Donald nodded. 'Yes, she did. She came over straight from work at about seven. I cooked a Thai meal, we had a few glasses of Chardonnay, and watched *Scream* on the TV. We went to bed about midnight.'

Bovalino scribbled the details in his notepad.

'Can we have her contact details, please?'

'Of course,' said Donald, as he got up from the chair. He walked over to a large office desk positioned against the wall just beyond the lounge. After rummaging through a couple of drawers for a moment, he found what he was looking for. 'Here it is.'

As he returned, Jones and Bovalino stood up from the sofa.

'Her business card,' said Donald, handing it over to Jones, who read the details aloud.

'*Shelley Hamilton – Corporate Insurance Broker, HM Parsons Ltd.*'

'That's her. Their offices are on Portland Street, up near Piccadilly.'

Jones tapped the card against his fingers. 'Thank you for this, Mr Donald.'

Donald checked his watch, then folded his arms against his chest. 'Are we done, gentlemen? I'm afraid I must be getting on.'

'Yes,' said Jones, 'I think we have everything we need.'

'I'll show you out, then.'

Donald ushered them to the door and bade them farewell.

Back in the safety of the descending lift, Jones and Bovalino debriefed.

'Well, he was a bit of a wanker, wasn't he?' said Bovalino, with a chuckle.

'Grade A, Bov. Grade A.'

'Do you think he's involved?'

Jones rubbed his chin. 'I dunno. There's something not right about him, but is he a kidnapper? I'm not so sure.'

'Time to check out his alibi,' said Bovalino.

'Yeah. We may as well head over there now. Although something tells me that, by the time we get there, Shelley Hamilton will be expecting us.'

Bovalino chuckled again. 'Yeah. I'd put *your* money on it, Jonesy.'

20

PHILLIPS WALKED BACK TOWARDS HER OFFICE FROM THE SMALL kitchen situated at the end of the incident room. She held a cup of instant coffee in her hand as she approached Entwistle. 'How you getting on with Donald's finances?'

Entwistle blew out his lips and tapped the screen on his laptop with his pen. 'This guy is up to his eyeballs in debt, Guv.'

Phillips leaned in to get a closer look.

Just then, Jones and Bovalino walked in.

'Here they come, Bonnie and Clyde,' joked Entwistle.

Phillips chuckled and stood upright as they approached. 'So, how was Mr Donald?'

'A grade-A wanker, boss,' said Bovalino.

'Really? I am surprised,' Phillips replied sarcastically as she took a mouthful of coffee.

'He has an alibi, Guv,' said Jones, 'but, conveniently, it's his girlfriend. We've just been to see her at work, and she backs up his story. The night Hollie was taken, she claims she went to Donald's apartment straight from work. He cooked, they drank, watched a movie, and went to bed.'

'And do you believe either of them?'

Jones pursed his lips for a long moment before responding. 'In all honesty, no. That said, I'm not sure they were involved in the kidnapping either. But there's definitely something about the pair of them that I don't like.'

'And she's *way* too hot for a guy like him, Guv,' Bovalino chimed in. 'She's a petite, dark-skinned goddess. And, well, he's just a prick with lots of cash.'

Entwistle shook his head. 'More like a prick with lots of debt. He's up shit creek without a paddle at the moment.'

Jones raised an eyebrow. 'Really? He certainly doesn't live like that. You should see the place – a huge penthouse overlooking the water – it's like something out of that movie, *Wall Street*.'

'And you're right,' said Entwistle. 'They're both lying. Unless, of course, someone used his car that night – *or* it was stolen.'

Phillips's interest was piqued. 'Why do you say that?'

Entwistle passed a document over to Phillips, which contained a number of CCTV photos. 'These were taken from the ANPR cameras on Ashton Old Road, at 7.30 p.m. on the 31st of October. That's Donald's car.' He pointed with his pen.

Jones craned his neck to see the images. 'I knew they were bloody lying.'

Entwistle passed over another printed picture. 'This is CCTV footage taken from one of the fixed road cameras outside the Northern Snooker Centre in Openshaw.'

Phillips examined the printout. 'There's Donald's car again.'

'And guess who happens to be the owner of the Northern Snooker Centre?' said Entwistle.

'Go on,' said Phillips.

Entwistle flashed a wide grin. 'The wife of Manchester's most elusive gangster, Adders Bahmani.'

Phillips eyes widened. 'You're bloody kidding me!'

'I am *not*, Guv,' said Entwistle, and pointed at the picture once more. 'Look. The car next to Donald's belongs to Bahmani. I've checked the DVLA database.'

Bovalino moved round to stand beside Phillips. 'Can I see that?'

Phillips passed him the image.

'Entwistle's right,' said Bovalino nodding 'A white Range Rover. I remember seeing it at Bahmani's yard. It was there when we questioned him about the canal murders case. It's a great big thing with blacked-out windows'

'So what the hell is Donald doing hanging around with a gangster like Adders Bahmani?' said Phillips.

Jones shrugged his shoulders. 'Could *he* be behind the kidnapping?'

Phillips chewed her lip for a moment as she considered that as an option. 'It seems a bit high-profile for a slug like Bahmani. He usually prefers to stay in the shadows. Having said that, he's certainly capable of kidnap. Sex Crimes and Trafficking have been after him for years on suspicion of kidnapping young girls from Eastern Europe.'

'Yeah, but he puts *those* girls to work on the streets, Guv,' said Jones. 'Whoever took Hollie wants four million quid to give her *back*.'

Phillips nodded softly. 'Good point.'

'I do have another theory, Guv,' said Entwistle.

'And what's that?'

'Bahmani could be Donald's business partner.'

'Go on,' said Phillips.

'Well. Having looked into his records, in the last twelve months Donald has been refused finance by every major bank in the city. He wanted money for a development project he's been trying to get off the ground near the airport – a hotel and leisure complex. He then tried the smaller banks, but they turned him down too. It seems that, after the public lawsuit he and Hawkins got themselves into, he's considered a big risk. As of today, Gerry Donald is in debt, and I mean *serious* debt.'

'How much?' asked Jones.

'Just shy of one million, sterling.'

Bovalino whistled. 'Wow.'

Entwistle continued, 'On paper, Bahmani owns very little, as we know. Every business he's involved in is registered in his wife's name. But, talking to one of the guys in Sex Crimes earlier today, they believe he's super cash-rich. Maybe Donald wants him to finance the development deal?'

'That's a very dangerous game to be playing if he does,' said Jones. 'Bahmani's hardcore. If things go south in a deal with him, he won't just walk away like Hawkins did. He'll make sure Donald ends up *in* the development, if you know what I mean.'

Phillips nodded.

At that moment, PC Lawford approached, looking a little sheepish. 'I'm sorry to interrupt Ma'am, but Chief Superintendent Fox has just called.'

'And *you* spoke to her?'

'Yes, Ma'am. The phone in your office has been ringing off the hook for the last five minutes, so I picked it up from my extension.'

'And what did Fox say, exactly?' asked Phillips.

'She wants to see you right away, Ma'am. In her office.'

Phillips rolled her eyes. 'Ok. Thank you, Lawford.' She turned back to the team. 'Right, guys. Finding the link between Donald and Bahmani is our new priority. See what you can find as a matter of urgency.'

Each of the men nodded.

'In the meantime, I'd better go and find out what our beloved leader wants.'

21

FOX'S PERSONAL ASSISTANT, MS BLAIR, KNOCKED ON THE DOOR to the chief super's office, then waited. A moment later, Fox shouted, 'Come!'

Blair opened the door and ushered Phillips inside.

Fox sat typing into her PC at her desk. She didn't look up or acknowledge Phillips, who took a seat without being asked.

When her task was complete, Fox turned to face Phillips. Her expression was grave as she peered over her spectacles. 'What the hell is going on, Phillips?'

Phillips recoiled slightly, in her chair. 'I'm sorry, Ma'am?'

'DCI Saxby informs me that Sir Richard is less than impressed with the progress MCU has made on finding his daughter. It's three days since we received the ransom demand and we have nothing to go on.'

Phillips's brow furrowed. 'I must have missed a meeting. Are we reporting to Sir Richard now?'

'Don't be facetious,' said Fox. 'You know full well how connected he is. He's been on the phone to the chief constable, raging about how incompetent we all are.'

Phillips shook her head. 'Bloody Saxby's been stirring the pot again.'

'That may very well be the case, but the truth of the matter is, Sir Richard's daughter's been missing for four days now and we're still no closer to finding her. Has there been any further contact from the kidnappers?'

'No, Ma'am. Nothing.'

Fox let out a loud sigh. 'This investigation is going nowhere fast. You don't need me to tell you, it doesn't look good for MCU, Phillips.'

'I know, Ma'am. And I was sure Sam Cartwright was the connection to the gang, but whatever she knew died with her.'

'You're referring to the junkie found dead the other day?'

'Yes, Ma'am.'

Fox let out a loud sigh and leaned back in her chair. 'Well, as you say. Whatever this Cartwright woman did, or didn't, do, we'll never know, now. *She's dead.* So it's time to move on from that one.'

'I hear what you're saying, Ma'am, but with your permission, I'd like to canvass her neighbours and see if they saw anything suspicious the night she died. We had planned to do it the day we found her body, but you told us it was a waste of time.'

'And I'm telling you the same thing now. Cartwright was a junkie who died of an overdose. We will not be wasting any more time investigating her death. I want all your energies focused on finding the girl.'

Phillips knew there was no point arguing.

'So, what else have you got to go on?' said Fox.

'Well, Ma'am. It looks like Hollie's uncle – Sandra Hawkins's brother – Gerry Donald, could be a person of interest,' said Phillips.

'Really? How so?'

'He's in serious debt. Almost a million pounds.'

Fox's eyes widened. 'Go on.'

'Entwistle has been digging into his finances, and it turns out he and Hawkins were in business together, on a deal that went south. Hawkins pulled the plug and cut his losses – easy to do when you're worth millions. Not so for Donald, who lost everything. His financial situation, and the fact he blames Hawkins for it, means he has motive. Plus, he lied about his whereabouts on the night Hollie was taken. He says he was at home with his girlfriend, but we've tracked his car to a snooker club in Openshaw.'

'An interesting development indeed.'

Phillips sat forwards now. 'What's even more interesting is the fact the snooker club is registered to the wife of Adders Bahmani.'

Fox's eyes appeared to glisten. '*Bahmani* could be involved?'

'It's possible, yes. But then again, it's not his usual caper. It seems quite high-profile for a man used to operating in Manchester's underbelly.'

Fox appeared excited now. 'Well, well, well. If we could finally nick that reptile, it'd be a feather in MCU's cap, for sure. And Chief Constable Morris would be royally pissed off it was my team that nicked him. Every copper in Manchester knows Bahmani's crooked, but no one's been able to prove anything despite years of trying.'

'If you're in agreement, Ma'am, I'd like to search Donald's home,' said Phillips, 'see if we can find anything that could lead us to Hollie.'

Fox nodded eagerly. 'Of course. Based on the danger to life, and the fact he lied about his alibi, you should have no issues with the search warrant.'

'Thank you. I'll sort the paperwork and we'll go in at dawn.'

'Excellent. I want a full debrief as soon as the raid's complete,' said Fox.

'Yes, Ma'am,' said Phillips, and stood. 'I'd better get back downstairs and brief the team.'

Fox appeared lost in her own thoughts now as she shooed Phillips away. 'Adders-Bloody-Bahmani,' she muttered under breath, and her Cheshire Cat grin reappeared. 'We might finally have got you,' she added, as Phillips left the room.

22

NOVEMBER 5TH

Presented with the warrant to search Donald's apartment, the overnight concierge had no choice but to allow Phillips and the team access to the elevator. As instructed, there was no call ahead, and a uniformed officer remained in reception to ensure this instruction was strictly adhered to.

As Phillips, Jones, Bovalino, Entwistle, and a number of uniformed officers gathered in the cramped hallway outside Donald's penthouse, Phillips checked her watch; it was 5.30 a.m. Jones and Bovalino had explained the layout of the apartment, in detail, during the briefing just over an hour ago. The plan was that she and Bovalino would take the bedrooms, whilst Jones, Entwistle and the uniformed team would take downstairs.

Phillips ensured her stab vest was secured in place, then whispered final instructions. She gave the uniformed officers the green light. The heavy metal battering ram slammed into the wooden frame, and the door burst open at the first attempt. Phillips led the team inside and rushed towards the staircase.

The apartment was cavernous. By the time Phillips reached the top of the stairs – with Bovalino in tow – Donald stumbled out of his bedroom, having clearly been woken by the noise. He wore pyjamas, and his hair was dishevelled, eyes puffy.

'What the hell is going on?' he shouted, an incredulous look on his face.

Phillips flashed her ID. 'DCI Phillips, from the Major Crimes Team.' She handed him a copy of the warrant, 'We have authority to search these premises in relation to the disappearance of Hollie Hawkins.'

'You've gotta be joking!' said Donald. Phillips pushed passed him and headed for his bedroom. Donald followed her. 'Look, I told your officers the other day, I haven't seen my niece for almost two years. *I* didn't bloody kidnap her!'

Phillips turned to face him and looked him dead in the eye. 'Are you alone, Mr Donald?'

'Yes. Yes, I am.'

'So no one else is in the apartment?'

'What? Apart from ten tooled-up coppers, you mean?' said Donald, in a sarcastic tone.

Phillips scanned the room. 'Your girlfriend, Shelley Hamilton. She's a regular visitor, isn't she?'

Donald dropped onto the end of the bed. 'Sometimes, yes. But not tonight. Tonight I'm all alone, as my bed will testify.' He waved his arm across the enormous mattress, which did indeed appear to have been slept in by just one person.

'Can I have your phone, please?' said Phillips.

'What?'

Phillips took a step closer and held out her hand. 'Your phone. Where is it?'

Donald ran his fingers through his matted hair. 'Why do you need my phone?'

Phillips was in no mood to explain every detail of the search. 'Read the warrant. It explains the scope of what we can, and can't, have access to. If you do, you'll see your phone now belongs to me. Hand it over.'

With some obvious reluctance, Donald stood up from the bed and retrieved his iPhone from his bedside cabinet. He handed it to Phillips.

'Thank you,' said Phillips with a thin smile. 'Bov, can you escort Mr Donald downstairs and have one of the uniformed team sit with him, out of the way?'

'Yes, Guv.' Bovalino stepped forwards and locked his thick hand around Donald's bicep. 'This way, sir,' he said, and yanked him out of the room.

A few minutes later, when Bovalino returned, Phillips had already begun her search. With hands protected by latex gloves, she was rummaging through his sock drawer.

'I've left him with PC Lawford, Guv.'

'Good,' Phillips said, without turning round. 'You can start in the en suite.'

Bovalino headed into the en suite and started his search. For the next twenty minutes, Phillips checked every drawer, cabinet and hanging rail in the room, but came up with nothing. After a thorough search of the space under his bed, she stopped to take a breath and scrutinised the room. 'What are you hiding, Donald?' she whispered.

At that moment, Bovalino reappeared from the en suite. Phillips could tell by the look of disappointment on his face that he'd had no luck either.

He shrugged. 'Sorry, Guv. Nothing in there.'

Phillips let out a frustrated sigh. 'Nothing in here, either. Let's check the next bedroom.' She got to her feet.

Bovalino nodded, and followed her through to the second bedroom.

As Phillips opened the large wardrobe doors, a voice from downstairs shouted, 'Guv!'

She stopped what she was doing and walked out onto the mezzanine balcony to peer over the rail.

It was Jones, who stood looking up at her. 'You'd better come and see this.'

Phillips instructed Bovalino to continue his search, then headed downstairs to where Jones was stood waiting. As she moved closer, he leaned in and whispered – so Donald couldn't hear – 'I think we might have found the link to Bahmani.'

Phillips raised an eyebrow.

'It's in the downstairs toilet.'

Phillips followed Jones into the surprisingly large WC. Entwistle stood in front of a mirrored wall, holding a large object covered in foil. He presented it to her as she moved closer.

'Looks like heroin, Guv,' Jones said. 'We removed the side panels on the bath and found it taped to the underside of the tub. Entwistle is just about to run a mobile test on it.'

Phillips took a closer look. It did indeed look like a large pack of uncut heroin, probably about two kilos. She allowed a wide grin to spread across her face. 'Who's been a naughty boy, then?'

Just then, one of the uniformed team knocked on the toilet door. 'Ma'am, have you got a second?'

A moment later, Phillips entered the utility room, where Donald kept his washing machine and other laundry paraphernalia.

'I found it down here, behind the washing machine,' said the officer, who took a knee and pointed his finger at a black leather bag lying on the floor against the wall.

Phillips knelt next to him and opened the bag with a gloved finger. Inside were bundles of twenty-pound notes. 'Jesus. There must be fifty grand in here,' she said. She picked up the bag and got back to her feet. 'Let's see what he has to say about this lot.'

Phillips strode into the lounge area where Donald sat, with PC Lawford keeping a watchful eye on him. She dropped the bag on the glass coffee table and opened it wide enough for him to see some of the notes poking out. 'Where did you get this?'

Donald's eyes darted in the direction of the money, then back to Phillips. 'I've never seen that before.'

Phillips scoffed. 'Oh, come on, Donald. Don't piss us about.'

'I'm telling you the truth. I've never seen that bag in my life.'

Phillips shouted for Entwistle to join her.

A moment later he appeared, still holding the packet of heroin. 'It's heroin, Guv.'

Phillips nodded. 'We found it taped to the bottom of your bathtub. Is that not yours, either?'

Donald stared at the package in silence for a long moment before he finally spoke. 'I'd like my phone call, please.'

Phillips chortled. 'This isn't bloody *Law and Order*, mate.'

Donald appeared indignant. 'I know my rights.'

'Funny you should say that,' said Phillips, as she cast her eyes towards Entwistle, 'because I'm arresting you for possession with intent to sell class-A narcotics. Entwistle, caution him, then help him get dressed.'

Entwistle stepped forwards. 'You do not have to say anything, but it may harm your defence if you do not mention, when questioned, something which you later rely on in court. Anything you do say, may be given in evidence...'

SOMETIME LATER, Phillips and Jones stood in the interview room observation suite, staring at the monitor feed from Interview Room Two.

'How the hell can he afford Nic Johnson as his counsel?' said Phillips, with considerable irritation. 'She's a bloody nightmare.'

Jones nodded his agreement as the door opened and

Entwistle entered, followed by Bovalino, who made straight for the monitor.

'Jesus. I heard he'd got Johnson as his lawyer,' said the Italian.

Entwistle looked puzzled. 'What is it with everyone and this chick?' He stared at the monitor. Nic Johnson was dressed impeccably in a designer black suit, her stair-rod-straight jet-black hair cut into a sharp bob.

Jones folded his arms and hitched his buttocks onto the desk behind him. 'You've clearly never had the pleasure of doing battle with Nic Johnson then, Entwistle?'

'No, I haven't.'

Jones continued, 'Well, if you had, you'd know she's as tough as a cat's head, and strikes fear into almost everyone in the CPS. She rarely loses her cases. And if I were you. I wouldn't let her hear you refer to her as "a chick" either. She's likely to cut your balls off and feed them to you on a silver platter.'

'As you can see, Jones is a big fan,' Phillips commented. 'He met her for the first time when she represented Marty Michaels. As you know, he was up for murder a few years back.'

'The case where you got shot?' asked Entwistle.

'That's the one,' said Phillips, without feeling.

'She's a piece of work, I can tell you,' added Jones.

'Yes, she is,' said Phillips. 'Not long after that case, she used the fact *I* broke the law to help Michaels – her own bloody client, I might add – to discredit me in court on another case. The jury bought it and her client got off on a rape charge. He was a mega-rich footballer who was sleeping with a fifteen-year-old girl. He was found not guilty and went straight back to his old life. In fact, he's still playing.'

'Do you think she'll try that one again here, Guv?' asked Jones.

Phillips shook her head. 'The CPS will be prepared for it

this time. They were blindsided in that case.' She turned her attention back to the monitor. 'How is the lab getting on with the full test of the heroin?'

'We'll have the results back this afternoon,' said Entwistle.

'Good,' said Phillips. 'Okay. So, aside from the suspected heroin and a bag of cash, there was no trace of Hollie in the apartment. *But* we do know Donald's broke, he has serious beef with Richard Hawkins, and lied about where he was the night Hollie was taken. If he is involved, we need to use his current predicament to get him to talk – *and fast*. Time is running out for Hollie.'

The team around her nodded.

'Jonesy, I want you in there with me.'

'Yes, Guv.'

'You two, stay here and make notes. If you spot anything we miss, pull us out. Ok?'

Bovalino and Entwistle nodded again.

Phillips picked up her leather-bound notepad from the desk and took a deep breath. 'Right then, Jonesy. Let's do this.'

As PHILLIPS and Jones entered Interview Room Two, Gerry Donald remained seated behind a small desk, arms folded against his chest. He said nothing, instead fixing them both with an icy stare.

Nic Johnson followed her usual strategy of trying to assume control of the room from the outset. She stood and offered her hand to both Phillips and Jones before she returned to her seat and started in on the defensive. 'My client fully intends to cooperate with your investigation. We are very confident that all of this can be explained quite simply.'

Phillips nodded, but said nothing – her own tactic that helped her gain control. She placed her notepad on the table and busied herself as she set up the DIR – digital interview recorder. When she was finished, she turned to look directly at Johnson. 'I must say, Ms Johnson, I'm surprised to see you representing Mr Donald. Especially when I consider *your* considerable fees and your client's *financial* issues.'

Johnson didn't flinch. 'Whoever settles my client's account is none of your business, Inspector.'

'*Chief* Inspector, actually,' Phillips shot back.

'Oh? You were reinstated?' said Johnson, obviously feigning surprise. Phillips was sure there was little gossip Johnson did not know of in the Manchester criminal justice system.

Phillips ignored the comment and pressed on. 'Now then, Gerry. We found a large quantity of uncut heroin in your apartment, along with a hold-all containing almost fifty thousand pounds in cash. Can you tell us how they came to be in your possession?'

Donald opened his mouth to speak, but Johnson cut in before he had chance to answer. 'My client has shared with me the fact he has a drug problem. The heroin was for personal use.'

'Two kilos? That's some habit, Gerry,' Phillips scoffed.

Johnson continued, 'And he won the money playing poker.'

Phillips snorted loudly. 'That must have been a high-stakes game.'

'It was,' said Johnson.

'I'd like to hear it from Gerry. If you don't mind?' said Phillips.

Johnson beckoned Donald to move in close, and whispered in his ear. Donald nodded, and turned his attention back to Phillips. 'Like Nic said. It was a high-stakes game. Five grand buy-in.'

'If you won the cash playing poker, why did you say you'd never seen it when we found it this morning?'

'I panicked. That's all.'

'Ah, right, you panicked,' said Phillips.

'Yes, I did. It's pretty bloody scary having a load of coppers kicking your door down and going through your stuff, I can tell you.'

Phillips continued, 'We've checked your finances and you're flat broke, Gerry. In fact, you're worse than broke – you have debts of close to a million quid. If that's the case, where did you get five thousand pounds for the buy-in?'

Donald shrugged. 'I borrowed it.'

Phillips raised her eyebrows. 'And who would be stupid enough to lend you money?'

'My sister,' said Donald.

'Sandra?'

'That's right. You can check with her. She gave it to me last week,' said Donald.

'And does Sir Richard know he's funding your gambling habit?'

Donald screwed his face up. 'It's not a habit, but I very much doubt it. And besides, that bastard owes me a lot more than five grand.'

Phillips latched on to Donald's obvious irritation. 'That's right. You and he were business partners, weren't you?'

'If you can call it that. In my world, a partner doesn't walk away and leave you in the shit!'

Johnson placed her hand on Donald's wrist – a silent cue used by lawyers when they felt their client was sharing too much information. It worked. He stopped talking.

Phillips continued. 'Is that how you feel? That Richard Hawkins left you in the shit?'

Donald looked at Johnson, who cut in now. 'Chief Inspector. How are my client's business dealings relevant to why we're here?'

Phillips ignored the question and changed tack. 'Where did you get the heroin, Gerry?'

Donald glanced at Johnson, who nodded. 'Just some guy I met in the pub.'

Phillips eyes narrowed. 'You bought two kilos of heroin from a guy in the pub?'

'Yes.'

'And does this guy have a name?' asked Phillips.

'He never told me. And I didn't ask.'

Phillips reclined in her chair and folded her arms across her chest. 'So how did you meet this guy in the pub, then?'

'He walked up to me at the bar and asked me if I wanted any gear. I said yes. He said, "How much?" and I said as much as he could get.'

'And which pub was this?'

Donald shrugged again. 'I can't remember.'

Phillips produced a wry grin and allowed herself a chuckle. 'That's convenient, isn't it?' She signalled for Jones to take over.

Jones leant forwards in his chair. 'Where were you on the night of the 31st October, Gerry? Halloween?'

Donald tutted. 'You know where I was. I've already told you this yesterday.'

'You may have told me, but DCI Phillips hasn't heard it from you, yet. Could you share your movements with her?'

Donald released an exasperated sigh. 'Like I told you and that big fella that was with you, I was at home with Shelley, all night. We had dinner, watched a movie, then we went to bed.'

Jones opened a Manila folder on the desk. 'So you never left the apartment?'

'No, I didn't.'

'And Shelley stayed the night?' Jones continued.

'Yes. She came to mine straight from work, and then went back to work the following day.'

Jones glanced down at his own notes. 'Ah yes. She confirmed that when we spoke to her yesterday.'

Donald flashed a lopsided grin, evidently pleased with his alibi.

'Which seems a bit odd, really,' said Jones, as he pulled an A4 print from the folder. He turned it to face Donald and Johnson, and slid it across the table. 'Because we came across this ANPR footage of your car in Openshaw, on the night you and Shelley claim to have been at yours all evening. Are you familiar with automatic number plate registration cameras?'

Donald's mouth fell open, but no words came out.

'They're all over the city,' said Jones, 'and each time your car drives past one, it registers on our database. It means we can track cars twenty-four hours a day. Do you know where this picture was taken?'

Donald's eyes darted towards Johnson, who cut in. 'How is any of this relevant to my client's arrest this morning?'

Phillips rejoined the fray. 'It's relevant to your client's credibility regarding his whereabouts on the night of October 31. Now answer the question, Gerry. Where was your car parked when it was caught on this ANPR camera?'

Johnson nodded for Donald to answer. 'The Northern Snooker Club in Openshaw,' he said, his voice cracking as he spoke.

'Bingo,' said Jones theatrically. 'And what were you doing there on Halloween, when you told us you were tucked up in bed with your girlfriend?'

'Playing snooker,' said Donald, regaining his composure.

'Who with?'

'On my own,' said Donald.

Jones nodded. '*Of course you were.* Do you by any chance know who owns the Northern Snooker Club?'

Donald's nose twitched. It was obvious enough for Phillips to see it, so she was sure Jones had seen it too.

'No. I can't say that I do.'

'Adders Bahmani,' said Jones, and tapped the picture with

an index finger. 'That's his Range Rover parked next to your car.'

Johnson interjected. 'As fascinating as this is, again, how is any of it relevant?'

Jones stared at Johnson. 'Adders Bahmani is a suspected serious criminal. He's been implicated in all manner of crimes, including drug trafficking and kidnapping.'

'So?' said Johnson.

'So. You have to admit, it does seem a little convenient. We find two kilos of heroin and fifty grand cash in Gerry's apartment the same week his car is spotted, parked next to a suspected drug dealer and kidnapper's car. Especially as he lied about being there when we questioned him yesterday.'

Phillips cut back in before Johnson could respond. 'Why did you lie about where you were on the night of your niece's disappearance, Gerry?'

Donald stuttered.

Phillips pressed on. 'Is it because you were involved in her kidnap, along with Adders Bahmani? Did you help him get into the Marstons Club on the night she was snatched? Are the drugs and the money your cut of the ransom?'

'No!'

'It's time to stop lying, Gerry,' said Phillips. 'Where is Hollie? What has Bahmani done with her?'

Donald's complexion had turned ashen. He stared blankly at Phillips and Jones.

'Can I have a moment alone with my client, please?' asked Johnson.

Phillips forced a thin smile and stood. 'Of course. We'll find another room until you're ready.'

Jones followed her out, and the door closed behind them. They made their way to the observation suite, where Bovalino and Entwistle waited.

Following the correct protocols, the monitors and speakers

had been switched off whilst Johnson held counsel with Donald.

'What do you reckon, Guv?' asked Bovalino.

Phillips rubbed the back of her neck for a moment before answering. 'He's as dodgy as all hell, but I'm still not sure he's involved in the kidnapping.'

'Me neither,' said Jones. 'But, based on his lifestyle, he's definitely involved in dealing drugs – *and* with Bahmani – in some capacity.'

Phillips nodded. 'One hundred per cent. I mean, does he look like a man with a smack habit that requires him to buy two kilos of heroin at a time?'

'Not one bit,' said Entwistle.

Phillips tapped her tongue against the roof of her mouth for moment as she considered her next move. 'Right. Well, if I know Johnson like I think I do, she's about to produce a client statement that'll bear as much regard to the truth as a bloody fairy story. So whilst she creates her work of fiction, I'm off to get a cuppa. Shout me when she's ready to share her masterpiece.'

Sometime later, Jones appeared in the canteen, where Phillips was sat cradling the remains of her black tea. He smiled as he approached. 'They're ready, Guv.'

Phillips drained her mug and followed him back towards the interview suite. A few minutes later, she led the way into Interview Room Two. She and Jones took a seat each, opposite Donald and Johnson.

'My client would like me to read a statement he has prepared regarding the night his niece was taken,' said Johnson, who produced a hand-written statement. 'It also explains the drugs and money found in his apartment this morning.'

'Go on,' said Phillips.

Johnson began reading aloud. '*On the evening of the 31st of October, I visited the Northern Snooker Club in Openshaw, where I* *played snooker, alone, from 7.30 p.m. until approximately 10 p.m., at which time I left and made my way home to my apartment in Salford Quays. I did not speak with anyone at the club, or on my way home. I did, however, speak to the concierge on my return to the apartment block at approximately 10.30 p.m. He can verify this fact. The money that was found in my apartment was winnings from a poker game. The drugs recovered from my home were for my own personal use. I have a significant drug habit, and it was never my intention to sell the heroin to anyone else. I do not know anyone named Adders Bahmani, nor do I have any knowledge of his alleged crimes. The fact my car was parked next to his at the Northern Snooker Club is nothing more than a coincidence. I have nothing further to say on the matter. Gerry Donald.'* Johnson passed over the statement to Phillips, who didn't bother looking at it.

'If this is all just a coincidence, then why did you lie about your whereabouts on the night Hollie was taken, Gerry?'

Donald folded his arms and stared Phillips dead in the eye. 'No comment.'

23

JONES HAD HANDLED THE FORMALITIES AND CHARGED DONALD for possession of the heroin, and he was now safely locked away in the custody suite of Ashton House. He would remain there until morning, at which point he would be transferred to Manchester's Magistrates' Court, and then remanded into HMP Hawk Green until his trial.

Back in her office on the third floor, Phillips closed the door, but remained standing as she placed a call to Dr Chakrabortty's mobile. The pathologist answered after a few rings.

'Jane. What can I do for you?'

Phillips wandered over to her desk and glanced at the lab report displayed on her computer screen. It was a full analysis of the drugs seized from Donald, and had arrived in her inbox less than half an hour ago. 'I want to know if the heroin you found in Cartwright's system is a match for a batch we seized this morning. Do you have the compositions report?'

'It's on my laptop,' said Chakrabortty. 'Give me a minute to find it.'

Phillips took a seat in front of her PC while she waited. She could hear Chakrabortty tapping away at the other end of the phone before she rejoined the call.

'I'm sending it to your email now,' said Chakrabortty.

'Ditto,' said Phillips. 'I've just sent you my lab report on the drugs from this morning's raid.'

Phillips's PC pinged, signalling she had incoming mail, and a moment later the message icon appeared in the bottom of the screen. Through the phone, she could hear the same thing happening on Chakrabortty's side. They opened their respective documents at the same time.

On the screen, Phillips placed her own lab report next to the one Chakrabortty had sent over. Side by side, it was evident they were pretty much identical, but Chakrabortty was the first to comment.

'The compositions are carbon copies. The biggest component in each mix is heroin, with large traces of fentanyl, quinine, manganese, calcium, copper, iron and zinc.'

'So they've come from the same source?' asked Phillips.

'It's difficult to say for sure but, looking at the samples side by side, it would seem highly likely. I must say that, compared to other samples I've tested before, it looks like a relatively pure batch as well.'

'Yeah. And people pay a premium for purity. I'm guessing this stuff was never destined for the sex workers and smack-heads of Manchester's underbelly. This looks like the heroin of high-rollers.'

'Based on its purity, I would say that's probably a fair assumption,' said Chakrabortty.

Phillips reclined in her chair, thinking aloud. 'If that's the case, then how did a low-paid security officer get hold of it?'

'I'm afraid that's your area of expertise, Jane,' said Chakrabortty.

Phillips nodded, her head now awash with questions.

'Jane?' Chakrabortty prompted.

'What?' said Phillips. Clearly she had missed something.

'I asked you if there was anything else you needed from me?'

'Sorry. I was miles away.'

'I could tell.'

'No. Thank you. That's all I needed to know.'

'Right, well, it's time I was going home. You know where I am if anything else comes to mind.'

Phillips checked her watch. It was 6 p.m. and she had lost track of time. 'Of course. I forget that not everyone keeps the same hours as me. You get yourself away.'

'Take care, Jane,' said Chakrabortty, and ended the call.

Phillips sat in silence for a few minutes and stared at the lab reports. 'Where did Cartwright get such pure heroin?' she whispered into the now-dark room. Her gut told her that, somehow, it had to be connected to Hollie's kidnapping.

24

NOVEMBER 6TH

THE MAJOR CRIMES UNIT'S CORE TEAM ALL ARRIVED AT ASHTON House at 7 a.m. the next day. Phillips was keen to piece together the events from the hours leading up to Sam Cartwright's death. To that end, Bovalino and Entwistle had been tasked with searching CCTV footage from the streets and shops surrounding Cartwright's house, whilst she and Jones paid a visit to Gerry Donald in the ground-floor custody suite.

Phillips led the way to the charge desk, where the Custody Sergeant sat behind a screen, working at his computer. Mike Allinson was a seasoned copper with just a few years remaining before he was obliged to retire. Considering the abuse he endured on a daily – or nightly – basis from drunk or high criminals, he maintained a jolly demeanour, which perfectly matched his round face and greying beard.

He looked up as they approached. 'Morning Ma'am, morning Jonesy,' he said, as he flashed one of his trademark smiles. 'What brings you down here so early?'

'Gerry Donald,' said Phillips. 'We'd like to ask him a few more questions before he heads off to court.'

'Is he in?' joked Jonesy.

Allinson chuckled. 'Last time I looked.'

The sergeant made his way round to the other side of the desk, and Phillips noted his uniform was a tight fit against his rotund belly. 'Follow me,' he said, and headed in the direction of the cells, his keys jangling on a chain against one of his thick legs.

When they reached Donald's cell, Allinson opened the small observation hole in the door and peered inside. 'Mr Donald. You have some visitors,' he said with a cheerful tone that sounded more guest-house manager than detention officer. He turned to Phillips and Jones. 'Looks like he's awake,' he said, before unlocking the door and pulling it open. 'You can use the small room at the end of the cells. It's empty at the moment.'

'Thank you,' said Phillips.

'Cheers, Mike,' added Jones, as he patted him on the shoulder.

Allinson nodded and headed back to the charge desk as Phillips stepped inside Donald's cell. 'Morning, Gerry,' she said with false enthusiasm. 'You ready for your stay in Hawk Green?'

Donald screwed his face up when he saw his visitors. 'What the bloody hell do you two want?'

'A little chat,' said Phillips. 'DS Jones, please escort our guest to the meeting room, will you?'

'My pleasure, Guv,' said Jones, and stepped forwards and hauled Donald up from the blue plastic mattress and onto his feet. 'This way, *sir*.'

A few minutes later, Phillips and Jones took seats at a small table opposite Donald, who now took tentative sips from a mug of hot tea. He looked dishevelled, and his eyes were red and puffy, as if he hadn't slept. His dark stubble cast a shadow across his jaw.

'Rough night?' asked Phillips.

'What do you think?' sneered Donald.

Phillips cut to the chase. 'Have you ever met a woman called Sam Cartwright?'

Donald shook his head. 'The name doesn't ring a bell.'

'You sure? She worked at the Marstons Club, where your sister and brother-in-law are members.'

Donald took a mouthful of tea. 'I know what the Marstons Club is. I used to be a member there myself.'

'Used to be?' said Jones. 'When did you leave?'

'I dunno. About a year ago, I suppose. It was an expense I didn't need.'

'I see,' said Phillips.

'Anyway,' said Donald, 'if you're asking me questions, shouldn't Nic be here?'

Phillips shook her head. 'This is just a chat. Off the record. You'll notice there's no recording device and we're not taking notes.'

Donald leant back in his chair and placed the cup down on the table between them. 'Nope. I'm not having it. Either my lawyer is present, or I'm saying nothing.'

Phillips continued, unperturbed. 'You see, the thing is, Gerry, Sam Cartwright died of a heroin overdose just a few days ago. We tested what was in her system, and guess what?'

Donald stared at Phillips, his gaze unflinching.

'It was the exact same heroin as we found in your flat. The compositions are identical.'

Phillips spotted Donald's nose as it twitched – in the exact same way it had during yesterday's interview, when she'd mentioned Bahmani's name.

'So what?' he said.

Phillips looked at Jones for added effect before exhaling loudly. 'Well, Gerry. If we can prove the heroin in Cartwright's system came from, then we'll be looking at adding secondary murder to your charges...manslaughter at the very least. And that, coupled with the possession charge, means a very long time in Hawk Green for you.'

Donald's eyes widened.

Phillips was stretching the bounds of the law, and she knew it. But she also knew her best and only chance of getting a lead on the heroin – and potentially finding a connection to Hollie – was off the record. If Nic Johnson became involved, she would destroy this line of questioning in a nano-second. 'Tell us who sold you the heroin. Let *them* take the blame for Cartwright's death instead of *you*.'

Donald opened his mouth to speak, but no words came out.

Phillips continued to push. 'Was it Adders Bahmani? Did he sell you the heroin?'

Jones joined in too. 'Come on, Gerry. You shouldn't have the spend the rest of your life in prison for a man like Bahmani. Tell us off the record what we want to know, and we'll have a quiet word with the CPS. Tell them you cooperated. Help you get a reduced sentence.'

Donald folded his arms across his chest and cleared his throat as he looked first at Jones and then at Phillips. 'No comment.'

25

AFTER CONTINUING HIS 'NO COMMENT' ANSWERS TO THEIR questions, Phillips and Jones gave up trying to elicit any information from Donald, and left him to Sergeant Allinson to prepare him for his trip to the Magistrates' Court.

Stopping at the canteen on her way back to the incident room, Phillips ordered a round of bacon sandwiches and hot drinks for the team. It was 8.30 a.m. and the incident room was still empty, with most of the wider team not due to start work for another thirty minutes. Phillips and Jones joined Bovalino and Entwistle at their desks and tucked into their quarry.

'Any joy with Donald?' Bovalino asked through a mouthful of food.

Phillips swallowed what she was chewing. '"No comment".'

'Smart boy,' said Bovalino.

'Whoever his supplier is,' said Jones, 'Donald must be sufficiently terrified of them to want to take his chances in Hawk Green rather than grass them up. That place is horrific.'

'Do you think it's Bahmani?' asked Entwistle, taking a bite of his sandwich.

'Has to be,' said Phillips. 'Has to be.'

Bovalino finished his food and threw the wrapper, with a loud clatter, into the metal wastepaper bin against the wall. He mock-celebrated his victory, and grinned. 'In that case, I'm not surprised he'd rather go to prison. Bahmani's an animal.'

Phillips nodded, and wiped her mouth with a napkin. 'Yeah. He is. So, did you find anything of interest on the CCTV?'

'Nothing on the cameras that I checked,' said Entwistle, 'but Bov had better luck, didn't you?'

Bovalino turned his monitor to face the team. 'I had a look at the junction of Poundswick Lane and Broadwood Road, where Cartwright lived. There's a bunch of shops on there, and the indoor market. Chakrabortty's post mortem confirmed she died at approximately 2 p.m. on Saturday the 2nd of November, so I scanned through footage of that morning and found this.' He pressed enter on the keyboard and the footage played on screen.

The team watched as Sam Cartwright appeared at the end of Broadwood Road. She stopped, looked for traffic, then crossed Poundswick Lane. 'We pick her up again here,' Bovalino said as he opened another window on the screen and pressed play. 'This is the camera from the shopping precinct.'

Phillips leaned forwards to get a closer look.

'She goes into the small supermarket for about ten minutes,' Bovalino continued to narrate, 'and reappears with two bags of groceries.' He switched windows once again. 'And then we see her here again, heading back across Poundswick Lane and home.'

'What time was this?' asked Phillips.

'Eleven a.m., Guv.'

'And is there any footage closer to her house?'

'I'm afraid not,' said Bovalino as he pulled up a different image on his screen, 'But I did have a look at the cameras from 11 a.m. through to 2.30 p.m., and spotted this guy at 1.45 p.m., heading towards Broadwood Road. He's wearing a cap to cover his eyes, and is the only person all day who never once let his face be seen on camera. It struck me as odd.' Bovalino pressed play, and again the team watched the footage unfold.

'You're right, Bov,' said Phillips after a few moments. 'It's as if he knows he's being watched. Look at that there; he's in the middle of the frame, but keeps the peak of his cap down so we never see his eyes.'

'We lose him after that on this camera. He's gone for about fifteen minutes, but then he's back just after 2 p.m.,' said Bovalino, 'walking at pace in the opposite direction. He stops at the junction to take a call.'

At that moment, on the screen, the mystery man pulled his phone from his pocket and spoke into it for approximately twenty seconds before he ended the call and stepped off the curb to cross the street.

'Is there any more footage of him in the shopping precinct, where we see his face?'

Bovalino shook his head. 'Not that I've found yet, Guv, but I'll contact the different retailers and see if they have anything from their own cameras.'

Jones stood up from his chair and moved towards Bovalino's computer. 'Play the bit where he answers the phone again, will you?'

Bovalino complied.

'Pause it there!' Jones said.

With the screen frozen, Jones moved closer to the screen, studying it before tapping it with his index finger. 'Look at that, Guv.'

Phillips frowned. 'Look at what?'

'The tattoo poking out of his jacket, on his left arm. Do you recognise it?'

'Should I?'

Jones nodded with enthusiasm. 'Yes, Guv. It's a dead ringer for John Robbins's tattoo. I had a really good look at it each time we talked to him, as it kept popping out of his shirt sleeve. And I'm telling you, that's *his* wrist. Either that, or it's a bloody big coincidence.'

Each of the team smiled, clearly expecting Phillips's next words. 'And you know how I feel about coincidences, don't you, Jonesy?'

'You don't believe in them, Guv,' Jones said with a wide grin.

Phillips clapped her hands together. 'Bloody hell, what an amazing spot. Pull Robbins in and let's see what he has to say for himself. Well done, guys. Great work.'

At that moment, Phillips's phone began to ring. She checked the display and her heart sank. She rolled her eyes in the direction of the team and stood, answering it as she strode back to her office. 'DCI Saxby. How can I help?'

26

PHILLIPS WAS BUSY AT HER COMPUTER WHEN JONES KNOCKED ON her open office door.

'He's downstairs, Guv. Do you want me and Bov to interview him, or do you want to do it with me?'

'I'll do it with you,' said Phillips. 'Bov can watch from the observation suite. Does Robbins know what we want to talk to him about?'

'No, Guv. I thought it best not to give him any time to prepare. He thinks he's just here to help with our enquiries. Seemed quite pleased to be helping us, in all honesty.'

'Not quite the reaction I would've expected.'

'Me neither,' said Jones. 'So how was Saxby?'

Phillips let out a frustrated sigh. 'Oh, you know. Arrogant, pompous, condescending. Would you like me to go on?'

Jones chuckled. 'Sounds about right.'

'He was lecturing me on the speed of the investigation – or as he put it, "the lack thereof". I mean, what kind of a copper uses phrases like "the lack thereof"?'

'He's got a bloody cheek, hasn't he? We've hardly seen him

since he was drafted in. I mean, he's the supposed expert. What exactly is he supposed to be doing?' asked Jones.

Phillips, reclining in her chair, used her pen as a pointer. 'Well, that's just the point Jonesy. As Saxby was at pains to tell me the other day, and I quote, "I'm not a bloody beat copper!"'.

'So what *is* he, then?'

'*His* job is liaising with the family – in this case, with Sir Richard and his wife. He was very quick to pass on Sir Richard's apparent and growing frustrations at our lack of progress. Seems the good knight is not that keen on handing over four million quid.'

'It's his bloody daughter's life that's at stake. No amount of money would be too much to protect my girls.'

'And most *normal* parents, I dare say. But Richard Hawkins isn't normal,' said Phillips.

Jones moved farther into the room now, his brow furrowed. 'Do you think Hollie's still alive, Guv?'

Phillips breathed in deeply, and shook her head as she exhaled. 'I honestly couldn't say, Jonesy. It really does seem odd to me that they gave the Hawkinses a week to find the money. Why so long? Why not send the ransom video on day one and the drop details on, say, day three. Why be so specific as to give him a week?'

'Beats me, Guv.'

'Saxby thinks it's not significant,' said Phillips, 'but I'm sure it is.'

'And how is he so sure it's not significant?'

'God knows. He didn't expand on his theory. I even pushed him again on the call today. He just kept ducking the questions and moved back to talking about "how unhappy Sir Richard was", and how "it would be better for all involved if the kidnappers could be caught before the money is handed over". He's a slippery bugger, I can tell you. Won't be drawn on anything.

Just hangs around in the background, waiting for an opportunity to do his best seagull impression.'

Jones screwed his face up at the statement. 'Seagull
impression?'

'Have you never heard of someone "Doing a Seagull?"'
asked Phillips with a wide grin.

'No, I haven't.'

'It came from my old boss, DCI Campbell, back in the early
days. It's when someone waits for their moment to swoop in –
shits all over you – then swoops out again.'

Jones burst out laughing. 'I love it. Sounds like Saxby all
right.'

Phillips nodded. 'And someone else we've worked for, hey?'
She was, of course, referring to their former boss, DCI Brown,
now a superintendent and climbing the ladder, fast. Considered by many to be the most disliked senior officer, he currently
worked as part of the Greater Manchester Police Force.

'Shall we go down and see Robbins?' said Jones.

Phillips sat forwards in her chair and drummed her fingers
on the desk. 'Yeah. Let's find out if it was him on the CCTV, and
if it was, what the bloody hell he was doing so close to
Cartwright's gaff the day she died.'

As Robbins wasn't under arrest, he did not require a solicitor
to be present. He had, to all intents and purposes, come to the
station of his own accord.

Phillips placed her laptop on the table between them and
took a seat opposite him. Jones took the seat next to her, and
she explained the formalities and the various ways that their
conversation would be recorded. She then asked if he was
happy to continue – he was.

With the clock ticking louder than ever in the hunt for clues to Hollie Hawkins's whereabouts, Phillips wasted no time. 'Did you visit the home of Sam Cartwright on the day she died?'

Robbins recoiled a little in his chair. 'I beg your pardon?'

Phillips's tone was deliberately harsh. She wanted to shake him, to see what would fall out. 'You heard me, John. Were you at the home of Sam Cartwright on the day she died?'

Robbins stumbled over his words. 'Er, no. I wasn't.'

'I think you're lying to me, John.' Phillips opened her laptop and turned it to face him, then tapped the screen with her finger. 'Because I believe this is you, captured on CCTV, walking towards Sam Cartwright's house just moments before she died.'

Robbins stared at the screen, his eyes wide.

'Is that you, John?'

Robbins's mouth fell open as his eyes switched from the screen back to Phillips.

Phillips brought up another still image taken from the CCTV footage. 'Here you are again, on the phone, a few minutes after Cartwright died.'

'That's not me,' said Robbins. He sounded panicked.

'Would you mind rolling up your left shirt sleeve for me, please?'

'What?'

'Your left shirt sleeve,' repeated Phillips. 'Can you roll it back? I'd like to see your wrist.'

'I don't understand. Why do you want to see my wrist?'

'Well, the thing is, John,' said Phillips, 'the man in this picture has a tattoo on his left wrist that looks just like yours. It's a very distinctive design. A lion motif, intricately inked, within a dark leaf ring and a globe. DS Jones looked into that specific design and found out all about its origin, didn't you, Sergeant?'

'I did, Ma'am,' said Jones, playing his part to perfection like he had in so many interviews before. 'It's the symbol for the Royal Marines.'

'You're an ex-commando, aren't you?' said Phillips.

Robbins's breathing was shallow now. His eyes darted between the image on the screen, Phillips and Jones. Phillips could sense he was on the edge and about to open up, so she pushed on. 'You may as well tell us the truth – *while you still can.* You see, we also found traces of DNA at Cartwright's house that belonged to someone else. A male,' she lied. With no suspicion of murder, Evans and his team had not needed to look for detailed forensics. 'A simple swab of your mouth will tell us whether that DNA belongs to you, John. And my money's on the fact that it will. So I'll ask you again, were you at Sam Cartwright's house on the day she died? A simple yes or no will do.'

Robbins shoulders sagged and he dropped his head. He stared at the table for a long moment before he looked up at Phillips and nodded.

'For the tape. John Robbins has just nodded, indicating he was at Sam Cartwright's house on the day she died,' said Phillips.

'What were you doing there, John?' asked Jones.

Robbins's words came out all at once. 'I was there. But I didn't go inside. I rang the doorbell. Tried the front door handle and looked through the front window. But she wasn't at home.'

'Did you go round the back?' asked Phillips.

'Yeah. I checked the garden, and tried the back door, but I couldn't see anything.'

'Why were you there?'

Robbins seemed eager to please now. 'Sam suffered from depression and anxiety. A lot of veterans do. And she's been quite down, lately. I hadn't seen or heard from her for a few days since the kidnapping. I got the sense she felt responsible in some way. So I figured I'd go round and check on her. You know. To make sure she hadn't done anything stupid.'

'You mean suicide?' said Jones.

Robbins focused his full attention on Jones. 'Yeah. It's the silent killer among veterans. We all saw, and did, things in active combat that changed us forever. Sam was no different, and that stuff can eat away at you if you're not careful.'

'So how do you explain being there at the exact time she took an overdose?' said Phillips.

'I can't. Just a coincidence, I guess.'

Phillips glanced sideways at Jones. She was sure he was thinking the same thing. *There's no such thing as a coincidence.* She turned her attention back to the laptop screen. 'I'm intrigued, John. In your role in the Marines, were you trained in surveillance and counter-intelligence?'

Robbins's brow furrowed. He seemed surprised by the question. 'Yes, to some degree.'

'You see, John,' said Phillips, 'we've watched every piece of CCTV footage that features you around Cartwright's house, and you never once showed your face to the camera. Do you not think that's a bit odd?'

Robbins shrugged his shoulders. 'Not really. I was wearing a cap with a wide brim.'

Phillips forced a thin smile. 'It's a bit convenient, isn't it?'

Jones cut in now. 'Do you know what that says to me, John?'

'No,' said Robbins, his eyes narrow.

'That says to me that, because of your military training, you knew the cameras were there, and how to avoid being seen.'

'That wasn't the case at all. I just chose to wear a cap that day.'

'Bollocks.' Jones pressed on. 'I think you went to see Cartwright because you and she were involved in the kidnapping of Hollie Hawkins.'

'Don't be ridiculous.'

'You knew she was flaky, that she had a drug habit. And that if we put pressure on, she'd crack. Tell us where the girl is. Tell us how you did it—'

'Seriously,' said Robbins as he cut Jones off, 'you're living in cloud cuckoo land, mate.'

Jones continued unabated, 'So you went to her house to make sure she didn't say anything to us. But when you got there, you spotted her lying on the floor, just like we did. But instead of forcing your way in to help her, you realised your troubles were potentially over. So you legged it, leaving her to die.'

Robbins slammed his fist down on the table. 'That's just not true!' He clenched his fists and took a deep breath. 'Look. I went round to see Sam because I was worried about her. I cared about her. I should have looked through the window at the back, but for whatever reason, I didn't. And I can't forgive myself for that. If I had, maybe she'd still be alive. You have to believe me. I had nothing to do with the kidnap of Hollie Hawkins. Nothing.' Robbins pointed an index finger at Jones now. 'In fact, if you remember, *I* was the one who showed you how the kidnappers got in. Now why would I do that if I was working with them?'

Phillips folded her arms across her chest. 'To throw us off the scent.'

'Do me a favour,' scoffed Robbins. 'I'm a retired, highly decorated Royal Marine with an unblemished service record. Not to mention, I've got kids of my own. I couldn't kidnap a young girl. It goes against *everything* I believe in. I've risked my life in combat to protect the people of this country. Because that's what I do; I protect those that cannot defend themselves. *I don't hurt them.*'

Phillips eyed Robbins for a long moment before she responded. 'Did you know Sam changed her name?'

Robbins's brow furrowed. 'She what?'

'She changed her name. She was known as Sam Blackwood when she was in the Army, but changed it to Sam Cartwright after she left. Were you aware of that?'

Robbins shook his head. 'I had no idea.'

Phillips continued. 'We think she did it to hide her past; the fact she had a record for drugs possession and assault.'

Robbins's mouth opened, but he said nothing for a moment. Then, 'Assault?' he breathed, in a wondering tone.

Jones interjected now. 'Don't you do background checks on your staff at Marstons?'

'Yeah we do,' said Robbins. 'But Green does them. I just get given the names once they've been appointed.'

'Well, looks like he needs to be a bit more thorough in future, doesn't it?' said Jones.

'Yeah. I guess he does,' said Robbins.

Phillips decided now would be a good time to regroup with Bovalino, get his take on what they'd just heard. She glanced up at the clock on the wall behind Robbins's head. 'Right. I think we should take a short break. I'm suspending this interview at 5 p.m.' She stood and signalled for Jones to follow her out.

'Do we think he's involved?' Bovalino asked as they walked into the observation suite.

'He seems genuine enough. And seemed shocked when we told him Cartwright had a record,' said Phillips. She shook her head. 'But the timing of his visit, plus the fact he hid his face? That's what's bothering me at the moment.'

'Me too,' said Jones. 'Should we arrest him? Scare him a little, see if we can crack him?'

'On what grounds? We can't prove he's done anything illegal,' said Phillips. 'According to Chakrabortty, Cartwright died of an overdose, and we have absolutely nothing to tie him to the kidnapping.'

Jones nodded. 'And to be fair, he's right. He *was* the one who spotted how the gang got into the Marstons Club.'

Phillips stared at the monitor displaying the video feed of Interview Room Two, and watched Robbins for a long moment, sitting alone at the table. She turned back to Jones and Bovalino. 'Release him for now, but let's keep an eye on him. Get Entwistle to dig into his background. Run his bank accounts, previous jobs, friends and family, the works. If there's anything dodgy about this guy, Entwistle will find it.'

'Agreed,' said Jones. 'I'll give Robbins the good news and drive him home.'

27

IT HAD BECOME A WELL-WORN ROUTINE AT MEALTIMES, AND IT seemed that Blue had been selected to deliver her food. Like clockwork, the lock being released would signal someone was about to enter, then the door would open slowly and Blue would walk into the room. Sometimes – as was the case this time – if Hollie managed to get to the small table in the middle room before Blue entered, she could catch a glimpse of the world beyond her makeshift cell: a long, concrete corridor lit with what appeared to be temporary lights. But the space was always empty. Never a soul in sight.

Blue carried the tray in and was careful when he placed it on the table so as not to spill any of the precious cargo. 'I've made you carrot and coriander soup,' he said.

The softness of his voice took her by surprise, and she detected an accent of some kind; Scottish or Irish, but she couldn't be certain.

Hollie opened her mouth to thank him but, as ever, Blue appeared keen to remove himself from the room as quickly as possible. He turned on his heels, and marched back towards the door.

'If my dad doesn't pay, are you really going to kill me?' Hollie asked, even though she feared the answer.

Blue turned to face her, and for a moment it appeared as if he would answer the question. Instead, he swivelled and yanked the door wide open, forgetting to knock.

Without warning, Hollie found herself staring into the cold, black eyes of a tall, muscular woman. Her face was scarred and distorted down the entire left-hand side, as if it had been burned.

The woman, angry with Blue's error, shot out of sight. 'The door! Shut the door, you stupid old bastard!' she cried.

Blue lurched through the open door and slammed it shut behind him.

A chorus of shouts erupted outside Hollie's room, and she rushed to the door in an attempt to hear what was being said. But by the time she got there, all she heard was a door slam and the muffled argument as it continued, fading away from her room.

28

NOVEMBER 7TH

With time running out, and the pressure mounting by the minute, Phillips was beginning to feel a touch of claustrophobia in her office. She decided to decamp the core MCU team of Jones, Bovalino and Entwistle, to the conference suite at the far end of the incident room.

When she arrived, carrying her early morning coffee, Entwistle had just finished connecting his laptop to the projector that hung down from the roof. This made it much easier for the whole team to view the background information he'd found on John Robbins.

With everyone seated, Entwistle began. 'I pretty much worked all night to find this information—'

'What d'ya want, mate? A medal?' joked Bovalino.

'Ignore him, Entwistle,' said Phillips with a grin. 'Carry on.'

'I've dug into every file I could find on John Robbins. Turns out he's a bloody war hero.'

A grainy picture of a younger Robbins appeared on the large screen fitted to the wall. Dressed in desert fatigues with full body armour, Robbins stood in front of a military vehicle. His skin was heavily tanned, and he carried an SA80 automatic rifle in his gloved hands. 'This is John Robbins in Afghanistan in 2011. He was a sergeant in the Royal Marines, 3 Commando Brigade. This was taken during his second tour of Afghanistan, where his bravery earned him the Conspicuous Gallantry Cross. Apparently he and another member of his team took on the enemy at close quarters so that seriously wounded casualties from their section could be medivacked to safety.' Another picture of Robbins, looking a little older and in civilian clothing – but still armed – appeared. 'He was also part of a highly successful reconnaissance unit that deployed around the globe. I'm not sure where this was taken, but it would seem, from the fact he's in civilian clothes, that he was working undercover at this point.' Next on the screen was a collection of pictures with Robbins in sports gear. 'He retired from the Marines in 2015, but remains a reserve. He's big into charity work to support veterans whose lives have been changed through their experiences of combat.'

'Seems like a thoroughly decent bloke,' said Jones.

'He really does,' said Entwistle. 'No criminal record, not even a speeding offence. And his finances are in great shape too. He receives a full navy pension each month, as well as his salary from the club, which is thirty-eight grand a year before tax. Basically, he's as clean as a whistle.'

Phillips took a deep breath and let it out loudly through her nose. 'Jesus. If it wasn't for bad luck, I'd have no luck at all.'

'Sorry Guv,' said Entwistle. 'I looked everywhere for even the slightest hint that he could be crooked, but he's a bit of a living legend.'

'But that still doesn't explain why he was at Cartwright's house when she died.' said Phillips.

'Maybe it *was* just a coincidence, Guv,' said Jones.

Phillips nodded reluctantly. 'Yeah. Maybe.' She placed her hands on the sides of her head and her elbows on the desk.

'Doesn't help us though, does it? We're still no further forward, and we've been at this for almost a week now.'

It was Jones's turn to open his laptop. 'I think I may have found something, Guv.'

That drew Phillips's full attention. 'Really?'

'Entwistle, I'm emailing you the ransom video. Can you pull it up on the big screen?'

A moment later, the team found themselves looking at Hollie Hawkins's face, staring at them from the video message sent to her father six days earlier.

'Press play, and I'll tell you when to stop it,' said Jones.

The video played for a few minutes, up to the point where Hollie broke down and one of the kidnappers forced her head sideways with the gun.

'Stop there!' said Jones.

Entwistle paused the video.

'Do you see that, there? To the left of her head.'

Phillips leaned forwards and focused in on the image. 'What are we looking at, Jonesy?'

Jones stood up and walked to the screen, pointing to the area of the footage he was talking about. 'This here. Can you make it out?'

'It looks like a block of metal,' Bovalino said.

Jones returned to his laptop, but remained standing. 'It is, Bov. Entwistle, I'm sending you another image. Can you pull it up for me?'

Entwistle's screen pinged, and the email notification with Jones's name appeared in the bottom corner of the screen. He opened it and clicked on the attached image.

Jones walked back to the screen and used his pen as a pointer. 'See this picture of Salford Baths? Look closely at the steel structure that spans the apex of the ceiling. Now look back at the metal block behind Hollie's head.'

Entwistle put both images side by side on screen.

Jones continued, 'They're not identical, but very, very similar.'

'When was Salford Baths constructed?' asked Phillips.

'Eighteen-fifty, Guv,' said Jones.

'So, based on that structure, the building they're holding Hollie in is likely Victorian and derelict,' said Phillips. 'And out of the way of any prying eyes.'

'Looks that way,' said Jones.

'Bov, you're a Mancunian. Where would we find a building like that?' asked Phillips.

Bovalino rubbed his stubble for a moment. 'Probably around the parts of Salford that are still to be developed. Or over where I grew up, in West Gorton. There's a bunch of buildings I remember scrambling round in when I was a teenager. I've not been back home for a while, but last time I was there, they were still standing – and still derelict. Could be worth a look?'

'Bit of a needle in a haystack, isn't it?' said Phillips.

'It's something, though,' said Jones.

Phillips nodded. 'You and Bov, check them out.' She turned to Entwistle. 'You're a graduate, aren't you?'

'Yes, Guv.'

'Right, well, while these two are in West Gorton, I want you to go back to uni.'

Entwistle's brow furrowed. 'Hey?'

'Get up to Manchester University. They've got a huge school of architecture there. See who you can find that knows about Victorian buildings – especially those in Manchester. They might recognise that particular structure and be able to match it to a specific architect. That could help us narrow the search considerably.'

'Yes, Guv,' Entwistle said with alacrity.

Phillips checked her watch. It was coming up to 8.30 a.m. 'Right. Well, I'd better prep for my morning debrief with Fox.

No doubt I'm up for another bollocking. Let's stay in contact and aim to reconvene this afternoon, ok?'

A chorus of 'Yes Guv' filled the room.

'Let's get to it. We're running out of time,' said Phillips, and headed back to her office.

29

As Phillips strode into her office, she was surprised to see Chief Superintendent Fox standing there, examining a framed photo she'd picked up from the desk.

'Morning, Ma'am. I wasn't expecting you for another thirty minutes,' said Phillips.

Fox turned and flashed her trademark Cheshire Cat grin. 'How long did you live in Hong Kong?'

'Sixteen years,' said Phillips. She walked towards her office chair. 'I was born there, and we moved back to the UK when it was handed back to the Chinese.'

Fox replaced the picture on the desk. 'Your father was a policeman, wasn't he?'

'Yes. The Royal Hong Kong Police.'

'Is that what inspired you to join the force?'

'Amongst other things. I guess I always had a sense of right and wrong, of wanting to see justice done.'

Fox took a seat. 'That's you all over, isn't it? Out for justice at every turn.'

'Aren't we all, Ma'am?'

Fox didn't answer, choosing instead to glance around

Phillips's small office. 'Looks like you could do with a new carpet. And the walls could do with a lick of paint.'

Phillips bit her lip. 'I'll speak to the maintenance team. I'll make it a priority as soon as I've found Hollie Hawkins.' Her tone was borderline sarcastic, and she held her breath for a moment, expecting a reprisal. It wasn't forthcoming.

'So. Since you brought her up, what's happening with Hollie Hawkins? Did you get anywhere with the head of security at Marstons? Robbins, wasn't it?'

Phillips never ceased to be amazed at how much information Fox absorbed when, most of the time, she appeared to be paying little attention. But then again, it was also well known that she had spies everywhere in Ashton House.

'I'm afraid that one looks likes a dead end. He's something of a war hero. As clean as a whistle, and has no ties to anyone of a criminal nature. And, I must admit, he doesn't seem the type.'

'So, according to the ransom video, we're expecting the kidnappers to tell us the location of the money drop when? Tomorrow?'

'That's correct.'

'And we still have not one clue who they are or where they might be holding the girl?'

'The team is working on a couple of leads as we speak, Ma'am.'

'Really? What leads?' said Fox.

'Jones spotted something in the background of the ransom video that looks like she is – or was – being held in a Victorian structure. The team are out trying to find its location.'

'This is Manchester, for God's sake. The bloody place is full of Victorian architecture. What are you going to do? Search every old building in the city?'

Phillips could feel her blood beginning to boil. 'If we have to, yes.'

'Oh, get real, Phillips,' said Fox, losing her temper. 'Even with a hundred officers, that could take months. We have *one day*! The chief constable called again last night, complaining that Sir Richard is threatening to go to the Prime Minister. He says that, with the amount of tax he pays, the police should be working much harder than we are to find his daughter. And he's really not very happy about having to pay the ransom.'

'He's worth close to a hundred million. What's four million to him?'

'That's not the point, Phillips. No one should be expected to pay money to see their child safe. That's what we get paid for.'

'I know that, Ma'am. And I agree with you. But this gang left nothing behind. The only lead we had was Cartwright, and she's dead.'

'She wasn't a lead; she was a junkie. An ex-squaddie who couldn't handle civilian life. The world's full of them, all moaning about having PTSD. They knew what they were signing up for when they joined the military. There's no use complaining about it now.'

It took all of Phillips strength not to reach across, grab Fox by the hair and smash her face into the desk. Instead, she took a silent breath and reminded herself that Fox was more than likely a sociopath; she had no heart. 'With respect, Ma'am—' Those three words almost stuck in her throat as she said them. '—PTSD is killing more of our veterans than the active combat in Iraq and Afghanistan combined. It's a serious issue for a lot of our ex-forces. Addiction is one of the many symptoms—'

'Oh, spare me the public service broadcast, Phillips,' said Fox cutting her dead. 'Just find me the fucking girl, and quickly. The last thing I want is another call from the chief constable with more complaints from Sir Richard.'

'What about Saxby?' said Phillips.

'What do you mean, "What about Saxby?"'

'Isn't he supposed to be liaising with Sir Richard, keeping him off our backs?'

Fox scoffed. 'Have I taught you nothing about police politics, Phillips?'

'Ma'am?'

'Do you really think someone like Saxby is on *your* side, that's he's in and out of his meetings with Sir Richard, telling him what a great job you're doing here at MCU? Not a chance. He's a self-serving, snivelling little prick from the Met who is here purely to further his own reputation in Whitehall. As you have no leads, I can guarantee you the only thing he's telling Sir Richard right now is how shit you lot are, how it would be different if the Met were handling it.'

'But that's bullshit,' said Phillips. 'He couldn't catch a cold, never mind a kidnap gang!'

Fox stared at Phillips now, her eyes black and cold. 'That's as maybe, Phillips, but he's got the ear of the people that matter – including the chief constable. So stop being so bloody naïve and find the girl before this damn case damages the reputation of Major Crimes for good. Got it?'

Phillips swallowed down her hatred for Fox and the likes of Saxby. 'Yes. Got it.'

'Good,' said Fox, and stood. 'I want an update by the end of the day.'

With that, she took her leave.

Phillips sat and stewed for a few minutes after Fox had left. She wanted to scream and shout out her frustration, but that wouldn't be a good look for a DCI in a glass office.

At that moment, there was a knock on her office door, followed by it being opened. Phillips turned to see PC Lawford.

'Sorry to disturb you, Ma'am.'

'What is it?' said Phillips, annoyed by the interruption.

'It's John Robbins.'

'What about him?'

'He's in reception and he's asking for you,' said Lawford.

Phillips raised an eyebrow. 'Is he, now?'

'Yes, Ma'am. Says it's urgent.'

30

PHILLIPS DIDN'T FEEL THE NEED TO SPEAK TO ROBBINS IN THE formal surroundings of an official interview room. So instead, she showed him into one of the ground-floor meeting rooms usually reserved for community group sessions and the occasional staff presentation. The lights came on as they entered, and Phillips suggested he take a seat at one end of the u-shaped conference table. He did so, and produced his laptop as she sat down next to him.

'I wanted to show you something that proves I had nothing to do with Sam's death,' said Robbins as he opened the laptop and logged in.

Phillips's interest was piqued. 'Really? What?'

Robbins kept his eyes on the screen as he tapped away at the keyboard. 'CCTV from her neighbour's house, from the day she died.' He turned the screen to face her. 'This is time-stamped, and clearly shows the comings and goings at Sam's house on November 3rd.'

'Where did you get this?' asked Phillips.

'Like I said, from her neighbour, Mrs Elliot. She lives at number thirty-eight, which is attached to Sam's house. The camera is positioned to capture their front door, but because of the angle, it also covers Sam's. For expedience, I've prepared an edited version for you, but I'll also give you a copy of the whole, unedited, video as well. That way, you can check for yourself that it's not been doctored.' Robbins pressed play, and the screen came to life.

Phillips watched as the footage unfolded.

'Nothing happens until 10.55 a.m., when Sam leaves the house,' said Robbins. 'You'll notice she locks the door before she heads off, turning left at end of her path and heading towards the main shopping precinct. She's away for approximately thirty minutes, and returns carrying two bags of shopping. She unlocks the door and goes inside. We don't see anything else of her after that. Then, just after 1.45 p.m., I arrive – which matches the timeline of your own footage. The stuff you showed me the other day.'

'Carry on,' said Phillips.

'I ring the doorbell and try the door. Then, when I don't get a response, I look through the lounge window. Because I can't see anything, I head round the back to try the back door, but again get no response. I'm gone for no longer than a minute before I'm back at the front of the house, where I walk straight onto Broadwood Road and back down to the shops, where your cameras picked me up again.'

'How did you get this footage?' said Phillips.

'I met Mrs Elliot once, when I went to a barbecue at Sam's. She joined the party for a gin and tonic, and we got chatting. Turns out her nephew is in the Navy, so when she found out I was a retired Royal Marine, well, she took a real shine to me.'

'But how did you explain why you needed the footage?'

'I just told her that Sam's death had been a real shock to me – which it was – that you lot were investigating how she died, and that I wanted to do what I could to help you,' Robbins said. 'She said that Sam had always been a good neighbour, and was more than happy to give me whatever I needed. I downloaded it straight from her PC.'

Phillips sat in silence for a moment, processing what she had just seen. It appeared that Cartwright had died of an overdose after all. 'So why come all the way out here to show this to me? We released you without charge.'

Robbins fixed Phillips with a steely glare. 'Because I lost so much of myself in Afghanistan and even more when I left the military. I won't lose my integrity now. I needed you to know that I wasn't lying the other day. I did go to her house to check on her, but I never went in. I just wish I'd looked through the kitchen window. She might still be alive.'

'I doubt it,' Phillips said, her voice soft. 'The heroin was exceptionally pure, plus it had been mixed with fentanyl, which is lethal. On top of that, she had a heart condition. There's little chance she would have lived.'

Robbins's eyes widened. 'A heart condition? I never knew.'

'I doubt she did either , to be honest. It appears as if it was an underlying problem,' said Phillips. 'The pathologist believes she would've had to become quite ill before it was picked up in testing. So, don't blame yourself.'

Phillips glanced at the clock on the wall. It was approaching 10.30 a.m. 'Look. I really appreciate you going out of your way to bring this to me.'

'Not a problem.' Robbins passed across a USB stick. 'It's all on there. Your tech guys will be able to verify that it's not been tampered with.'

Phillips took it and nodded. 'Thank you. I'm sure that won't be necessary.'

Robbins glanced at his watch now. 'Well, I'd better get going. My shift starts at eleven.'

'Of course. I'll show you out,' said Phillips.

They stood in unison and walked towards the door.

As Phillips opened it, Robbins touched her arm. 'I meant

what I said the other day, Inspector. I swore to protect those who cannot protect themselves. If there's anything I can do to help you find Hollie Hawkins – or the people that took her – just name it. It really pisses me off that she was taken on my watch.'

Phillips smiled and nodded. 'Of course. And thank you, Mr Robbins.'

31

Professor Fiona Levin had just finished giving her first lecture of the day when Entwistle arrived at the Manchester School of Architecture. He waited patiently as her students filed out of the lecture hall before he stepped inside. Her back to him, she packed her files into a large, brown attaché case.

'Professor Levin?' Entwistle said into the cavernous hall.

Levin spun on her heels to face him. She was younger than Entwistle had expected – mid-thirties at a guess – tall and long-limbed, with curly brown hair, and smartly dressed in a white shirt and black trousers. 'Yes?' she said as she looked him up and down.

Entwistle produced his credentials and stepped close enough for Levin to read them. 'I'm Detective Constable Entwistle, with the Major Crimes Unit. Your office told me you'd be here.'

Levin's brow furrowed. 'Did they? And why would the police be looking for me?' Her tone was clipped, her accent neutral and unmistakably public-school.

'I understand you're the leading expert on historical Manchester architecture—'

'Who told you that?' Levin cut him off.

Entwistle felt his cheeks flush slightly. 'Er, well, I googled it.'

'Ah Google, the tool of the idol generation.' Levin sounded decades older than her years. 'Whatever happened to using the library?' she added wistfully.

Entwistle bit his lip. He really didn't have time for a lecture on learning styles from an academic. 'I don't mean to be rude, Professor, but I'm working on an urgent case and I need you to look at some images for me.'

Levin raised an eyebrow as she locked the buckle on the strap of her attaché case in place. 'What case is that?'

'A missing person. A fifteen-year-old girl, actually. We're very concerned for her safety, and I was hoping your expertise might help us find her alive.'

Levin's whole body appeared to soften in an instant as a grave look spread across her face. 'Oh dear. That's terrible. How can I help?'

Entwistle moved over to where Levin stood, and opened the file he was carrying. Inside were several close-up stills taken from the ransom demand video, carefully edited to ensure Hollie could not be seen. He pointed to the metal structure Jones had identified. 'We're looking to locate a building that might contain this kind of metal joist. We believe it's Victorian.'

Levin inspected the images for a long moment in silence, then nodded. 'It's definitely Victorian. Mid-nineteenth century, I would say.' She looked up at Entwistle, and he saw pity in her eyes. 'I'm afraid there are quite a number of buildings in and around Manchester that still contain this kind of metalwork. I would be more than happy to compile a list for you, but I'm afraid it could take a few days to complete.'

'I don't have that kind of time, and neither does she,' said Entwistle, as he struggled to conceal his disappointment. 'Would you mind taking another look? Even the tiniest of differences could help us narrow down the search.'

Levin offered a soft smile. 'Of course.' She picked up the images once more.

Entwistle watched in silence as she studied the images with forensic detail, her face contorting in concentration. A couple of minutes later, Levin's face changed and her head moved back a fraction. 'Do you have a magnifying glass?' she asked out of the blue.

The question caught Entwistle off guard. 'I'm sorry?'

Levin switched her focus to him now. 'A magnifying glass. Do you have one?'

Entwistle shook his head. 'No. I'm afraid I don't.'

Levin passed the images back to Entwistle and grabbed her attaché case. 'Follow me.' She headed to the door at pace.

Levin moved quickly along the corridor, Entwistle struggling to keep up, until she stopped and pushed open a door marked 'Staff Room'. He followed her inside. The room was empty. Levin dropped her case on the floor and began rummaging through a cupboard situated next to a small kitchen area containing a kettle, cups and an array of teas and coffees.

'I'm sure it's in here somewhere...' mumbled Levin, her back to Entwistle.

'What is?' he asked.

'Ha! Got it,' said Levin, then turned and presented him with her find – a large magnifying glass. 'It's Dr Bannister's. He never uses it, but he also never throws anything away. I knew it had to be in here. Pass me those images again, will you?'

Entwistle handed them over, and watched with anticipation as Levin pored over the images through the magnifying glass.

'That looks familiar,' she said at length.

Entwistle's heart lifted. 'What does?'

Levin ignored him, instead moving across the room to a computer, where she began to type furiously.

Entwistle followed her. 'What are you looking for?'

'This,' Levin said with a satisfied grin, as she turned the monitor to face him. 'Gorton Monastery. The building you're looking for is potentially close by.'

'How do you know that?'

Levin handed Entwistle the magnifying glass and one of the stills. 'Take a look at the shadow in the background of the picture,' she said, indicating the spot with an index finger. 'Note its shape and the bulbous edges at the base.'

Entwistle could see it clearly.

'I'm sure that shadow has been cast by the spire of Gorton Monastery,' she explained, pointing to the computer, where an image of a large church filled the screen.

Entwistle moved closer to compare the two images. They looked almost identical. 'Bloody hell! That's amazing!'

'Thank you,' said Levin. 'Obviously, I can't be a hundred per cent certain, but it looks like the building you're looking for is somewhere in the vicinity of the Monastery. The time of day, and the position of the sun, will affect the direction of the shadow, so I'm afraid I can't be more specific on the exact location.'

Entwistle felt his pulse race as adrenaline surged through his body. Without thinking, he grabbed Levin and hugged her. 'Thank you, Professor.'

The action clearly took her by surprise. As Entwistle pulled away, Levin stared at him, eyes wide, face frozen. For a split second he feared he had overstepped a mark and would soon find himself on the end of an official complaint, but, much to his relief, Levin eventually blushed and produced a warm smile. 'You're very welcome, detective.'

'I must call my boss,' Entwistle said as he backed out of the room. 'Once again, thank you. This could be a life-saver. Literally.' He lurched through the door and out into the long corridor. He immediately pulled his phone from his pocket and called Phillips.

'Entwistle. Tell me you have something,' she said, her tone eager.

'I do, Guv,' said Entwistle. 'I think I know where they're holding Hollie.'

32

HOLLIE WOKE WITH A START AND SAT UPRIGHT ON THE BED. HER heart pounded in her ears, and the back of her neck was soaked with sweat. She had no idea what time it was, but guessed it was somewhere between breakfast and lunch. Mealtimes were now her only reference point each day.

From beyond the door came raised voices; another argument between the gang. Taking care to not be heard, she climbed out of the bed and tiptoed across the room, where she placed her ear to the ice-cold door. The voices were muffled through the metal and it was difficult to make out which of the gang was speaking at first, but it was obvious they were talking about her.

'Even if he does pay, we've got no choice now.' It was a woman's voice. Black, thought Hollie, as she continued. 'Thanks to this bloody idiot, she's seen my face!'

'Look, I just think we need to look at all the options,' said another gang member. It sounded like the man who had pointed the gun at Hollie during the ransom video – Red.

'Sorry, Red, but I'm with Black on this.' Hollie recognised

the next man's sinister tone immediately; White. 'If we're gonna get out of this in one piece, the girl has to go.'

'What about you, Blue?' asked Red.

'Who cares what that stupid fuck thinks,' shouted Black. 'He's the reason we're in this bloody situation in the first place!'

There was a moment of silence before Hollie recognised Blue spoke. 'We don't kill kids.'

'Oh yeah? And I didn't think we showed our faces either, but I was wrong about that, wasn't I?' said Black.

'Give it a rest, will you? I told you, she caught me off guard,' Blue shot back.

'I knew he was too old for this job, Red. But you wouldn't bloody listen, would you?'

'I'll show you who's too old, you stupid bitch!' shouted Blue.

'Come on, then!' screamed Black.

Hollie heard as they came together for a moment, before Red broke it up. 'Pack it in, the pair of you. If we've got any chance at pulling this off, we need to stick together, not start fighting with each other. So, can everyone please shut the fuck up, and get on with the job in hand? All right?'

A muffled chorus of responses filtered through the door, and a moment later, Hollie heard the gang's footsteps moving away down the corridor.

HOLLIE HAD no idea how much time had passed whilst she sat in silence and stared at the door, overwhelmed by fear. The sound of the lock being released caused her to jump with fright. A moment later, Red entered the room carrying a plate of food.

Hollie had only spoken to him once before, whilst the gang had filmed the ransom video. He terrified her. Physically, he was much bigger than either Blue or Black. Hollie guessed he was about the same as White. He placed her tray on the table, but she had no interest in food.

'Please don't kill me,' she blurted out.

Red stared at her in silence.

Hollie continued, 'I won't tell anyone I saw the woman's face. I promise. I'll never say a word to anybody.'

Red turned his masked face towards the door, then back to Hollie. 'What made you say that?'

'I heard you all arguing about the fact I saw her face. White said I had to go, and *you* said you'd "take care of me". That means you're going to kill me when this is all over, doesn't it?'

Red took a seat on the bed next to Hollie and spoke in a low whisper. 'I don't kill kids, Hollie. You have to believe that.'

'But what if my dad doesn't pay?'

'He'll pay,' said Red, without emotion.

'But what if he *doesn't?*'

'You're his fifteen-year-old daughter. Of course he'll pay.'

'I'm his *stepdaughter*, and we don't get on at all,' said Hollie, through her tears,

'It can't be that bad that he'd let you die.'

Hollie nodded. 'It is. He's such a shit to my mum and I won't let him get away with it. We argue all the time.'

'I'm sure he'll pay,' repeated Red, then stood up.

Hollie stared down at the bed and sobbed. 'I think about dying all the time.'

Red thrust his hands into the pockets of his black combat trousers. 'How old are you?'

'Fifteen,' Hollie said as she wiped her nose on her sleeve. 'Sixteen next month.'

'And you think about dying?'

Hollie nodded. 'Sometimes I think it'd be better than my life now.'

Red let out a sardonic chuckle. 'Seriously. What fifteen-year-old thinks like that?'

Hollie flicked the hair away from her face indignantly. 'You'd be surprised. A lot of girls at my school have talked about suicide.'

'I thought you went to a posh private school?' said Red. 'Aren't all your mates, rich?'

'Sure they are. But it doesn't mean they're happy. Most of us have rich parents who are more interested in making money than making time for us.'

'Poor little rich kids, hey?' said Red, his tone sarcastic.

'Go ahead, make fun of me, but I'd rather be broke and happy than live like I do now.'

Red laughed hard, which rattled against the mask. 'What a load of bollocks. You've got to be rich in the first place to talk like that. Take it from me; growing up broke is shit. Especially when your parents don't give a toss either. Trust me, your life ain't so bad.'

'You don't know anything about my life!' shouted Hollie.

'I know a lot more than you think, Hollie *Marie* Hawkins.'

Hollie was taken aback by the fact he knew her full name. *Nobody* knew her middle name.

'We've been watching you for a long time,' said Red. 'We know your family very well indeed, including all your mother and father's dirty secrets.'

Hollie stared at the masked face. 'Do you mean the fact he hits her? And that he's cheating on her?'

Red nodded. 'Amongst other things.'

'I've seen the bruises, you know. On my mum's arms and back. She tries to hide them, but I've caught her coming out of the shower. She's always saying she fell over, or she slipped playing tennis, but I don't believe her.'

Red shook his head. 'Any man who lays his hands on a woman is a coward.'

Hollie continued, 'And I've seen the emails he sends to his nasty little sluts. Disgusting sex emails to girls that are just a few years older than me. Telling them what he'd like to do to them in bed. It's sick.'

Red's head cocked to one side slightly. 'Where have you seen his emails?'

'On his computer. I sneak into his office when he's not there.'

'Really?' said Red. 'I would have thought someone like Sir Richard Hawkins would have his computer password-protected?'

'He does,' said Hollie. 'He changes it every week. But, because it has to be unique each time, he's always forgetting what it is. So he writes it down in a notepad that he keeps in his top drawer. He doesn't know I know it's there. And when he goes out, I use it to log in and take a look at what he's been up to. It's sickening.'

Red chuckled and stood up again. 'There's nothing so cunning as a teenager, is there?'

Hollie continued, 'Everything about him is vile; even his business is monstrous.'

'What makes you say that?'

'Because he sells guns to terrorists.'

'Why do you think his guns are going to terrorists?' asked Red.

'Because he's always taking private planes to Islamabad. He never tells me or mum where he's going – says it's confidential government stuff – but I've seen loads of emails and flight details from the jet operator he uses. I also saw an email from a security company he pays a lot of money to, to take him to Peshawar.'

'Does he now?'

Hollie nodded. 'Yeah he does. And do you know what's in Peshawar?'

Red didn't answer.

'The Taliban headquarters in Pakistan,' Hollie said proudly. 'I googled it.'

'Well, well, well. Maybe the rumours are true, then?' said Red.

'What rumours?'

'Exactly what you just said. That your father has been selling guns to the Taliban in Afghanistan, via Pakistan. He's denied it for years, but the British military have been finding his munitions in Taliban compounds all over Afghanistan. He claims they must have been passed on, after he sold them legitimately to the Saudi and Pakistan governments, but I've always been sure that's a lie.'

'All my father ever does is lie. All day, every day.'

BY THE TIME ENTWISTLE CALLED, Jones and Bovalino had searched two derelict buildings in Gorton. Armed with the additional information, they narrowed their search to the immediate vicinity of Gorton Monastery. There were two specific buildings Bovalino remembered from his childhood, so they decided to check those out first.

Bovalino pulled the squad car up next to the first building. A former workhouse, it had also been a warehouse, a factory and eventually an illegal nightclub before finally being abandoned and left to decay. Located off the main drag, its large second-floor windows – some of which sat in the shadow of Gorton Monastery – made it a strong contender for the location where the ransom video had been filmed. As the car stopped, Jones leaned forwards in his seat and surveyed the building.

'Should we wait for back-up, Jonesy?' asked Bovalino.

'Nar, mate. Let's have a look around first. If we see anything dodgy, we can get TFU in. I don't fancy calling in the tactical team if the place is empty. We'll never live it down.'

'Good point,' Bovalino said as he opened his car door.

Once out of the car, they collected a heavy-duty torch each from the boot, then followed the high wall round to the rear of the building, where they found the old wooden entrance gates standing slightly ajar. They stopped for a moment and Jones took a tentative look through the gap in the large hinge.

'Looks clear,' he said, then beckoned for Bovalino to follow him through the gates.

A few moments later, as they stood outside the entrance. Bovalino tried the door handle; it was locked up tight.

Jones craned his neck back to survey the structure. 'Does anyone actually own this place, Bov?'

'I dunno. It was on the market for years, but the For Sale sign seems to have disappeared.'

'In that case, do you think anyone would mind if we kick the door in?' Jones had a knowing grin.

Bovalino tapped his torch on the rotting wooden frame. 'Looks like it needs replacing to me, Jonesy. And if it helps save a young girl's life, I'm sure any owners would understand.'

Jones nodded. 'Off you go then, big lad. Do what you do best.'

Bovalino smiled and took a step back, then turned his body at an angle so his shoulder would lead the way. A split second later, he ran headlong at the ancient door. It was no match for the big Italian's size and speed, and splintered open at the first attempt.

Inside, two corridors led off the central entrance hall in opposite directions.

'You take that side,' Jones said as he switched on his torch, 'I'll take this. Shout if you find anything.'

Bovalino nodded. 'Will do.'

RED HAD TURNED to leave when the door to Hollie's room flew open and Black rushed in. 'The silent alarms going off,' she said. 'We've got company.'

Red grabbed Hollie by the arm. 'Come with me.' He pulled her up from the chair and they followed Black out of the room.

Out in the corridor, Red handed Hollie to Black. 'How the hell did they find us?'

'God knows.'

'How many are there?'

'Two. One in the east wing, and one just on the other side of the wall.'

Hollie didn't need any encouragement. 'I'm in here!' she screamed. 'Help me!'

'Shut up, you silly little bitch,' Black snarled in a low voice as she wrapped a gloved hand over Hollie's mouth and pushed Hollie's arm painfully up her back.

'You and the guys, head to the ERV,' Red said. 'I'll meet you there later. Right now, I've got a job to do.'

Black nodded, then dragged Hollie down the corridor. Blue and White stood ahead of them, armed and ready.

BOVALINO ARCED his flashlight and carefully checked each empty room as he passed along the dark corridor. With no windows on the ground floor, the space was almost pitch black but for a few shafts of light streaming through holes in the dilapidated brick walls. As he approached the last door, he noticed it looked as though it had been recently repaired. New hinges and a hook for a padlock had been added, although the padlock itself was not in place. His pulse began to quicken as he reached for the door handle and gently pushed it open, then stepped into the dark room beyond.

Holding his torch like a spear, he scanned the space. The flashlight revealed what appeared to be an old storage room, relatively empty aside from a few dusty old drums of what looked like engine oil, or some kind of lubricant. Bovalino tapped lightly on the side of one of the drums. It was pretty much empty. He inspected it with his flashlight, and it was then that he noticed an oily boot print on the floor. Moving closer, he realised it was fresh. Adrenaline coursed through his body, and his heart began to beat like a drum in his head.

In spite of his considerable height and physical ability, Bovalino knew the guys they were hunting were more than likely highly trained ex-military – with the added risk of weapons – whereas he and Jones were just a couple of coppers with a flashlight each. The absurdity of his situation hit home, and he reached for his phone to call in the Firearms team. A noise from behind startled him.

Acting on instinct, he spun on his heels, torch in his hand, and came face to face with a man wearing a mask. He opened his mouth to shout for Jones, but his words were silenced as the masked man rushed him and slammed shoulder-first into Bovalino's solar plexus. The impact took his breath away and he dropped to the floor like a stone. In an instant, the masked man was upon him, wrapping muscular arms around Bovalino's neck and legs around his torso. Bovalino tried to cry out for Jones once more, but the man's grip on his throat prevented him making any noise.

A moment later, Bovalino was pulled onto his back in a move he recognised from his time in the octagon as a mixed martial arts hold. The masked man was soon underneath him, and used Bovalino's considerable weight against him. Black dots began to appear in his vision as the breath was squeezed out of him. He knew he had to make a move or die.

Mustering every ounce of strength he could, he raised his head, then slammed it backwards onto the man's mask. He repeated the move over and over until, finally, the mask dislodged. His attacker let go for a split second and Bovalino seized the moment. He rolled his heavy body to the side and jumped to his feet. The masked man was soon back on his feet, but struggling to refit the mask. Bovalino charged at him, wrapped his thick arms around the man and lifted him off his feet, then slammed him down onto the floor, using his twenty stone to crush his attacker, who – clearly winded – gasped for air.

Bovalino grabbed at the mask and yanked it off.

Staring back at him was a face he recognised. 'Fuck. It's you!' Bovalino exclaimed as he grabbed the man's arms and held them against the ground.

A heavy kick to the groin stopped Bovalino in his tracks and he fell forwards onto the floor in agony.

In an instant, the masked man was out from under him and back on his feet.

By the time Bovalino had pulled himself up onto his hands and knees, his attacker had replaced his mask and headed out of the door.

Bovalino struggled to his feet and gave chase. 'Jonesy! I've got him!' he shouted as he lunged out into the corridor.

Much to Bovalino's surprise, Bovalino's assailant headed upstairs instead of back towards the exit.

Just then, Jones sprinted into the corridor.

'He's gone upstairs, Jonesy. I'm going after him,' Bovalino said, his voice echoing around the space.

'Wait for back-up, Bov!' shouted Jones.

Bovalino chose to ignore his partner. If he could catch the masked man, it might just save Hollie's life, so he set off, taking the steps two at a time.

Bovalino could hear the man climbing higher and higher. Behind, Jonesy was trying to catch up.

As he reached the top floor, Bovalino found himself bathed in sunlight from a large window to his left. He found he had a clear view of the entire floor. Ahead of him, the masked man had stopped, and appeared to be trapped, his only exit point behind where Bovalino now stood. 'Give yourself up!' said Bovalino, his words echoing around the open space.

The masked man didn't respond. Instead, he swivelled left and ran directly towards one of the metal pillars that held up the roof. With the speed of a monkey, he used the protruding rivets to climb the metal structure, and a moment later he was up on the beam that ran across the apex of the cavernous pitched roof, at least thirty feet above the ground. It appeared he was heading towards a hole in the roof where a skylight had once been.

Bovalino ran after him and attempted to climb the metal pillar himself. However, his large, wide feet struggled to gain traction against the rivets, and it was with some difficulty that he eventually reached the apex beam. By now, the masked man had already moved halfway across, and positioned himself under the broken skylight.

'Bov! Stop!' Jones shouted when he arrived at the top of the stairs. 'You'll bloody kill yourself.'

Bovalino wasn't listening. He was focused on stopping the masked man from making his escape. He took a tentative step out onto the narrow beam, and Jones shouted again.

'Jesus, Bov! Wait for the tactical team. They're on their way.'

Ahead of him, the masked man stood motionless, watching Bovalino as he edged closer, step by step.

'Tell me where the girl is,' said Bovalino.

The masked man laughed. 'Not today, mate. Not today.' He leapt from the beam and grabbed the metal frame of the skylight with both hands.

Bovalino rushed forwards and tried to grab his leg, but lost his footing. Time seemed to stand still as his large body fell forwards. His arms windmilled, and he clutched at air in an attempt to save himself.

He could hear Jones's screams as he hurtled towards the ground.

A second later, he hit the concrete with a sickening thud and the world went black.

33

By the time Phillips arrived on scene, paramedics were working to stabilise Bovalino in the back of an ambulance. Jones stood to the rear of the vehicle, staring blankly in through the open doors. Phillips placed a reassuring hand on his shoulder, and he turned towards her. His face was ashen, his eyes fighting away tears.

'How is he?' asked Phillips.

Jones shook his head. 'Not good, Guv. He fell almost thirty feet onto concrete. His body's all smashed up, and he's unconscious.'

Phillips stepped forwards and took in the scene. For once, Bovalino looked small and frail, laid out on the gurney with a neck brace in place. Splints wrapped both legs, and several drips and tubes came out of his arms. Two paramedics worked on him methodically.

The one nearest to Phillips offered a faint smile. 'He's in good hands. We're doing everything we can for him.'

Phillips flashed a weak smile in return, then turned back to Jones. 'Have you let Izzie know?'

'Yes. I called her just now.'

'How was she?'

Jones swallowed hard. 'Devastated. They've been together since they were teenagers. You know how much she loves him.'

Tears welled in Phillips's eyes as she imagined what Bovalino's wife must be going through. It reminded her why she had remained resolutely single for so long. The job they did was dangerous, and having someone at home who worried about you was a big responsibility to carry every day.

'She's heading to the hospital as we speak,' added Jones.

Phillips took a deep breath and gestured for Jones to follow her away from the ambulance.

Out of sight and earshot of anyone, she drew him into tight hug. 'He's gonna be ok, you know,' she said into his ear. 'Bov's a fighter,'

After a long moment, Jones pulled away. 'It's my fault. I tried to stop him, but he wouldn't listen. I should have *ordered* him down.'

'And do you think he would've listened to that? *Bov*, really?'

Jones's shoulders sagged and he shook his head.

'Exactly. He was doing what he thought was best for Hollie,' said Phillips.

Jones covered his face with his hands for a moment before rubbing his eyes and exhaling loudly. 'Fuck. I could do with a cigarette right now.'

Phillips offered him a warm smile, knowing how hard he had fought to give up the habit, a little over a year earlier. 'Are you feeling up to showing me inside, or would you prefer to stay here with Bov?'

Jones's nostrils flared and his jaw tensed for a moment. His eyes went steely. 'No. I want to catch these bastards. There's nothing I can do for him just now. And this is now personal. They messed with the wrong team today, Guv.'

'Good. In that case, let's get inside and take a look.'

194 · OMJ RYAN

EQUIPPED WITH HEAVY-DUTY FLASHLIGHTS, and wearing latex gloves, Phillips and Jones moved slowly through the east side of the building, where Bovalino had battled his attacker.

A few metres in, Phillips spotted a small plastic block attached to the wall. She stopped and trained her flashlight on it. 'Jonesy. Look at this.'

Jones moved next to her and waved his hand in front of it, but nothing happened. 'What the hell is that?'

'No idea.' Phillips pulled out her phone and took a picture of the block. 'Let's see if Entwistle can figure it out,' she added, as she emailed it through to him.

They continued down the long corridor. It wasn't long before they found a room containing oil drums. They took their time checking for any clues that Hollie had been held there, which wasn't easy with just the flashlights for illumination. Once the SOCO team arrived and set up their gear, the place would be lit up like a Christmas tree, but for now, they inspected the room one metre at a time.

Phillips spotted an oily footprint next to one of the drums. She stopped for a moment and attempted to gather her bearings.

'From where I'm stood now, where is the door where we came into the building?' she asked.

Jones turned to face her, then looked left and right. 'That way,' he said eventually.

Phillips followed his pointed finger and shifted her body so she was standing facing the same direction. She said nothing for a long moment, as she worked out where she was positioned in relation to the structure of the overall building.

'What you thinking, Guv?' said Jones.

'This is the last door on the corridor. Right?'

'I think so.'

'And there's no more doors?'

'Not that I know of,' said Jones.

'But, if you think about the size of this building and where we're stood, we're only about halfway down its length. Right?'

'Which means?'

'Which means, Jonesy, that either there were other doors that have since been bricked up...'

'Or?'

'Or this room is *the entrance* to the rest of the building.'

'Do you mean, like a false wall?'

'Exactly,' said Phillips, and turned to face the wall behind her. 'Exactly like a false wall.' She moved forwards and placed her hands on the exposed brickwork. 'Jesus, Jonesy. This isn't brick, it's bloody plasterboard covered in wallpaper. Come and feel.'

Jones followed suit, and ran his hands over the surface of the wall. 'It is too. Jesus. From a distance it looked just like brickwork.'

Phillips banged her fist on the wall, which sounded hollow. 'Flash that light over here, will you.'

As Jones trained his flashlight on the false wall, Phillips began to run her fingers across the surface until she found what she was looking for – a small indent that housed a semi-circular handle. She pulled it out and turned it anti-clockwise, which produced a satisfying click. A second later, she pushed open the hidden door, and stepped into a brightly lit space, Jones tucked in behind her.

She was shocked by what she saw. The place was kitted out like a military bunker; a number of rooms ran off a central corridor, there was a small mess hall, and a bunk room with four camp beds and a chemical toilet.

'I think it's fair to say that whoever was here has a military background, don't you?' said Phillips.

Jones nodded. 'Certainly looks that way.'

Phillips pressed on, and they walked farther into the building. They found another room, accessed by a heavy-duty metal door that had been left ajar. Phillips pushed it open but didn't enter the room. Inside stood another camp bed, complete with a sleeping bag and pillow.

Phillips stepped inside and found a chemical toilet positioned behind the door. In the middle of the room was a small table with a plate of uneaten food – some form of salad – and cutlery. Next to the bed stood a raft of books written for teenagers, and music magazines piled high. Phillips knelt and inspected the pillow, on which lay multiple strands of blonde hair.

'What colour was Hollie's hair?' she asked.

'Blonde, Guv,' said Jones.

Phillips nodded. 'It appears that she was here, then.'

'Let's just hope she's still alive,' said Jones.

At that moment, Phillips's phone began to vibrate. She pulled it from her pocket. The incoming call was from Entwistle. She switched it on to speaker. 'What you got for us?'

'It looks like some kind of motion sensor, Guv.'

'Which explains how they knew we were here,' said Jones.

'Any idea of its origins?'

'Sadly, no. I couldn't find the exact model you sent me, but it's very similar to a bunch you can get online from any one of a hundred retailers.'

'So no use in helping us track the gang?'

'I'm afraid not.'

Just then, Phillips's phone began to beep, which indicated another call coming in, this time from Fox. 'Ok, thanks. I'd better go.' She switched calls, took it off speaker, then placed the phone against her ear. 'Chief Superintendent Fox?'

'When exactly were you going to tell me that one of my officers had been seriously injured?'

'I'm on scene now, Ma'am. I was just about to call you.'

'*Don't bullshit me, Phillips.*'

'I promise you, Ma'am, I'm not. I was about to call—'

'*I want you and Saxby in my office within the hour.*'

'But Ma'am, surely finding Hollie is my priority right now,' said Phillips.

'*I don't think you heard me, Chief Inspector. I want you and Saxby in my office! No excuses, and no more bullshit. Understood?*'

'Yes, Ma'am.'

Fox ended the call without saying goodbye, and Phillips let out a frustrated sigh. 'Well, Jonesy, it looks like a bollocking from Fox is *actually* my priority.'

Jones shook his head.

'You may as well head to the hospital. I'll go and take one for the team.'

34

Ms Blair ushered Phillips through the door and into the chief superintendent's office, where Fox was already in discussion with Saxby.

Fox's eyes fell on Phillips. 'Chief Inspector. Take a seat.'

As she sat, Saxby nodded, but said nothing.

'Any news on Bovalino?' asked Fox.

'Nothing at this stage, Ma'am. Jones was following the ambulance to the hospital when I left. It took them over an hour to stabilise him at the scene.'

'That doesn't sound good.'

'No, Ma'am, I'm afraid it doesn't. He's in a very serious condition.'

'Tell me what happened,' said Fox.

Phillips relayed the events of the day, from Entwistle's visit with Professor Levin to Jones and Bovalino's search of the old workhouse in Gorton. How they had split up as they searched the two sides of the building, and then how Bovalino had clashed with one of the kidnappers and chased him into the rafters of the building, resulting in his accident.

'So, your men let our best chance of catching the kidnappers slip away, then?' said Saxby, when Phillips had finished.

As thoughts of Bov and his wife, Izzie, flashed through her mind, Phillips was possessed with an urge to rip Saxby's head off and feed it to him. It took all her strength to maintain a civil tone when she answered. 'And what would *you* have done differently, then?'

'Well. If this was my investigation, I can guarantee I'd be further forward in the search for the girl by now—'

'Based on what evidence, exactly?' said Phillips.

'Let's just call it a hunch,' replied Saxby. 'And I'd have sent a fully armed tactical team into the building. Not just a couple of bobbies with flashlights for protection.'

'They're *seasoned* detectives, and they went into the building based on the danger to life. Jones *did* call in the TFU, but by the time they arrived, the kidnappers had escaped.'

'Yes. But only because your heavy-handed amateurs bundled in and made so much noise. Have they ever heard of a covert operation, Chief Inspector?'

Phillips was starting to lose her temper now. 'Well, if you'd bothered to check out the scene, as opposed to just kissing Sir Richard's arse—'

'I beg your pardon?' said Saxby, clearly affronted.

Phillips ignored him and continued, '—then you'd have known that the gang had filled the place with motion detectors. They knew we were coming the moment Jones and Bovalino entered the building.'

Fox watched on, but had yet to enter the fray. She was no doubt trying to decide which horse to back.

'The fact of the matter remains, DCI Phillips,' said Saxby, 'that in the last week, your team has failed to create a single tangible lead as to Hollie's whereabouts.'

'*Are you for real?* Thanks to the tenacity and skill of *my team*, we found the kidnappers hideout. And from what we can ascertain, Hollie is still alive.'

'As long as your bungled raid hasn't panicked them into cutting their losses and killing her,' said Saxby.

'These guys don't panic,' said Phillips, her tone assured. 'They took everything they needed when they left. It was clear they had a well-drilled plan for escape. The guy who attacked Bov knew exactly how to get out of that building through the roof. It wasn't an accident that the skylight was missing. He used a classic military tactic – drawing the enemy away from his team, enabling them to escape. With your military background, I would have thought *you'd* have recognised that.'

Before Saxby could reply, Fox finally stepped in. 'So you're *sure* they're military?'

'Almost certain, Ma'am. I'm no expert, but everything points to them being a well drilled, well trained team. And if that is the case, there's a good chance they served together – most likely in active combat.'

'Sounds like more assumptions to me,' said Saxby.

Fox continued. 'So what about the ex-military leads you explored? Any further developments on those?'

'Well, Ma'am,' said Phillips, 'Robbins was working and very visible at the club on the night Hollie was taken, so it looks like he's out, Cartwright's dead, Baker has CCTV footage that proves he was at work when she was snatched, and Holmes and Matthews are each other's alibis – along with another dozen or so of their colleagues at Hawkins's factory. Plus they have CCTV to vouch for their whereabouts as well.'

'So. *No leads* there, either?' sneered Saxby.

Phillips had heard enough. 'So what about you? You're the *expert*. What have you come up with?'

Saxby bristled. 'Like I said many times before, I'm here in an advisory role, at the request of Sir Richard and the Home Office. I'm not here to be a foot soldier.'

'Well, why don't you do that?' snarled Phillips. '*Advise* me. You've been here a week, and so far all I've seen you do is fawn over Sir Richard or sit up here on the fifth floor, drinking tea.'

Saxby opened his mouth to speak, but Fox cut him off. 'DCI Saxby. Would you mind leaving us for a moment?'

Saxby turned to face Fox. 'May I ask why, Ma'am?'

'No, you may not,' said Fox, her tone flat.

Saxby pursed his lips, and fixed Phillips with a cold stare. 'As you wish, Ma'am.' He got up and left the room.

When the door had closed behind him, Fox turned her attention to Phillips. 'As much as you dislike him, what Saxby says is correct. Jones and Bovalino didn't follow protocols—'

'I know, Ma'am, but—'

'They didn't follow protocols, they took too many risks, and because of that, the girl is in even graver danger – and an officer is seriously injured.'

'Ma'am, I understand what you're saying, but—'

'That's just it, Phillips. I don't think you do. As Saxby rightly says, it's been over a week since the girl was snatched, and so far the MCU is no further forward. If anything, by losing one of the team, we've gone backwards. Sir Richard is bitching and moaning to everyone in Whitehall. The chief constable is getting it in the neck – which means yours truly here is also copping a load of flack. If the girl dies, this will be a very public scandal, and that's not something I want attached to my department. So, with that in mind, I've made a decision...'

Phillips's pulse quickened, in anticipation of what was to come.

'...if – as you suggest – your failed attempt today *hasn't* panicked them, then tomorrow we can expect the kidnappers to send Sir Richard details of the money drop.'

'Yes, Ma'am.'

'With that in mind, I've decided that DCI Saxby will take

control of the ransom drop, and *he* will decide how we proceed tactically.'

Phillips was aghast. 'You can't do that. The man's inept.'

'I can, and I will. If this thing goes south, then it can take the Met down with it. Not MCU.'

'With respect, Ma'am, if it does go south, the girl could end up dead.'

'*If* that happens – *if* – then it'll be Saxby's neck on the line. Not mine – and not yours.'

Phillips couldn't believe what she was hearing. 'Please, Ma'am. Let me handle the drop. I can bring Saxby into the team. But letting him run the op...that's madness.'

Fox fixed Phillips with her black, cold eyes. 'Are you suggesting I've lost my mind?'

'No Ma'am, of course not.'

'Good. In that case, I've made my decision. Saxby is in charge.'

Phillips swallowed her hatred for Fox deep into her belly. How could she risk Hollie's life just to save her own reputation?

'So, unless there's anything else...?' said Fox.

'No, Ma'am.'

'That's settled then. Dismissed.'

35

After her meeting with Fox, Phillips was tempted to head home and drink herself numb. It had been a long time since she had done that, but today she felt very thirsty indeed. As she approached her car, she came to her senses. The only place she should be was at the hospital. In the car, she pulled up Jones's number on screen and called him handsfree as she set off in the direction of the MRI.

It took a number of failed attempts, but she finally managed to get through.

'Hi, Guv,' said Jones.

'How is he?'

'They're preparing him for surgery. Looks like he has a fractured skull, swelling on the brain, a fractured pelvis and internal bleeding. There's also some potential damage to his spine.'

'Jesus,' said Phillips, almost lost for words.

'Izzie's here, but they won't let her see him. Judging by the state of his injuries, that's probably for the best, to be honest.'

'What about Entwistle?' asked Phillips.

'On his way over, Guv.'

'So am I. Are you still in A&E?'

'*Yeah. Just sat in the waiting room.*'

'Right. I'll be with you in fifteen minutes.'

Phillips ended the call, her mind awash with images of Bovalino and the times they'd shared over the years; good, bad and, in some cases, deadly. Filled with a sense of foreboding, she was impatient to get to the MRI. 'Sod it,' she said out loud, switched on the siren and blue lights, then accelerated into the outside lane. In the world of Major Crimes, this was a real emergency.

The remaining journey took a little over seven minutes, and after she had parked in a spot reserved for police vehicles, she made her way through the main doors of the Accident and Emergency department. Inside, she soon found Jones, Entwistle and Izzie Bovalino, huddled together on a row of plastic seats screwed into the polished concrete floor.

As she approached, Jones and Entwistle stood.

'Guv,' said Jones.

'Guv,' repeated Entwistle.

Phillips nodded to them both, and approached Izzie with open arms, who stood and allowed her small, petite frame to be enveloped in a hug. After a long moment, Phillips pulled back and stared into Izzie's elfin face. 'How are you holding up?'

Izzie's eyes and nose were red and swollen, and her mascara had left black streaks, which matched her long dark hair, down her cheeks. 'I'm ok. Just praying for Lorenzo.'

It was strange to hear Bovalino called by his first name. He was – and always had been – Bov to the team, and it was easy to forget his wife and family referred to him by something else.

'How's he doing?' asked Phillips.

Izzie opened her mouth to speak, but no words would come out.

Jones stepped in. 'He's just gone into surgery. They need to stop the internal bleeding, then fix his broken bones. The doctor reckons it could take a few hours.'

'Every day since he became a policeman, I've prayed for him, you know,' Izzie said softly, 'I prayed to God to keep my Lorenzo safe, to bring him home to me each night. But I was always terrified...' Her words tailed off as tears streaked down her cheeks once more. 'I can't lose him, Jane. He's my life.'

Phillips wrapped an arm around Izzie's shoulder. 'You're not going to lose him. He's a fighter.' She said the words, but, deep down, she was worried too. Judging by his injuries, even if he did survive, the chances of making a full recovery looked slim. 'Do you have anyone who can come and sit with you?'

Izzie nodded. 'My sisters are on their way now. They'll be here soon.'

Phillips squeezed her tightly again. 'Good. We'll sit with you until they get here.'

Sometime later, Izzie's sisters arrived en masse, making a noisy and heart-warming – Italian-style – entrance. In a flash, Izzie was surrounded, wrapped up in her family's love.

Phillips signalled to Jones and Entwistle that it was time they took a break, and together they headed for the Colombian Bean Cafe on the ground floor of the main hospital building.

Ten minutes later, armed with a strong black coffee each, they regrouped around a table in the corner of the cafe.

'I'm really scared, Guv,' said Jones. 'He's my best mate. What if he dies?'

'We can't think like that, Jonesy. We have to be strong for Bov – and for Izzie,' said Phillips.

Jones dropped his chin and nodded.

Phillips waited patiently for him to gather his thoughts.

After a long moment, he exhaled sharply and lifted his head. 'So, how was the meeting with Fox and Saxby?'

Phillips sat back in her chair and blew her lips. 'Far worse than I was expecting, I'm afraid.'

'How so?' asked Jones.

'She's not happy that you and Bov broke protocol by not waiting for back-up.'

Jones eyes widened and his jaw clenched. 'If Bov had caught the guy and saved Hollie, he'd be a hero. But because he got away, *we're* the villains now?'

Phillips nodded sagely. 'I'm afraid so. You know how Fox works, Jonesy. She's the queen of the "self-preservation-society".'

'She's a fucking bitch,' spat Jones under his breath.

Phillips took a sip of her hot coffee. 'Yes. She's that too.'

'But how can she say Jonesy and Bov messed up?' asked Entwistle. 'They found the kidnappers' hideout based on a single shadow in the background of a grainy video. That's amazing detective work.'

Phillips let out an ironic chuckle. 'You've got a lot to learn about police politics, Entwistle, but then again, I've been at this for twenty years and I'm still getting it wrong.'

Jones banged his fist on the table, drawing anxious looks from patrons at the nearby tables. 'How can she stitch Bov up like this when he's fighting for his life?'

Phillips reached across and placed a reassuring hand on Jones's wrist. 'Because that's what she does. I know it's easier said than done, but don't take it personally. Fox is looking after Fox. It's what she does best, and it's what she's always done.'

Jones's lips formed a snarl. 'Well, all I can say is, she better watch where she's walking alone at night. One of these days, someone might give her what she deserves.'

Phillips had worked with Jones for long enough to know he was just venting. As much as he hated Fox, Jones was as straight a copper as you could find. But she understood his anger and frustration. It was tough for her to swallow too.

She said nothing for a few minutes to allow him to calm down. Then she took a deep breath and blew it out. 'Look. I know this will go down like a shit-sandwich too, but Fox has decided that Saxby will take the lead on the ransom-money drop.'

Both men recoiled in their seats. Unsurprisingly, Jones was first to speak. 'Are you fucking kidding me?'

His language again drew disapproving looks from those seated nearest to them.

Phillips quietly apologised on Jones's behalf before she turned back to face him and Entwistle. She leaned forwards and spoke in hushed tones. 'Look. I don't like it any more than you do, but she's made up her mind. She's worried it's all gonna go tits up, and wants to distance MCU from any fallout. She reckons the Met can carry the can.'

Jones's eyes were wide and wild now. 'But that's nonsense. The man is a buffoon. He hasn't a clue what he's doing.'

'I know. I know. And I made the exact same point to Fox this evening, but she's not having it. Saxby's in charge of the operation, and all strategy related to it.'

'So, we have to do what he says then, Guv?' asked Entwistle.

'Yep. I'm afraid so.'

Jones sat back and rubbed his hands down his face, causing the skin to redden. 'In that case, the girl's dead, plain and simple. If Saxby's in charge, she's a gonner.'

Phillips had no reply for Jones, because she too feared the worst.

'So, we're still expecting the ransom drop details tomorrow?' said Entwistle.

'I think so, but Saxby has other ideas. He reckons us discovering their hideout could panic them into killing Hollie and making a run for it. But I don't see it. They've been one stop ahead of us the whole time. Plus, as I pointed out to him and Fox, these guys don't panic. They knew we were coming, and had a plan to escape. No. I'm sure they'll be back in touch. They've got four million reasons to, after all.'

Jones shrugged his shoulders. 'So what do we do now? What's next?'

Phillips drained her coffee and stood. 'Now? Now, Jonesy, we go back and check on Bov. He's our priority tonight. We can deal with Saxby and Fox in the morning.'

36

NOVEMBER 8TH

PHILLIPS WAS GETTING OUT OF THE SHOWER WHEN SAXBY CALLED.

'*Sir Richard has received another video from the kidnappers. I want you over there immediately.*' His tone was more than a little superior. She mused he must be smug after the conversation with Fox the previous day.

Phillips bit her tongue. Naked, apart from a towel, this wasn't the time to get into the semantics of the new chain of command. She checked the alarm clock on her bedside table – 6.27 a.m. 'I'll be there by 7.15.'

'Very good,' said Saxby, and ended the call.

Phillips threw her phone onto the bed and took a couple of deep breaths to calm her growing anxiety. Saxby wasn't going to get the better of her.

Twenty minutes later, dressed in her usual charcoal grey suit with a white shirt and black boots, and carrying her overcoat on her arm, she stepped out of her front door. Because she always wore her hair tied back, she'd had no reason to waste time blow-drying it.

The drive from her Chorlton terraced house to the Hawkins's Altrincham mansion took just twenty minutes, and as she pulled up on the street outside the large metal gates, she spotted Saxby's car coming from the opposite direction. The gates opened and she drove in before him, and up to the house.

As she stepped out, Saxby parked up behind her. He seemed as keen as ever to be first to the front door, and almost threw himself out of his car in order to catch Phillips before she walked up the front steps. He tugged at her arm, and she turned to face him.

'From now on, we follow the correct procedure.' He stepped uncomfortably close, his face just a few inches from hers.

Instinctively she took a step back, but he followed her. Personal space was clearly not something he valued. 'Listen, Saxby. As I understand it, you're in charge of the ransom drop. Not the investigation. I'm still the SIO on that, so cut the senior officer crap, will you?'

Saxby flashed a thin smile. 'After the ransom drop, there won't *be* an investigation.'

Phillips opened her mouth to respond, but was stopped in her tracks by Sir Richard, who opened the front door. 'It's about time you lot arrived.'

Saxby turned and thrust out his hand. 'Sir Richard,' he said as Hawkins shook it, 'how are you holding up?'

'I'm fine. It's my money and my daughter I'm worried about.' He turned and walked back into the house.

Saxby raced in after him, and Phillips fell in behind.

Once again, Sir Richard directed them to the kitchen, where Sandra Hawkins sat at the large kitchen island. The scene was identical to their first meeting. Hawkins turned his laptop to face them. 'This came in at 5 a.m. today.' He pressed play on the video.

As before, Hollie appeared in the middle of the screen, but the location was different – a good indicator that it had been recorded in the last twenty-four hours, thought Phillips.

'*My name is Hollie Hawkins. The time is now 1 a.m. on Friday* the 8th of November. I am being well treated and remain unharmed. To ensure that continues, and to secure my safe return, my father, Sir Richard Hawkins, is to pay four million pounds in cash tonight. The location where the money is to be left can be found at the following grid reference: Sierra Kilo 1-4-2 9-0-1. The money is to be left at this exact location at twenty-three hundred hours, in eight waterproof bags, half a million pounds in each. My mother, Sandra Hawkins, is to deliver the cash, alone. If my captors seen any sign of police involvement – or trackers on the money – you will never see me again.'

Phillips noted the change in Hollie's delivery. In comparison with the first video, she appeared a lot calmer, certainly less frightened of the situation. Phillips recalled the vast array of books and magazines in the room where Hollie had been held captive, and was filled with hope that the gang was actually treating her well – that perhaps the first video had been made to look worse that it was in order to shock Richard and Sandra Hawkins into paying the ransom.

'So. It looks like we have no choice but to pay the money,' said Hawkins, fixing Phillips with an icy glare.

'Do you have the cash?' asked Saxby.

'Yes. It's in here.' Hawkins beckoned them into his home office, situated just off the kitchen. On the floor were several bags, each stuffed with packets of bank notes.

'Can your wife lift that kind of weight? That's a lot of money,' said Phillips.

'I know it's a lot of money,' said Hawkins. 'It's a lot of *my* money.'

Sandra Hawkins appeared at the door. 'If it's split up into eight bags as they've asked, I should be able to lift them out of the car. That's all I have to do. I won't be carrying them anywhere.'

'I've told her she's not going,' Hawkins barked. 'One of you lot can do it instead.'

Phillips made to answer him, but Saxby beat her to it. 'Sir
Richard. I understand your concern, but our priority has to be
the safe return of your daughter. As the kidnappers have made
clear, we cannot be seen to be involved.'

'But you *will* be involved, won't you?' said Hawkins.

'Of course. We'll follow Mrs Hawkins at a safe distance,
using surveillance experts. We'll also have teams of specialist
firearms officers on standby. The goal is to let the kidnappers
take the money, then follow them to where they're keeping
Hollie. We go in, grab Hollie, and get your money back.'

'It sounds so simple when you say it, DCI Saxby,' said
Phillips, only just able to mask the sarcasm in her voice.

If Saxby noticed her tone, he didn't show it. He continued
his grandstanding. 'You'll be glad to know that I am taking
control of the operation tonight. I am very confident that, by
morning you'll have your daughter, *and* your money, safely
back where they belong, and we'll have the kidnappers in
custody.'

Phillips closed her eyes for a moment. This guy really had
no clue. There was no way this team would make life so easy
for them. She pulled out her phone and opened up the web
browser, then began to type into it.

'Are we boring you, Chief Inspector?' said Saxby.

Phillips looked up. 'No. I'm just checking the location
attached to that grid reference. Seems prudent to know where
we're going, wouldn't you agree?'

Saxby bristled, then forced a thin smile. 'Quite.'

'Here we are,' said Phillips, turning the phone to face the
room. 'It's up near the Snake Pass, in the High Peak.' A winding,
narrow road, Snake Pass cut through the rough terrain of the
Peak District, a cluster of unforgiving hills that connected
Manchester to Sheffield and the rest of Yorkshire.

'That seems like an odd place for the drop,' Hawkins
observed. 'I mean, it's open country up there.'

'Well, as we've discussed before, Sir Richard,' said Saxby, 'I do believe the kidnappers to be ex-military. That is the *exact* kind of landscape they are trained to operate in.'

Phillips couldn't believe what she was hearing. *He believed?* It was her team that had ascertained the military link! 'I know I'm no expert on these things,' she said, 'but even with their military training, isn't using a location, with just a handful of roads in or out, a huge risk?'

Saxby scoffed. 'Never underestimate the cunning of a military man.'

'I wouldn't. And that's why it seems odd to me. These guys don't take risks.'

'Well, it's a good job I'm in charge of the operation then, isn't it?' said Saxby.

'So how will all this happen tonight?' Hawkins cut in.

Saxby almost stood to attention as he answered. 'How long does it take to get from here to the Snake Pass, Chief Inspector?'

'About an hour.'

'Ok. In that case, Mrs Hawkins, I would like you to leave here at 21.45 and drive to the location, which we will pre-programme into your GPS. You will be followed by a number of surveillance officers, in various vehicles, throughout your journey. Once you get there, leave the money on the ground, as advised, and drive home. Do not look back, and no matter what you see, do not stop. You will be watched and monitored by my officers at all times – *as will your money*, Sir Richard.'

Hawkins blew his lips and ran his fingers through his hair. 'Will she have air support?'

'I'm sorry?' said Saxby.

'Will there be an eye in the sky? Like a police helicopter?'

Saxby shook his head. 'No, I'm afraid not. They are far too loud. The kidnappers would know we were watching them. No. We'll be using well practiced metropolitan police, surveillance techniques utilising cars and motorbikes, as well as officers on

the ground in the surrounding terrain. Don't worry, Sir
Richard, Lady Hawkins, we'll catch them.'

Phillips wanted to scream. The golden rule of surveillance
was to expect the unexpected. Plan for the worst and hope for
the best. In this instance, Saxby was already planning his
victory parade. Somehow, she had to find a way to mitigate the
damage his over-confidence was in danger of causing.

'Right then,' said Hawkins, looking at his watch.' I'm afraid I
have some calls to make.' It was clearly time for Phillips and
Saxby to leave.

'Of course, Sir Richard. I know how busy you must be,'
Saxby said, almost bowing.

Phillips smiled warmly as she passed Sandra Hawkins,
whose eyes were wide, filled with fear. She wanted desperately
to comfort her, tell her everything was going to be ok, but with
Saxby in charge, she couldn't make that promise. *Her* daughter's
life was now in the hands of an idiot's ego.

Outside on the drive, as Phillips was about to get into her
car, Saxby grabbed her by the shoulder, forcing her to face him.
Once again he stood up close, and she could smell his pungent,
stale coffee and nicotine-laced breath. 'As of now, I have total
control of this operation. I want you and your team in *my* office
at 11 a.m., ok?'

Phillips nodded, but remained silent as she held her breath.

Saxby checked his watch theatrically. 'Right. Well, as the
chief constable is expecting me, I'd better be getting back.'
With a broad smile, he turned and marched towards his car.

Phillips watched him walk away and shook her head.
'Prick,' she muttered under her breath, then jumped into
her car.

37

Phillips sat, with Jones and Entwistle, waiting for Saxby in his temporary office. He finally arrived, fifteen minutes late for his own meeting. She was in no doubt it was deliberate, a power play to show who was in charge.

'Sorry. The *chief constable* kept me talking,' he said as he strode into his office with the air of a strutting peacock. He took a seat behind his desk. 'Right. Let's talk about tonight's drop, shall we?'

Phillips had called Entwistle as soon as she left the Hawkins's home, and in the last hour, he had used Google Earth to download detailed satellite images of the area. He passed the copies around now.

Saxby pursed his lips as he inspected his.

'Looks surprisingly open, sir,' said Jones, looking at the terrain. 'I have to say, it does seem an unnecessarily risky location the gang has chosen.'

'My thoughts exactly,' said Phillips.

Saxby laid the printout on the desk and reclined in his chair. 'Like I said to Sir Richard, they're military men, trained to operate in this exact terrain.'

'Yes, of course,' said Phillips, 'but only when the operation dictates it. Surely no unit would knowingly expose themselves in this way. Not if they were in control of the location. Not if they didn't have to.'

Saxby folded his arms across his chest. 'I'm sorry, Phillips. Are you basing that on your vast military experience?'

Phillips sat forwards in her chair and slapped the back of her hand on the printout. 'You don't have to be military trained to realise that a drop location, with limited roads in and out – *and* surrounded by woodland – is not a good place to pick up heavy bags of money. Even though they've explicitly said not to, the gang will know that Hawkins will bring us in. Which means they are expecting armed police. And where better to hide a sniper than in the forest? It just doesn't make sense. It's almost as if they're deliberately making it hard for themselves.'

'Nonsense, Phillips,' Saxby scoffed. 'They are doing what they're trained to do. The cover of woodland works both ways. Depending on their level of training and experience, they could easily use it to their own advantage.'

'I'm sorry sir, but I have to agree with DCI Phillips. It doesn't make sense to me either,' said Jones.

'Well you're hardly going to disagree with your boss, are you?' spat Saxby.

'Yes, he bloody well would,' said Phillips, 'because that's how we work in MCU. If one of us thinks something is wrong, we say it. We don't stand on ceremony. It's all about getting the right result.'

Saxby waved away her protest. 'Well, I can assure you, that's exactly what we're going to get tonight – *the right result.*'

Phillips felt her blood begin to boil. She was tempted to continue the argument for the hell of it, but knew it would be in vain. People like Saxby never listened to reason. This operation was just part of a game to him, a way to make a name for himself; to further his reputation in the Met. For a moment, she contemplated leaving him to hang himself with his own incompetence. But that could prove fatal for Hollie, and there was no way she could let that happen.

'I'd like Jones and I to be included in the surveillance team,' she said.

'That won't be necessary. I'm bringing in my specialist team from London. They're en route as we speak,' said Saxby.

Knowing how much he thought of himself and his buddies in the Met, Phillips had anticipated such a move and was ready with a counter-argument. 'Specialists or not, if they don't know the local area, they'll be at a serious disadvantage. That's where Jones and I can help. Having two coppers from Manchester on the team will improve your chances of this operation being the big success you want it to be,' she said, deliberately playing to his ego.

'So how *exactly* will having two locals on the team help?' said Saxby.

'Have you ever been to the High Peak?' asked Phillips.

'No.'

'Well, let's just say, it's pretty unforgiving terrain. Jones and I know it well, and we can help your boys navigate it.'

'That's why we have satellite navigation,' said Saxby.

Phillips chortled. 'You really haven't been up there, have you?'

'And what's that supposed to mean?' Saxby appeared affronted by the remark.

'It means that Sat Navs rarely work up in those hills. And at this time of the year, when the weather can change in a heartbeat, all it takes is one wrong turn and you could end up in the middle of nowhere. The bottom line is, you need people who know their way around, or your operation could easily go tits up.'

Saxby took a long moment to respond, then finally nodded.

He sat forwards again. 'Very well. You're in my team, but you follow my orders to *the letter*. Are we clear?'

Phillips nodded. 'Yes, we're clear.'

'In that case,' said Saxby, 'here's how it's going to play out...'

Fifteen minutes later, after hearing Saxby's plan for the operation, Phillips, Jones and Entwistle left his office on the fifth floor and made their way back to the incident room on the third floor. When they got back, they shut themselves away in Phillips's office.

'This guy's gonna get Hollie killed,' Jones muttered as soon as the door was closed.

'That's why I wanted us involved in the surveillance operation. I mean, what use is a bunch of guys from central London in an area like the High Peak?'

'Good call, Guv. I'm glad you did that.'

'Yeah. But I can't say that I'm very impressed with his plan for the op. His confidence that everything will go absolutely according to plan worries me.'

Jones nodded. 'Me too.'

'So while you're on the op, what can I do, Guv?' asked Entwistle.

Phillips sat down at her desk and took a moment to crystallise her thoughts. 'I've been starting to consider that we may be too focussed on the fact the team have military training. Is that blinding our judgement? I mean, there was a time when we suspected Bahmani was somehow involved.'

'Do you think he still is?' asked Entwistle.

'I really don't know, but it can't hurt to keep an eye on him.' Phillips looked at her watch. It was 12.30 p.m. 'Entwistle, you've got the whole afternoon to find out which of his lairs he's hiding out in today. Once you locate him, stay on him. If he's involved in this, I can guarantee he won't be able to stay away from four million quid for very long, and that may just lead us to Hollie.'

38

FOR THE PURPOSES OF THE SURVEILLANCE OPERATION, PHILLIPS and Jones borrowed a pool car from the fleet team. They had chosen a standard edition Volkswagen Golf, the best-selling and most common car on UK roads – the idea being to try and blend in as much as possible.

As the time approached 9.35 p.m., they waited on the long tree-lined street, approximately three hundred meters away from the Hawkins home. A motorcycle was stationed a few miles down the route, along with another car, both of which were manned by Saxby's team from London. It had started to rain heavily, and fog was forecast for later that evening.

Saxby, who was using the call sign 'Team Leader', was in a control vehicle near the drop site, and had been barking orders over the radio for the last half hour. Phillips had turned down their monitor for the moment. Nothing he had said so far had been of any value, and she was tired of hearing his voice.

'Any further updates on Bov?' she asked.

'Izzie says there's no change just yet, that the next forty-eight hours will be critical,' said Jones. 'They still can't get the swelling on his brain to go down. Until they can, the doctors want to keep him in an induced coma.'

'Jesus. I still can't believe it,' said Phillips. 'Especially not Bov. He always seemed indestructible.'

'Yeah, he did.'

At that moment, her mobile rang. It was Entwistle. As she answered it, she switched it to speaker so Jones could listen in.

'How are things at your end, Entwistle?' said Phillips.

'*Quiet as a mouse, Guv.*'

'Are you still outside the snooker hall?'

'*Yep. He's been in there for three hours. From where I'm parked, I can see the front and back of the building. A few cars have come and gone, but nothing out of the ordinary.*'

'Ok. Well, we're about to set off with Sandra in the next few minutes. If anything changes, call me immediately.'

'*Will do, Guv,*' said Entwistle, then ended the call.

Phillips and Jones sat in silence as they waited for Sandra Hawkins's car to emerge from the automatic gates.

'I still don't like this drop location, Jonesy,' said Phillips.

'Me neither. But what can we do? Saxby's acting as if he's bloody Montgomery chasing down Rommel in the desert.'

Phillips folded her arms across her chest. 'That's what I don't understand. Surely the fact that he's ex-military should mean he can see something's not right with this picture.'

'Not necessarily. He's an ex-officer, isn't he?' said Jones.

'What do you mean by that?'

'Well. A couple of my cousins were in the Army, and according to them, not all officers were made equal. Some were amazing soldiers with incredible leadership skills. Men you'd run through walls for. But then again, some, and I quote, "... were just a bunch of twats from university who liked getting dressed up for dinner."'

Phillips laughed out loud. 'Well, I think that just about sums up Major Harry Saxby, don't you?'

Jones chuckled along. 'Yeah.'

'Seriously though, I have a really bad feeling about this op. The kidnappers must know we're involved after what happened to Bov. I'm sure they're playing with us. We wait seven days for the details of the drop, then they send us out to the middle of nowhere. I'm not buying it. We're being led to that location for some reason – and it's not to find Hollie.'

'But that's where the money's going, so that *must* be the drop point.'

Phillips stared out of the window for a moment, then started scrolling through the contacts in her phone 'Screw it. We need some proper military expertise on this.'

Jones raised his eyebrows. 'Who are you calling?'

'Robbins.'

'Shit, Guv, that could get you in a lot of trouble. We still don't know for sure that he's not involved.'

'He isn't, Jonesy.'

'But how can you be sure?'

'Call it instinct. He's not the type,' said Phillips.

'Even if he's not, Guv, sharing confidential information with a member of the public? That's a career-ender.'

'Only if it gets out. And you and I aren't going to say anything, are we?' Phillips hit dial.

Once again she switched it to speaker to enable Jones to hear what was being said, but the phone eventually rang out and went to voicemail. She tried again, but got the same result. On the third attempt, she left a message. 'John, it's DCI Phillips. I need to speak to you urgently. Can you call me the moment you get this? Thanks.' She ended the call. 'I wonder where he is?'

'Well, let's hope he's not on his way to the High Peak,' Jones said with a wry grin.

'Piss off!' Phillips playfully punched his arm.

Just then, the gates to the Hawkins house began to open

slowly. Jones activated the windscreen wipers just as the large Range Rover edged out and stopped for a moment at the curb before pulling out onto the street. It headed off towards the M56, and the road to the ransom drop.

Jones pulled the car out and set off as Phillips reached over and turned up the volume on the radio. She grabbed the handset. 'Team Leader, this is Zero Four. We have eyes on the target. She is heading westbound on Netheredge Lane. We're following.'

'*Roger that, Zero Four,*' said Saxby over the radio.

39

For the next forty-five minutes, Phillips and Jones continued to take their turn at the head of the surveillance team, rotating with the second car and the motorbike, keeping Sandra Hawkins's car in sight – despite the heavy surface water on the roads. Throughout their journey, they had maintained constant contact with Saxby, plus the other team members, and there had been nothing to cause concern. Things were going according to plan. Still, Phillips could not let go of the foreboding in her gut, the sense that this drop was all wrong.

As the motorways turned to B roads, it became harder to tell if they were being followed, but as they moved through the small suburb of Brookfield, each operative reported a clear route and no issues. They edged closer to the market town of Glossop, at the base of the High Peak. Saxby had agreed that once the convoy reached that point, Phillips and Jones, with their knowledge of the terrain, would be responsible for following Sandra Hawkins for the final leg of the trip up Snake Pass.

'I'm still not happy about this,' said Phillips.

'All good so far, though, Guv.'

Phillips's phone began to ring. It was John Robbins. She answered it, and switched it to speaker. They had only a matter of minutes to spare before they took point, at which time she would need to narrate every step of their journey to the rest of the team. There was no time to waste.

'John, did you get my voicemail?'

'*Yes. Sorry about that. I left my phone in the car. I've just been to get it and—*'

'Are you near a computer?' said Phillips, cutting him off.

'*Yes, I'm at my desk.*'

'Right. I want you to key in some OS coordinates. Can you do that?'

'*Sure. Go ahead.*'

'They are, Sierra Kilo 1-4-2 9-0-1.'

Robbins repeated them back to her as he typed, then pressed return. '*Got it. They take you to a field in the High Peak.*'

'Yeah. We know. It's the location for the ransom drop. We're heading there now.'

'*Seems an odd place to choose.*'

'Why do you day that?'

'*Well, I can't speak for them, but I wouldn't choose a location like that. It's way too exposed, and there's very few ways in or out – unless they plan to yomp over the hills once they get the money, that is.*'

'Would you want to yomp ten miles with 50 kilos of cash on your back?'

Robbins chortled. '*Not a chance. That's a young soldier's game. Those days are long gone for me. Plus, in this weather, even the most experienced soldier could suffer exposure at that elevation.*'

'So *why* would an ex-military team send us up there?'

Robbins was silent for a moment, but Phillips could hear him rubbing his stubble close to the mouthpiece. '*The only thing I can think of is it's a decoy. That they have something else in*' *play. Or – maybe they're not actually veterans, and they don't know what they're doing, after all.'*

Phillips glanced at Jones as they approached the crossroads in the centre of Glossop. Ahead of them, Sandra Hawkins had stopped at a red light. Jones's forehead was wrinkled with uncertainty. They would take point from the crossroads as they ascended into the hills.

'Thanks, John. Look, I've got to go,' said Phillips, and ended the call. 'So what do we do now then, Jonesy?'

As their car came to a stop, Jones feverishly checked each of his mirrors for anything untoward. Heavy rain battled with the windscreen wipers, which moved back and forth at full speed. 'Like he said, could be a decoy, could be a cock-up on the gang's part. Or...we may have to consider that *he* could still be involved, Guv.'

'But if he is, then why tell us it's a potential decoy?'

'I haven't the foggiest. In truth, my head's all over the place with all this.'

Acting on pure gut instinct, Phillips picked up the radio. 'Team Leader, this is Zero Four. We have new intel that this could be a bad drop. I repeat. We have new intel that this could be a bad drop. I'm requesting we stand down and return to base.'

Saxby responded in a flash. *'Zero Four. This is Team Leader. What bloody intel?'*

Phillips knew she couldn't admit to sharing the details of the operation with Robbins without suffering serious consequences. 'The source wishes to remain confidential, Team Leader. But it is *good intel*. I believe we're heading into a trap. Sandra Hawkins could be in danger. I request that we stand down.'

'Zero Four. This is Team Leader,' said Saxby, his voice laced with anger. *'You will maintain your course, and you will not stand down. I repeat, maintain your course and do not stand down.'*

Phillips closed the radio link and blew out her lips in frustration, just as the lights ahead turned to green, and Sandra Hawkins began to pull away.

'Looks like we're going into the hills, Guv,' said Jones as he moved in front of the other surveillance car, and into the lead.

As they left the junction and headed along Sheffield Road, the road began to narrow, although it remained relatively well populated with shops, takeaways and houses. But once they'd navigated the final small junction and approached the start of what locals referred to as the Snake Pass, the road began to climb steeply. A thick fog was moving into the valley, and in a matter of seconds, visibility was severely reduced.

As they approached Hurst Road – the last turnoff for the next ten miles – Sandra Hawkins's brake lights flashed on unexpectedly and the big SUV came to a complete halt.

Phillips grabbed the radio as Jones accelerated up the hill. 'Team Leader, this is Zero Four. The target has stopped without warning—'

Before she could finish, the VW Golf hit something on the road. There was an almighty crash, Jones lost control of the car, and they skidded into a lamppost.

'Shit!' cried Phillips.

'*Zero Four. This is Team Leader,*' said Saxby over the radio. '*What is your position?*'

A split second later, there was another loud bang and thick red smoke enveloped their view. Phillips turned to check the rear window, but saw nothing but smoke mixing with the dense fog. 'We've been ambushed!' she screamed into the radio, before throwing it onto the floor.

As she opened the car door, torrential rain soaked her. She could hear shouting coming from the direction of Sandra Hawkins's car, where she could just about make out movement. Suddenly her eyes felt like they were on fire and her nose filled with mucous. She began coughing. She closed her eyes for protection, but could hear that Jones was suffering in the same way. They'd been attacked with smoke grenades and CS gas.

Shouts came from behind her, down the hill, where the trailing surveillance car had arrived, but they too were soon engulfed by the smoke and the CS gas.

Coughing uncontrollably, Phillips managed to feel her way around the car to where Jones should be. She found him on all fours, retching. An asthmatic and an ex-smoker, she knew his lungs were shot to pieces. She had to get him out of there fast.

Phillips opened her eyes long enough to grab Jones under his armpits and lift him up onto his feet. She dragged him down the hill, away from the gas and smoke, until at last they hit a patch of clean air and better visibility. As she looked back up the hill, she could see the remnants of the smoke floating up into the night sky. The heavy rain continued unabated.

DS Kevin Sharp, the motorbike surveillance officer, rushed towards them. 'Are you all right, Ma'am?'

Phillips nodded. 'It was an ambush,' she managed to say, and spat mucous onto the ground. 'They attacked the car carrying the money.'

In the distance, the sound of screeching tyres on tarmac filled the air for a moment, then faded. Phillips turned to see if she could make out a vehicle, but the smoke was too thick. The gang was getting away.

Next to her, Jones continued to retch and spit, eyes streaming.

'Are you ok, Jonesy?' asked Phillips.

Jones didn't manage to stop coughing for long enough to speak, so nodded weakly.

At that point, Phillips noticed DS Sharp was wearing a neckerchief along with his riding gear. 'I need your scarf.'

Sharp did a double take. 'I'm sorry, Ma'am?'

Phillips pulled at the material wrapped around his neck. 'I need your scarf. Give it to me.'

Sharp quickly removed the scarf and passed it over.

Phillips tied it over her nose and mouth. 'I'm going to get Sandra Hawkins.'

'I'll come with you, Ma'am,' said Sharp.

'No. Stay here and look after this one,' said Phillips, and patted Jones on the back.

Sharp nodded, and Phillips turned on her heels. She ran back up the hill towards the smoke and gas.

A second later, Sharp shouted her name. He was waving his radio in the air. 'Sorry, Ma'am. It's DCI Saxby. He wants to know what's going on.'

'Tell him I'll call him back,' Phillips shouted, and disappeared into the smoke.

40

NOVEMBER 9TH

PHILLIPS DRIED HER FACE WITH A PAPER TOWEL, THEN STARED AT her reflection in the mirror. The effects of the CS gas had finally worn off, but she looked like she'd been crying for a week, with her puffy red eyes and blotchy cheeks. It was approaching 1 a.m., and she was expected for an emergency meeting in Fox's office. It was unheard of for Fox to come into the building out of hours, so Phillips was dreading what lay ahead.

She took a deep breath, held it, and let it out with gusto. 'Come on, Jane. You can do this,' she said to her reflection. A moment later, she headed for the fifth floor.

Fox's door was ajar, and as Phillips approached, she could hear voices. Saxby was already in there.

'Take a seat, Jane,' said Fox as Phillips entered.

Phillips had never seen Fox dressed in anything other than her black and white uniform, and was taken aback by her casual attire of jeans, trainers and a sweatshirt. Her hair was tied back in a ponytail.

Saxby sat in a chair opposite Fox, an icy glare fixed to his face.

As Phillips sat, Fox locked eyes with her but said nothing, then did the same with Saxby. When an uncomfortable silence had been established, she finally spoke.

'So. *What exactly* happened, tonight?'

'We were ambushed, Ma'am,' said Phillips, 'just before we hit the Snake Pass.'

'And how did this happen?'

'DCI Phillips's incompetence, Ma'am,' said Saxby.

Phillips recoiled in her chair. '*My* incompetence? It was your bloody op, mate!'

'Exactly. And you messed it up.'

Phillips shook her head in disbelief. 'How did I mess it up?'

'You were distracted at a key moment and weren't close enough to Sandra Hawkins's car.'

'What? Because I told you it was a bad drop and we should stand down?'

'Yes. Exactly that,' said Saxby. 'If you hadn't been so focused on that, you'd have spotted the gang and Mrs Hawkins wouldn't have been ambushed.'

Fox had yet to say a word.

Phillips had expected Saxby to try and shift the blame, but this excuse was weak, even by his standards. '*I* told you it was a bad drop based on fresh intel. *You* didn't listen. DS Jones and I maintained our position throughout the operation. There was no way we could have stopped the ambush. It came out of nowhere and was over in a matter of seconds.'

Saxby bristled. 'Ah yes, the so-called fresh intel from your confidential informant. So who exactly was he? And how did he know it was bad?'

'Who he is is not important,' said Phillips.

Saxby lurched forwards in his chair. 'Yes it bloody well is!'

Fox cut in at last. 'I have to agree with DCI Saxby.'

Phillips turned to face her. 'Ma'am. I promised my informant I wouldn't say who he was.'

'Yes. Well, I promised I wouldn't fire anyone today,' said Fox, 'but we can't have everything in life, now can we?'

Phillips knew she had to come clean, but the truth could end her career, so she chose her words carefully. 'I spoke to John Robbins this evening. The head of security at Marstons—'

'You shared operational details with a civilian?' Saxby spat.

'No, I didn't,' she lied again. 'I simply asked him in a round-about way if a military team would ever pick a remote location, such as the High Peak, out of choice.'

'And what did he say?' asked Fox.

Phillips swallowed her rising anxiety. 'He said that if *he* was leading an extraction operation, even with all his combat experience, he wouldn't choose to operate in terrain such as that. Particularly at this time of year, when just the weather could very easily kill at that elevation.'

'And you believed him?' said Fox.

'Yes, Ma'am. I did.'

'Jesus Christ. I've heard it all now,' scoffed Saxby. 'He could be involved, for all you know!'

'Well, if he was, he can't be that clever, can he? I mean, he as good as warned me the ambush was coming, for God's sake.'

'She makes a strong point there, DCI Saxby,' said Fox, leaning forwards on her elbows. 'So what exactly happened, then, during this ambush?'

'Well, Ma'am. DS Jones and I were the lead car, following Sandra Hawkins,' said Phillips, 'We'd just started the ascent up Woodcock Road, towards the golf course, and the fog came in. Visibility was down to about thirty metres when suddenly Sandra slammed on the brakes. The next thing we know, our car hit something in the road – a stinger, we later discovered – and shredded our tyres. Jones lost control and we crashed into a lamppost. Then smoke grenades were set off, in front and behind us, and when we got out of the car, it became apparent some kind of chemical agent had been used. We suspect it was

CS gas. Jones and I were incapacitated. That was when the gang attacked Sandra's car and took the money. It all happened in less than a minute.'

Fox nodded. 'And did anyone see the attackers?'

'No, Ma'am,' said Phillips. 'The smoke made it impossible.'

'So, how is Sandra Hawkins?'

'She was unharmed, Ma'am, just a little shaken up. The paramedics checked her out at the scene and, once the effects of the gas and smoke had worn off, she was allowed to drive home.'

Saxby interjected now. 'Sir Richard is furious, Ma'am. I spoke to him *personally* and apologised.'

Fox fixed Saxby with her black eyes. 'Yes. So I'm told.'

'He's very upset about losing his money,' said Saxby.

'But not so bothered about his missing daughter, hey?' said Phillips, sarcastically.

'Enough,' said Fox with force. 'Well, between the pair of you, you've managed to create an almighty mess, haven't you? A mess that I'm now going to have to try and clear up. I'm sure, at this point, it's a case of damage limitation – where possible. Now we can only hope the girl is returned safe and well. If not, then I suggest you both prepare for the consequences that will be coming down the line. You were *both* culpable in this shit-show, and if anything happens to Hollie Hawkins, you can expect her father will want heads to roll.'

'But Ma'am. It wasn't my fault,' snivelled Saxby.

Fox glared at him now. 'It never is with you, is it, Saxby?'

Saxby sat to attention. 'Well, I must say—'

'No, you mustn't,' said Fox. 'What you must do is shut the fuck up and take what's coming to you when you get back to London, tomorrow. Your *expertise* is no longer required here in Manchester.'

'But what about Sir Richard? I'm his primary contact,' said Saxby.

'You *were*,' said Fox. 'From now on, I'll be dealing directly with the Hawkinses, so you're free to leave.'

Saxby clenched his jaw, but remained silent.

Fox turned her attention to Phillips now, whose pulse quickened in anticipation. 'And as for *you*, DCI Phillips. As I'll be spending most of tomorrow cleaning up this mess, I'd suggest that, as a matter of urgency, you come up with something substantive that I can give to the Hawkinses with regards to their daughter's whereabouts. That is the *only* thing that stands between you and a whole world of pain. Do I make myself clear?'

'Yes, Ma'am,' said Phillips with some relief.

Fox checked her watch. 'Well, as it's almost 1.30, I think we'd all better go home, so piss off, the pair of you.' She waved them away.

Phillips shot out of Fox's office and strode down the corridor in an attempt to get out of the building without being forced to speak with Saxby again, but her efforts were in vain, as he caught up to her at the top of the stairs.

'You're finished, Phillips,' he said to her back. 'With my connections in Whitehall, I'll make sure of that.'

She turned to face him. Once again, he stood uncomfortably close. Phillips edged backwards, but he mirrored her movement, keeping his face just inches from hers, his rancid breath more pungent than ever. She stared at him for a long moment, and then smiled. 'I've seen off bigger pricks than you, Saxby. You messed up tonight. Not me.'

'Well, I guess that depends very much on your point of view, doesn't it?'

Phillips nodded. 'Yeah, I guess it does.'

Saxby smiled thinly as Phillips held his gaze.

'Oh, and by the way,' she said, 'if you're gonna stand so close to people all the time, you should think about investing in a toothbrush.'

Saxby looked taken aback, and Phillips used the moment to retreat and head down the stairs and towards the car park.

'You're finished, Phillips!' Saxby shouted down the stairwell after her.

She didn't look back.

As Phillips unlocked the front door to her terraced house, situated in the bohemian suburb of Chorlton-cum-Hardy, she was greeted by her faithful Ragdoll cat, Floss, who instantly snaked around her feet. 'Well, you're a sight for sore eyes,' she said as she turned on the hall light and headed for the open-plan kitchen at the end of the hall.

She opened the large, double-doored fridge and inspected the contents; a microwave meal of spaghetti Bolognese, a full bottle of Pinot Grigio and a tin of cat food. Phillips picked up the bottle of wine and held it in her hands, staring at the condensation forming on the sides of the pale green glass. She was very tempted to open it and wash away all the bullshit of the last week, but then she caught sight of the clock on the wall; there was nothing positive to be gained from drinking at 2.30 a.m. She replaced the bottle and chose the Bolognese instead, which she nuked in the microwave whilst she fed Floss. Soon, they were both sat together on the couch in the lounge room, their bellies full. As usual, it wasn't long before Floss was fast asleep, but Phillips's racing mind kept her awake despite her exhaustion.

As Floss purred in her lap, Phillips began scrolling through her phone, looking for a distraction. For a reason she couldn't explain, she was drawn to the Facebook icon on her home screen. If truth be told, since its inception, she had never really been an advocate of social media, refusing point blank to allow her phone to send her notifications or updates. And ever since her very public demotion in the aftermath of the Marty Michaels case, she had avoided social sites almost entirely. However, in that moment, she felt compelled to open Facebook, so she pressed the icon and waited for the app to fill the screen. A second later, her feed updated itself and a loud ping indicated a new message. Intrigued, she pushed on the little red '1', and to her surprise was met by a name she recognised, but a face that, at first, she didn't. The message was from Daniel Lawry.

Suddenly she remembered. 'Bloody hell. Now there's a blast from the past,' she whispered aloud.

The message was short and sweet.

'HI JANEY.

Long time no speak. I can't believe it's nearly twenty-three years since you left Hong Kong! I've just been checking out your profile, and you're looking great. Even more beautiful than when we dated! I'm going to be in Manchester in the New Year with work. I was hoping we could maybe meet for a drink and catch up. Let me know. Love and Hugs, D.'

PHILLIPS CLICKED on Daniel's name so she could access his full profile, and began scrolling through his pictures. 'You're looking pretty good yourself, Daniel,' she said with a wide grin.

For the first time in years, she felt a tingle of excitement, and butterflies in her stomach. She and Daniel had dated briefly in their teens. They'd kissed and fooled around – as teenagers did – but nothing more than that. It had ended, before it really got started, when her family moved to Manchester. She wondered what they would find to talk about after so long, but she was intrigued to hear how life had turned out for him.

'One drink can't hurt,' she said, grinning. She closed her eyes and drifted off to sleep.

41

Phillips arrived at Ashton House at 7 a.m. with a coffee in one hand and a spring in her step. Despite spending the night on the couch with Floss, she had woken with renewed energy. The message from Danny last night had been at the front of her mind from the moment she had woken up, and thoughts of how their meeting would pan out swirled around her head.

She was surprised to see Jones and Entwistle already at their desks when she walked into the incident room.

Jones looked up from his computer. 'What's making you so happy?'

Phillips realised she was still beaming.

Entwistle glanced over. 'The meeting with Fox went well, then?'

Suddenly the memories of last night's failed operation crashed over Phillips like a rogue wave, dousing her good mood. Her face screwed up with agitation. 'Actually, no. It was bloody awful.'

'Sorry, Guv,' said Entwistle, now sheepish.

Phillips changed the subject. 'What are you guys in so early for, anyway?'

'I couldn't sleep,' said Jones.

'I didn't get home 'til 5 a.m., so had a shower, some break-fast, and came straight back in,' said Entwistle.

Phillips wandered over to Entwistle's desk. He appeared to be working on three different screens at once. She took a sip of her coffee as she stood at his shoulder. 'What are you working on?'

'I'm going back through articles and files on Sir Richard, trying to find any new military links that might help us identify the kidnappers. Bahmani stayed at the snooker club until 1 a.m. I followed him home and stayed outside his gaff until 4 a.m. It was all quiet. No one in or out.'

'Doesn't mean he's not involved, though.'

'No, Guv. But like you said, trafficking girls is one thing. Kidnapping the daughter of a major player with connections to the government? That seems a bit high-profile for him.'

Phillips took another drink. 'I have to admit, I've never really liked Bahmani for it, and after what happened last night, I'm convinced he's not involved. The gang that ambushed us was brutally efficient. I just can't see a team like that choosing to work for a cowboy like Bahmani.'

'So, based on that assumption,' said Entwistle, 'and the fact that all our potential suspects connected with the military have alibis, I'm going back through Hawkins's business history, trying to find anything that might shed some light on who these guys might be.'

Jones looked over. 'Well, based on the way they hit us last night, there's no doubt in my mind whatsoever that they're ex-military. If it hadn't been so bloody painful – in another life – I'd have to admire their skills. They blew us away in seconds.'

Phillips had to admit that, in the cold light of day, the execution of the ambush had been impressive. Catching Jones's eye, she nodded in the direction of her office. 'You got a minute?'

Jones got up and followed her in, closing the door behind him. 'So, what happened with Fox then, Guv?'

Phillips sighed and dropped into her leather chair. 'She says Saxby and I are both at fault for the failed drop last night. That if we don't find Hollie alive ASAP, we can both expect heads to roll.'

'But how can it be *your* fault, Guv? It was Saxby's op.'

'I know. And I tried to make that point. She wasn't having it. I'm the SIO in charge of the investigation, so in her mind, I'm as much to blame as him. Maybe more so.'

'So what about Saxby? What's happening with him?'

Phillips forced a faint smile. 'Well. That's the good news. She's sent him back to London. She says his expertise is no longer needed in Manchester.'

'She said that?'

'Yep. Straight to his face.'

Jones chuckled. 'I'd have paid good money to see that.'

'I have to admit, it was almost worth the bollocking just to see the little toad squirm.'

'So how long have we got before the shit hits the fan?' said Jones.

'The rest of today, I reckon. Maybe tomorrow, depending on how Fox's meetings go today with the top brass and Hawkins. But after that, if Hollie doesn't turn up, I think I'll be gone.'

Jones's eyes widened like saucers. 'Come on, Guv. They can't get rid of *you!*'

Phillips placed her elbows on the desk and her hands on the sides of her head. 'Yes they can. The truth is, I'm not Fox's type of copper, and there's no way she's gonna take the flack for me. If it comes down to it and Sir Richard and his cronies kick up a stink, I'll be under the bus in two seconds flat.'

'Well, we'd better get cracking and find Hollie then, hadn't we?' said Jones.

At that moment, Entwistle, holding his laptop, knocked on the door. 'Guv, I've found something. I'm not sure if it's connected, but I thought it was worth you taking a look.'

Phillips waved him in.

Just then, Jones's mobile began to ring, and he pulled it from his trouser pocket. 'Shit. It's Izzie. Why is she calling so early?'

'You'd better answer it,' she said.

As Jones left the room, Entwistle approached Phillips's desk and placed his laptop down.

'Like I say, Guv, it might be nothing, but I found this old story from 2011.' He turned the screen to face her.

Phillips found herself looking at an archive newspaper article.

Entwistle continued. 'Hawkins has been involved in a kidnap and ransom situation before.'

'You're kidding?'

'No. It happened when a team of contractors working for him in Syria were snatched by so-called ISIS freedom fighters. They demanded millions of pounds-worth of munitions in return for the group's safe return. Hawkins didn't pay, and they were publicly executed after four days.'

'Jesus,' whispered Phillips.

'At the time, Hawkins claimed he wasn't given enough time to meet the kidnappers' demands. There's a quote here, from him, saying, "they were unrealistic in their demands and killed the hostages after just four days. It is a huge regret for me that I wasn't more forceful and demanded a week. If I had, perhaps those hostages would still be alive today." It struck me that this might be why the kidnappers chose seven days, and the fact they said in the ransom video, "We will accept no excuses."'

'I can see the link, but it all seems a bit elaborate doesn't it?'

'Maybe it's their way of letting *him* know that *they* know about Syria?'

'Maybe. And if that's the case, then they must be somehow connected to him and know how he operates, how he thinks, the kind of bullshit he peddles.'

'Which means they've probably worked for him before, Guv.'

Phillips sat back in her chair. 'So who are we missing? Everyone we checked out had an alibi.'

Entwistle let out a frustrated sigh. 'I honestly don't know, Guv. I've looked at everyone remotely connected to him and found nothing.'

'In that case, it's time to start going back over those we've already spoken to. There must be something we're not seeing.'

'I'll get straight onto it,' said Entwistle.

'Good stuff. But, before you go. Why haven't I heard of this story before? I mean, I remember all those ISIS abductions and beheadings in Syria. They were all over the TV. Why not this one?'

'Because the team involved wasn't British. They were locals, working for Hawkins. He had a small factory there, which was heavily armed. They used to bus the employees in and out. These guys were admin staff who were snatched on their way home one night. No one in the UK was bothered about a bunch of Syrians being executed, so it never made the mainstream papers.'

'I can imagine that's why Hawkins refused to pay; no reputational damage back home if he didn't,' said Phillips.

'The same thought had crossed my mind, Guv.'

At that moment, Jones rushed back into the office, eyes wide.

'What is it?' asked Phillips.

'It's Bov, Guv. He's awake!'

Phillips's heart missed a beat. 'Oh. Thank God!'

'Izzie says he's been asking for us. He's insisting on it.'

Phillips jumped from her chair. 'Well, what are we waiting for? Let's get over there.'

HALF AN HOUR LATER, Phillips, Jones and Entwistle made their way into the spinal unit of the MRI. It was a sobering affair as they passed down the central corridor that fed rooms of up to six people, each with varying degrees of spinal injury and paralysis. Unbeknownst to the team, Bovalino had been transferred there from the ICU late the previous night.

Izzie was waiting for them outside a private room, and beckoned them over when they came into view.

Phillips gave her a hug as they met. 'How is he?'

Tears began to well up in Izzie's eyes. 'He's ok. In and out of sleep. Kind of lucid one minute, then totally incoherent the next. Apparently he has a urinary infection, which can cause problems with his speech. Come in and see for yourself. I'm afraid he's zonked out again at the minute.'

Phillips followed her into the room, with Jones and Entwistle close behind.

Bovalino lay in bed with his eyes shut. His back and head were raised to a forty-five-degree angle, and he was surrounded by a host of machines monitoring his vital signs. He looked frail, and even smaller than the last time Phillips had seen him, in the back of the ambulance. As Izzie approached, he opened his eyes slowly.

'There's someone here to see you, Leo,' said Izzie.

Bov turned to face Phillips and, after a long moment, smiled weakly. She squeezed his hand while Jones and Entwistle appeared at her shoulder.

'How are you, Bov?'

Bovalino's mouth and lips appeared bone dry. Phillips

guessed it was a side effect from being on the ventilator they had used during his induced coma. He was clearly finding it hard to speak. 'Ok,' he said, his voice croaky and barely audible. 'You had us worried there, pretending to be Spiderman. You silly bugger.'

Bovalino cracked a thin smile.

'No more climbing. Ok?'

Bovalino closed his eyes and nodded.

Phillips turned to Izzie now. 'What have the doctors said?'

'Some sensation has come back in his toes and feet, but he still can't move his legs. They're hoping that'll come back too – in time.'

Bov opened his eyes again and began trying to say something.

'What is it, Bov?' asked Phillips, but couldn't make out what he was saying. She leaned in closer, her ear next to his mouth. After a few more attempts, she turned to face Jones. 'I think he's saying something about a "breaker".'

Jones's brow furrowed. 'Breaker?'

Bovalino moved his head from side to side, then repeated the word. But it still wasn't clear.

'I'm sorry, Bov. I don't understand,' said Phillips.

Izzie interjected now. 'I think he's trying to say "the baker". He kept repeating it last night, when he came round, and then again when they were moving him, "Baker, baker". I didn't pay any attention to it then. I just figured he was drugged up and the effects of the infection. But this morning – before I called you, Jonesy – his speech was better and he was clearly saying "Baker". He kept saying, "Get Jonesy – the girl and baker."

Phillips leaned in close and spoke in a clear, slow voice. 'Bov, the man who attacked you – the man who took Hollie—' Bovalino opened his eyes. '—was it Marcus Baker?'

Phillips stood upright in anticipation. Bovalino nodded.

'So, you're saying that one of the kidnappers is Marcus Baker?'

Bovalino nodded.

'Jesus, Guv,' said Jones. 'He's the guy that punched Hawkins.'

Phillips squeezed Bovalino's hand tightly. 'Well done, Bov. You never stop being a detective, do you?'

Bovalino smiled and closed his eyes again.

Phillips turned to Jones and Entwistle. 'We need to find Baker *yesterday*. It's probably a long shot, Jonesy, but let's start with his house.'

'Got it,' said Jones.

'Entwistle, I want you looking into his background. Find out who he served with, where and when. John Robbins reckons one of the gang is female and, based on the way she moved when they grabbed Hollie, probably saw active combat. There can't be too many women who fit that description among his former colleagues. Finding her is crucial to narrowing down who the rest of the team could be. Also, find out which network Marcus Baker's phone is connected to. Let's see if they can track its most recent movements.'

'I'll get a cab back to the office and start digging,' said Entwistle.

'Good. As soon as you find anything, call me. Ok?'

Entwistle nodded, and Phillips turned back to face Bov. He was asleep again. 'Keep us posted, Izzie.'

'I will, Jane.'

Phillips walked around the bed and gave her a hug. 'He's gonna be ok, you know. He's a fighter. He'll come through this. You both will.'

As Phillips pulled back, tears were streaming down Izzie's face. She nodded and smiled. 'I'm sorry. We have to go. Are you gonna be ok?'

Izzie wiped her nose with a tissue. 'Yeah. My sisters will be here again in a bit. They'll look after me.'

Phillips squeezed her hand one last time before Jones stepped in and wrapped her up in a warm embrace.

A couple of minutes later, Phillips, Jones and Entwistle exited the spinal ward with renewed focus, on the hunt for Marcus Baker and his gang.

42

Jones drove to Marcus Baker's address in Hulme. It was a short trip, only a few minutes from the MRI to the densely populated suburb on the outskirts of the city centre. Baker's house had been part of the original development project that had regenerated Hulme in the late nineties and early noughties, a three-floored townhouse overlooking the park.

The MCU relied heavily on their uniformed counterparts when it came to kicking down suspects' doors. Thirty minutes later, a team of four uniformed officers stood ready to go into Baker's home, kitted out in protective helmets and stab vests. The lead officer held a small, but powerful, battering ram. Two more uniformed officers waited at the rear of the property in case Baker tried to make a run for it.

With no time to spare, Phillips gave the order to go in. Two deafening thuds followed, and the door swung open on its hinges. Shouts of 'Police!' filled the small hallway as the team rushed inside. Phillips and Jones, also wearing stab vests, followed them into the house and upstairs to the first floor. It was open plan and military clean, the furniture immaculate, and the space looked like a show-home. They moved up to the second floor, where they found two bedrooms and a bathroom in the same condition as downstairs. But no sign of Baker.

'Well, he's definitely not here, Guv,' said Jones.

'It was always a long shot,' said Phillips, 'but it's bloody annoying.'

Just then, Phillips's phone rang. It was Entwistle. She answered it and held it between her and Jones. 'You're on speaker. What have you got?'

'Ok,' said Entwistle. '*Baker's phone has been off-line for a week, so there's no way to track him from that.*'

'Always one step ahead,' said Jones.

'*But I have had a little more luck on identifying the female in the gang.*'

'Go on.'

'*Well, because we know Marcus Baker was a para, I looked to see which women had served in the Parachute Regiment.*'

'*And?*' said Phillips, already losing her patience.

'*Zero, Guv. They only allowed females into the elite forces in the last year or so, so when Baker saw active duty, it was male para-troopers only. However, women have served alongside men for decades as combat medics, in particular during the second Iraq war and in Afghanistan. And in Baker's case, having completed multiple tours alongside his unit, three female combat medics stand out. One is deceased, which narrows it down to two: The first is Caroline Fletcher. She has been living in Aberdeen since she left the military in 2011. She now works as an accountant, is married and with two kids.*'

'And the other?' asked Phillips, praying the second was a better match.

'*Much more promising, Guv. Her name's Michelle Spencer, a retired medic who lives in Salford. She has a criminal record for ABH, and is between jobs at the moment.*'

'That's her! It has to be,' said Phillips, feeling a rush of excitement. 'What's her address?'

Entwistle tapped into his laptop on the other end of the

phone for a moment. 'Er, looks like she's registered to pay Council Tax at 56 Gove Road in Salford. M5 5ZF.'

'Right. Meet us there in twenty minutes.'

'Consider it done, Guv.'

43

THIRTY MINUTES LATER, PHILLIPS, JONES AND ENTWISTLE STOOD
behind the uniformed team once more as they waited to go into
Spencer's home. Phillips gave them the green light and,
following more deafening thuds, the team rushed in through
the broken door.

Inside, on the doormat, was a multitude of takeaway menus,
a few direct mail flyers and a number of letters addressed to
Spencer.

After a few minutes, each room was declared clear. Based
on even a cursory inspection, it was evident Michelle Spencer
no longer lived at this address.

Phillips, Jones and Entwistle took a room each and worked
their way through the small two-bedroom council house,
looking for any signs of life. After ten minutes, they gathered
on the first floor, at the top of the stairs.

'Looks like she's long gone, Guv,' said Entwistle.

'Yep. And, like Baker's gaff, it's military clean apart from this
stuff that's been shoved through the letterbox,' added Jones,
holding the bunch of letters in his hand.

'Which means it was more than likely posted after she left. Let me see those,' said Phillips.

Jones passed them over, and Phillips quickly scanned the letters until she found one addressed to Michelle Spencer. She checked the postmark, and noted it was dated the 28th October. 'Looks like she left a few days before the kidnapping.'

'Getting ready for the operation, Guv?' said Jones.

Phillips nodded, then let out a frustrated growl. 'Yeah, but where the hell is she now?'

At that moment, the sergeant leading the uniformed team approached. 'We've checked the whole house, Ma'am. There's no sign of anyone. But we did find a bunch of stuff that had been burnt in the garden. Not sure if it's of any help.'

'Take us to it,' said Phillips, and a moment later she stepped out into the overgrown garden behind the sergeant, Jones and Entwistle in tow.

'This is it,' said the sergeant, standing over the charred remains on a large, blackened patch of grass.

Phillips knelt down and, with a gloved index finger, gently started to separate some of the remnants of the fire. It was difficult to make out what anything was – or had been – aside from a melted laptop, which had been burnt to a cinder.

Jones took a knee, picked up the computer and looked at Entwistle. 'Any chance you can tell us what was on this, then?'

Entwistle snorted. 'Even I'm not *that* good, Jonesy.'

At the edge of the burned area, something caught Phillips's eye. A charred stub of paper, which looked as if it had been ripped up before being thrown into the fire. On it was a sequence of handwritten letters and numbers. She inspected it closely and read them aloud. 'Four-two-nine-zero-one. Why do I recognise those numbers?'

Jones took the piece of paper. 'Four-two-nine-zero-one.'

'They're part of the ransom drop co-ordinates!' Phillips exclaimed.

Entwistle pulled out his notepad and flicked through the pages until he found what he was looking for. 'You're right, Guv,' he said, and presented his notes to Phillips. 'Sierra Kilo 1-4-2 9-0-1.'

Phillips, Jones and Entwistle began sifting through the charred remains for any more pieces of paper.

A few moments later, Jones found another bit of half-burnt paper with more handwritten letters and numbers, and handed it to Phillips. 'This one says Echo Romeo Victor, then on the next line, Sierra Juliet 8.'

'Echo Romeo Victor – ERV?' asked Entwistle. 'So what does that mean?'

Phillips smiled. 'In military terms, ERV stands for Emergency Rendezvous. It refers to a safe place to meet if things go tits up with an operation.'

'Which is exactly what happened when Bov and I stumbled into the old workhouse,' said Jones.

Phillips nodded. 'And the next line looks like the start of a grid reference. SJ 8-1. Keep looking. We need any sequence of numbers or letters that might go with them.'

For the next fifteen minutes, the trio carefully picked apart the remnants of what had clearly been a large fire, until Entwistle spotted another section of partially burnt paper, which he handed to Phillips. 'What about this, Guv?'

Phillips inspected it. It had not burnt completely, but was almost brown. It contained more numbers. 'Write these down. It's either 1-9-6-5, or Sierra 9-6-1.'

Entwistle scribbled in his pad.

'Read them back to me,' said Phillips as she pulled up the browser on her phone.

'Ok. Sierra Juliet 8-1-1 9-6-5,' said Entwistle.

Phillips keyed in the coordinates and read out the locations. 'This one refers to an address in Trafford Park.'

Entwistle continued, and read out the next set of coordinates, 'Sierra-Juliet 8-1-S 9-6-1.'

'That one doesn't exist,' said Phillips a second later. She then flicked back to the results of the first search, and zoomed into the map. She turned her phone so Entwistle and Jones could see what she was looking at. 'Looks like an unused building near Pomona, to me.'

'Which would fit with the gang's MO so far,' said Jones.

Phillips felt a surge of adrenaline rush through her body. 'I don't want to speak too soon, guys, but we might just have found where they're holding Hollie.'

44

HOLLIE COULD HEAR THE CHANGE IN THE GANG'S MOOD THROUGH the walls of her new room, which were much thinner than at the last place. This morning she could hear laughter and banter being thrown around. She pressed her ear to the flimsy wooden door to hear what was being said.

'So, what are you gonna do with your share, Blue?' said one of the gang. 'Off to Thailand to get yourself a Thai bride?'

'Piss off!' replied Blue. Hollie recognised his accent.

Her father must have paid the ransom money. Maybe he *didn't* hate her after all? She continued to listen, and could hear the sounds of boxes being packed up and bags being zipped.

'What about you, Red?' one asked, but it was hard to distinguish who was speaking.

'I'm gonna get a long way from here – and from *you lot*,' came the reply, accompanied by a chuckle. 'No offence, like. But if I ever see any of you again, it means something went badly wrong! So how about you?'

The next voice Hollie heard, she recognised as White's. 'Australia, I reckon. Got a sister down there.'

'The Dominican Republic for me,' said a woman's voice –

Black. 'There's no extradition treaty with the UK, so I don't have worry about Special Branch turning up at my beach party!'

Laughter erupted and the banter continued for a few more minutes, but it became harder to hear what was being said as they banged, dragged and pushed things around on other side of the door.

Sometime later, through the small frosted-glass window on the wall opposite her makeshift bed, Hollie heard voices outside. Then an eerie silence descended. She pressed her ear to the door, but could hear nothing. Hollie dragged the small plastic chair she'd been given over to the window and stood on the seat. The window had a small hole in the bottom corner, about the size of a pound coin, which allowed her to see and hear what was going on outside. As she peered through, she could see the gang – all still wearing their masks, which made them easier for her to identify – in the process of packing four cars full of heavy bags. They worked in silence for a few minutes until there was no more bags, then closed the boots on each car.

'That's it, then,' said Blue.

'That's it,' replied Red.

In turn, each of the gang embraced.

'What about the girl?' asked Black.

'You leave her to me,' said Red. 'I'll finish it.'

Hollie's heart rate spiked as she heard those words.

'You guys get going,' Red continued.

'You sure you're up to it, Red?' asked Black. 'I can do it, if not.'

Hollie stared out as Red placed his hand on Black's shoulder. 'You don't have to worry. Trust me, I'll take care of it. Now go on. You guys get yourselves away, and forget Hollie Hawkins ever existed.'

Blue, Black and White nodded in unison and pulled off their masks, but Hollie's limited view meant all she could see was the backs of their heads. They each jumped into a car and drove away in turn. Hollie continued to peer out through the window as Red – still wearing his mask – watched the rest of the gang leave. When they had disappeared from view, he walked to his car, opened the boot and pulled out a large black leather holdall. He unzipped it, checked the contents, then closed the boot and headed back inside with the bag.

Panic engulfed Hollie. Red had lied. He was coming to kill her. She jumped down from the chair, picked it up and clutched it in both hands. Then she moved next to the wall, so she would be hidden by the door when it opened. Red's footsteps drew closer, echoing through the old building. Her heart beat like a drum in her head. Tears streamed down her cheeks and her chest heaved as she fought to keep control of her breathing.

As the key turned in the lock, Hollie's whole body tightened. She lifted the chair as high in the air as she could, and waited. The door opened, shielding her from Red. As soon as he came into view, she screamed, and brought the chair down hard onto his back.

Red fell forwards but didn't go down. Instead, he turned, grabbed the chair and threw it across the room. Hollie made for the open door, but he was too quick and way too strong. He gripped his thick fingers around her arms and pulled her back into the room.

She kicked out as she tried to get away. 'Let me go! Please, let me go,' she screamed. 'I swear I won't tell anyone, anything. Just let me go!'

'Shut the fuck up!' Red shouted as he wrapped his left arm around her body and his right hand over her mouth. He dragged her over to the bed, threw her down, then used his considerable weight to trap her arms against the mattress on either side of her head.

45

TRAFFORD PARK IS A HEAVILY INDUSTRIALISED SUBURB FIVE MILES west of Manchester city centre. The building they were looking for was situated near Pomona. Following the grid reference, Phillips soon located a disused brick factory. When they arrived, she instructed Jones to park the car at a safe distance, underneath a railway arch that offered good cover whilst giving them a clear view of their surrounds. The building itself was typical of the area – red brick, with a slate roof and very few windows. Like the old workhouse, it too had fallen into some disrepair.

From their vantage point, they could see a car parked up outside – a ten-year-old Ford Fiesta. Entwistle checked its registration against the DVLA database.

'That's odd,' said Entwistle. 'It says here that the owner of that Fiesta is a Mable Tunnercliffe from Withington, who's eighty-one'

'And it's not been reported stolen?' asked Phillips.

'No, Guv. But it looks like it just passed its MOT in July.'

'Could be a clone vehicle,' said Jones.

'What's a clone vehicle?' asked Entwistle.

Phillips answered, 'It's when a car is stolen and given the plates of an identical, but legally owned, vehicle. It means that ANPR cameras don't flag them as nicked or using false plates.'

'Clever idea,' said Entwistle.

'Yeah. As soon as we come up with a system to catch them, the villains find a way to beat it,' said Jones.

Phillips sat in silence for a moment and surveyed the factory as she worked out what to do next. She opened the door and got out of the car. 'I'm gonna get a closer look.'

Jones tried to reply, but she shut the door before he had chance.

A few minutes later, as a bitter wind blew into her face, Phillips crept across the ancient cobbled yard to where the Fiesta was parked. As she moved next to it, she placed her hand over the bonnet. It was cold.

The entrance to the building was not visible from where she stood, so she moved round the corner to get a better look. The main door was ajar, and the faint sound of voices came from somewhere inside the building. She crept closer and peered inside, but it was pitch black. She was tempted to go in, but with her chequered history of walking into danger alone, she thought better of it and decided to head back to the car and call in the TFU.

As she moved back across the yard, she noticed several tyre tracks in the mud to the side of the cobbles, leading towards the main road. She knelt to get a closer look. They were fresh and, based on the different tyre treads, likely belonged to different cars. If she was right, at least two cars had driven away from this place very recently.

Phillips half ran back to the squad car but was careful to stay out of sight. She jumped in the front passenger seat and attempted to catch her breath.

Jones wasted no time in reprimanding her. 'Seriously, Guv. After what happened to Bov, you need to be more careful. If you don't stop bloody running into trouble on your own, they'll be sending *me* down – for murder.'

Phillips waved him away. 'Never mind all that. There are people in there. I couldn't see anyone, but I heard their voices. We need to call in Firearms.'

Jones shook his head, then picked up the radio and called control.

~

HOLLIE STARED up at the man she knew as Red. His masked face looked back at her. Her hands were still trapped in his tight grip, one on each side of her head.

'If you promise not to attack me again – or try to run away – I'll release your hands and let you up. Is that a deal?' he said.

Hollie nodded. True to his word, Red let go and stepped back. He picked up the chair from the other side of the room and placed it next to the bed.

Hollie sat upright. 'You've come to kill me, haven't you? Because I saw her face.'

Red shook his head. 'I told you, Hollie, I don't kill kids.'

'Liar!' said Hollie, as she began to cry. 'I heard you talking outside. You told them you were going to "finish it". That they should forget I ever existed. That means you're going to kill me!'

'That's not what I meant, Hollie.'

She was sobbing now. 'I heard you!'

Red sighed heavily. 'Look, Hollie. I told the guys what they wanted to hear. If they think that means I'm going to kill you, then so be it. By the time they find out I didn't, it'll be too late to do anything. Soon Black will be on a beach far away from here, and trust me, there's no way she's ever coming back to the UK.'

'But what about Blue and White?'

'As long as they have enough time to get out of the country, they won't care what happens to you. I meant what I said, Hollie, I won't kill kids – or *anyone* who's innocent, for that matter.'

Hollie stopped crying. 'So you're letting me go, then?'

'In time, yes. But first, I need to make sure I'm safely away from here when they find you.'

'When who finds me?'

'The police,' said Red. 'Once I'm out of the country, I'll let them know where you are. And you'll be free to go. Look, wait here.' He stood and left the room for a moment, then returned with the black leather holdall bag Hollie had seen him remove from his car. He dropped it on the bed in front of her. 'Open it.'

Hollie shuffled forwards and unzipped the bag.

'There's sandwiches, water, chocolate and magazines. It should be enough to keep you fed, watered and entertained for the next twelve hours. By then, I'll be long gone. An email will land in your dad's inbox, telling him where he can find you.'

Hollie's whole body softened. 'So I really am going home?'

Red touched her wrist gently with his gloved hand. 'Yes, you are.'

Hollie exhaled with relief, and giggled. 'I feel a bit bad, now.'

'What for?' asked Red.

'For hitting you with the chair.'

Red rubbed the back of his head for a moment. 'Yeah. I certainly wasn't expecting that when I walked in. That was a good shot, by the way.'

'I'm not as weak as people think.'

'I don't think you're weak at all, Hollie,' said Red. 'Quite the opposite, in fact.'

Hollie felt herself blush.

'That's why I think you should have this.' He passed her a handwritten note.

Hollie took it and stared at the words on the page: *OPERA-TION VOGUE.*

'If you ever get to a point where you've had enough of dealing with Sir Richard's bullshit and want him out of your – and your mother's – lives for good, google that,' said Red. 'It was an operation in Afghanistan where a lot of good men died. British soldiers were killed by the Taliban who – as it turned out – were using machine guns, mortars and rocket launchers manufactured and sold by your father – illegally. He's always said the munitions were sold legitimately to the Pakistani government, who must have then passed them on to the Taliban. But personally, I'm sure that's total bullshit.'

'Why?'

'I know your father well enough, and I know he's lying. The problem is, I can't prove it. But if *you* can access his emails like you say, then I'm sure you could find a trail that proves I'm right. Believe me, if that kind of information ever got out into the public domain, it would ruin him.'

Hollie swallowed hard and continued to stare at the words on the page. Her mind raced at the thought of exposing her stepfather for what he really was: a liar, a cheat, an abuser. It was an exhilarating thought, but one that also terrified her. If she exposed him, her life, and that of her mother, would never be the same again.

'Or alternatively, you can forget we ever had this conversation,' said Red. 'It's up to you, and I wouldn't blame you if you did; you've got a lot to lose.'

Hollie nodded, lost in her thoughts.

'Look. All I'm saying is, I'm certain the proof is out there. If you can find it and share it, then your stepdad's finished,' said Red.

PHILLIPS, Jones and Entwistle maintained their watch on the building as they waited for TFU.

Phillips drummed her fingers on her kneecap as she struggled to manage the nervous energy building inside her. 'How long 'til Firearms arrives?'

Jones checked his watch. 'Another eight minutes, Guv.'

Just then, a car pulled off the main drag and moved slowly along the battered, muddy track towards the old building.

'Looks like we've got company,' said Phillips.

'What's the make, model and registration?' asked Entwistle. 'I'll run a check on it.'

'Red, Vauxhall Corsa. Registration, Yankee Alpha 09, Charlie Echo Tango,' said Jones.

A minute passed before Entwistle pulled up the results. 'Looks like it could be another clone vehicle. This one is registered to Derek Whitehall who lives in Northenden. He's eighty-three. Again, no report of it being stolen.'

Up ahead, the Corsa slowed to a stop next to the Fiesta and a woman in black fatigues got out. She carried something in her right hand that appeared to be a handgun. She moved quickly and was soon out of sight, heading towards the entrance to the building.

'Looks like it could be Spencer,' said Jones, 'and she's tooled up.'

'Where the hell are the TFU?' Phillips grabbed the radio. 'This is Delta 4. I need an urgent ETA on the TFU we requested at the old brickworks in Pomona. We have a possible suspect on site, potentially in possession of a firearm.'

Silence filled the car as she waited for a response.

'*Delta 4. This is control. TFU is six minutes out.*'

'Six minutes? They could be long gone by then!' said Phillips. She slammed the radio against the dash, then reached for the door handle. 'Sod it. I'm going in.'

Jones's hand shot out and grabbed her wrist like a vice. He stared her straight in the eye. 'No, Guv. Not again.'

Phillips felt herself recoil. She'd never seen Jones look so determined.

He continued. 'No heroics on this one. That's what you said at Baker's house, and that applies to you too. We're all going home in one piece tonight, Guv. *All of us.*'

'WHERE WILL YOU GO?' asked Hollie.

'Overseas. Somewhere warm,' said Red. 'Somewhere where I can figure out how to help people with the money.'

'What do you mean?'

'All I need is enough cash to get away and set me up. The rest, I'm gonna give away over time.'

'Who to?'

'Well, veterans and their families, for a start. There are a lot of guys out there who need help dealing with life outside the wire. And I can't think of a more appropriate use of your father's money, can you?'

Hollie smiled at the thought of it.

'Maybe, then, I can finally sleep at night,' said Red.

Just then, the door to Hollie's room opened and the woman with the scarred face walked in, unmasked. Red appeared as surprised to see her as Hollie was.

'Well, this looks very cosy,' said Black.

'What the hell are you doing back here?' asked Red.

'I knew you didn't have the balls to go through with it,' said Black. She pulled a handgun from behind her back and pointed it at Hollie.

Acting on instinct, Hollie thrust herself against the wall.

'Jesus, Black!' shouted Red.

'And you can drop the codenames, Baker. I'll make sure she won't be telling *anyone* about us.'

'Come on, Spence,' Baker said as he stood up from the chair, 'don't do anything stupid. *We're* not killers.'

'Look at me,' said Spencer, and pointed to the large scar on the left-hand side of her face, 'Do you *really think* she won't be able to describe me in perfect detail?'

Baker stepped in front of Hollie, shielding her. 'We don't kill kids, Spence.'

'She's seen my face, Baker.'

'Trust me, Spence. She promised me she won't say anything.'

'Oh, well. That's all right then,' said Black, sarcastically. 'I mean, if she's *promised* you she won't, then we've got nothing to worry about then, have we?'

'I'm telling you, Spence, she's a good kid. She won't say anything.' Baker removed his own mask. 'And look. Now she's seen my face, too.'

Hollie stared at the handsome, scarred face that had finally been unveiled.

Baker continued, 'You won't say anything, will you Hollie?'

Hollie shook her head frantically. 'No. No. I promise. Not to anyone.'

'Get out of the way, Baker.' Spencer cocked the gun.

Hollie screamed with fright.

Baker raised his arms and took a step towards Spencer. 'Come on, Spence. Don't do this. This isn't right.'

'Yes it bloody is!' Spencer shouted in reply. 'People like *her* father set us up to fail over there. His greed put us in unnecessary danger, and look what happened to me. The day that IED went off, I lost everything that mattered to me; my best mate, half my face and my whole career. All gone, in an instant. I've been to some dark fucking places in the last few years, Baker.

But now I have a chance to start again, and I'm not gonna let anything, or anyone, stand in the way of that. *Not even you.*'

'Look. I get it. I lost people too. We all did,' Baker said. 'But whatever pain we've felt since, Hollie's not to blame. We don't need to kill her.'

Spencer thrust the gun towards Baker's chest. 'Get out of the way.'

Hollie's heart pounded like a bass drum in her chest. Her eyes darted around the room as she searched for an escape route. But the only way out was past Spencer.

'We've both seen too much killing,' Baker said as he opened his palm out flat in front of Spencer. 'Come on, give me the gun. No one else has to die. Not today.'

Hollie swallowed hard, her mouth dry with adrenaline.

'Baker, get out of the fucking way!' shouted Spencer.

Without warning, Baker launched himself at Spencer and knocked her to the ground. 'Run, Hollie,' he shouted as he fought for control of the gun. 'Run!'

Coming to her senses, Hollie scrambled from the bed and jumped over the two bodies as they grappled on the floor. She soon found herself in a darkened corridor, and took a second to get her bearings. She could see light coming in from her right, so set off running towards it, her footsteps echoing around the dark space.

An ungodly bang from behind stopped Hollie in her tracks. She turned to face the room she had just left, praying she would see Baker's face appear in the doorway. Her heart sank when Spencer staggered out, still holding the gun. For a moment, Spencer stared back into the room behind her, then turned and locked eyes with Hollie. She raised the gun and fired.

Hollie screamed as the bullet zipped past her head, then turned and ran for her life.

46

A GUNSHOT RANG OUT ACROSS THE BARREN LANDSCAPE. PHILLIPS jumped. 'Shit! We've gotta get in there, now.'

Jones grabbed the radio. 'Control, this is Delta 4. Gunshots fired at the old brickworks. How far out are TFU?'

'Delta 4, this is control. TFU are four minutes out.'

'We should wait, Guv,' said Jones.

Then a second shot was fired.

'No we bloody shouldn't!' replied Phillips as she pushed open the car door and jumped out. Jones and Entwistle followed.

Just then, Hollie appeared from the back of the brickworks. 'Help! Help! Somebody, help!' she shouted as she ran across the rough terrain. She was followed by the woman who'd entered the building ten minutes earlier. The woman raised the gun and fired at Hollie.

Hollie screamed and ducked, but continued to run away from the woman, who chased after her.

Phillips, Jones and Entwistle set off after them.

A moment later, Hollie disappeared into an adjacent dilapidated building that looked like it had once been connected to the brickworks. The woman raced in after her.

As Phillips, Jones and Entwistle approached the second building, Phillips signalled for them to slow down. They came to a stop just outside the entrance. Phillips listened intently. She could just make out the faint sound of footsteps within the old structure.

Jones stared at her, wide-eyed. 'We should wait for TFU, Guv.'

Phillips was still trying to catch her breath and said nothing for a moment.

'They'll be here in three minutes,' added Jones.

Phillips had never felt so conflicted. Every impulse in her body was telling her to go in and do whatever it took to save Hollie, but Jones was right. They should wait for the Firearms team. After all, she knew better than most how it felt to have your body torn apart by a bullet.

Just then, another shot rang out, and Hollie screamed in terror. That was all the incentive she needed.

'I'm going in. Entwistle, get back to the car and update TFU. Jonesy, you stay here. No sense in us both copping it from Fox,' she said with a faint smile, then headed in.

The old building was dark and wet from the recent downpours, and the chilly November wind blew through the open walls. Phillips soon found the concrete staircase that ran up the inside of the building. Footsteps and shouts came from above.

Jones arrived a second later.

'I told you to stay put,' whispered Phillips.

'Yeah, well, you're not the only one who can disobey orders, Guv,' he replied with a cheeky grin.

Phillips smiled and gave him a silent nod. Another shot rang out. She raced up the stairs, taking them two at a time. With each flight that passed, the woman's shouts and Hollie's screams grew louder.

As Phillips reached the top floor landing of the three-storey building, the ruckus stopped. She paused. The room in front of her was cloaked in darkness. Her heart pounded and her mouth was bone dry as she took a tentative step into the room.

Phillips heard the sound of the impact before she felt it. A moment later, her world went black.

～

As Jones turned to make his way up the final flight of stairs, he stopped in his tracks and watched in horror as Phillips tumbled towards him down the brutally hard staircase. She came to a stop on the landing in front of him. 'Guv!' he shouted, and knelt to check her for injuries. She was unconscious, and dark, viscous blood oozed from the back of her head onto the concrete.

'Get up,' a cold voice from above him said.

Jones looked up.

The woman they had been chasing stood at the top of the stairs, gun trained on him, left arm clutching Hollie tightly. At close quarters, he recognised her distinctive scarred face from the suspect files: Michelle Spencer.

'I said, get up,' Spencer repeated.

Jones did as instructed, lifting his hands in surrender as he did so. 'I'm DS Jones from the Major Crimes Unit. This is DCI Phillips.' He nodded towards her limp body. 'The Firearms team will be here any minute. Be sensible and give yourself up.'

'No surrender,' Spencer said as she moved down the staircase towards him. She stopped just a few steps from Phillips. 'Now, turn around.'

Again, Jones did as he was told.

'Move it,' Spencer ordered, then jabbed him in the spine with the pistol.

Jones took his time as he descended the steps, hoping to

buy precious seconds for the TFU to get into position. He prayed they would arrive before Spencer did anything stupid.

They moved down two flights of stairs, but as they turned onto the third, Jones spotted a large sliver of broken glass sticking out of the metal window frame on the landing ahead of him. His instincts urged him to try and reach for it, but his brain told him Spencer would shoot him dead first.

Spencer had obviously spotted the glass too. 'Don't even think about it,' she said, and again jabbed him in the back with the muzzle of her pistol.

Jones stopped and turned his body just enough so he could see her face. 'Seriously, Michelle. You don't need to do this.'

'Why does everyone seem to think they know what *I* need, hey?' she replied.

In a flash of movement, Hollie lurched forwards and sank her teeth into Spencer's left hand. Spencer screamed in agony and released her. In that instant, Jones rushed Spencer and grabbed the gun with both hands. As he did, Hollie squirmed past and raced away down the stairs.

Jones fought with everything he had to get the gun away from Spencer, but she was very strong, pushing him backwards. Then she slammed her foot into his crotch and he dropped to his knees in agony, gasping for breath. The woman was unrelenting and delivered a powerful kick to his ribs, which knocked him face-first onto the floor. He rolled around in agony, then a knee dug painfully in his back. Spencer's hand grabbed at what little hair he had and jerked his head backwards, away from the floor. The muzzle of the pistol dug into the back of his head.

'I'm tired of people always trying to fuck with me!' shouted Spencer.

Time appeared to pass in slow motion, and all Jones could think about was his wife and kids. How would they cope without him?

Suddenly Jones was aware of movement from above as a bloodied Phillips ran headlong down the stairs. A split second later, Spencer's knee left his back.

PHILLIPS LANDED HEAVILY on Spencer and grabbed at the gloved hand holding the gun. Using all her weight to hold Spencer down, she smashed the pistol against the concrete repeatedly, but Spencer stubbornly refused to let go.

The sound of sirens, as the Firearms team arrived, echoed around the hollow building.

Trapped flat against the concrete, and just inches from Phillips's face, Spencer – her pupils so wide her eyes were almost jet black – became feral, like a wild animal overwhelmed by the desire to survive. She threw a left hook with such force into Phillips's ribs that the crack of bone was audible. Phillips cried out in agony but, refusing to relent, continued to grapple for the gun. Spencer punched her again in the same rib. The pain was excruciating and too much to bear, and Phillips released Spencer's wrist.

Spencer thrust the gun up towards Phillips, who batted it away just as Spencer fired. The report consumed Phillips's hearing. Acting on pure instinct, she slammed her forehead down onto the bridge of Spencer's nose. The impact produced a sickening crunch and caused Spencer to cry out as the cartilage shattered and blood gushed from her nostrils.

As her head fell back onto the concrete, Spencer finally dropped the gun. Phillips grabbed for it, but Spencer instantly smashed her fist up into Phillips's solar plexus, stopping Phillips in her tracks. She slumped onto the concrete.

Grabbing the gun, Spencer jumped to her feet just as Jones rejoined the fray. He rushed her, but she side-stepped him and expertly smashed the butt of the gun into his temple. The blow knocked him clean out and sent him crashing to the ground with a heavy thud.

Phillips regained her feet as Spencer turned to face her. With blood still pouring from her broken nose, she trained the pistol on Phillips.

'It's over, Michelle. The Firearms team is here. There's no way out for you.'

Spencer's eyes, which remained black, glazed over. She said nothing for a long moment, then a knowing grin filled her face. 'You see, that's where you're wrong.' She retracted the gun and thrust the muzzle up under her own chin.

In that split second, Phillips threw herself at Spencer and pushed her backwards, just as another ear-splitting bang exploded into the space.

Phillips landed hard on the cold concrete floor, smashing her face onto the unforgiving surface. For a second, she lost consciousness. As she came to and opened her eyes, she became aware of silence. The unmistakable smell of gunpowder filled the air. She lifted her head and came face to face with Spencer's combat boots. As her gaze tracked up Spencer's legs, she realised Spencer was leaning against the window frame. Lifting herself up onto all fours, she took in the ghastly scene; Spencer stared back at her, motionless, impaled on a large glass spike, which stuck out through her right breastbone. Dark red blood poured from her open mouth.

Phillips jumped up and rushed to her. 'Hang in there, Michelle.'

Spencer coughed, and produced a blood-stained grin. 'I haven't got much choice, have I?' she said, then closed her eyes.

'Don't you fucking die on me, Michelle,' Phillips said as she pulled out her phone and called Entwistle.

The TFU had entered the building below and were making their way up the steps.

Entwistle answered almost immediately. 'Guv?'

'Call an ambulance!' shouted Phillips.

'Are you ok?'

'Never mind me. Just call an ambulance, now!'

47

THAT AFTERNOON, DURING HIS BRIEF VISIT TO THE MRI, SIR Richard Hawkins had insisted his daughter be kept in overnight for observation in spite of the consultant's confidence that Hollie could go home that day. But, as was usual where her stepfather was concerned, in the end he got his own way – which included a private room for Hollie. Then he left for yet *another* important business meeting. Hollie had overheard him on the phone outside her room, and knew that the meeting in question was with the chief constable concerning their plans to return to him whatever money had been recovered from the hideout. So, once again, it was left to Hollie's mother to be the parent. Sir Richard had, of course, apologised for how busy he was, and promised he would see her at home tomorrow. He really doesn't care, thought Hollie.

In contrast, Sandra Hawkins had not left her daughter's side since they had been reunited, and sat by her bedside now, holding her hand and brushing her hair from her face.

'What happened to my phone, Mum?' asked Hollie. She realised she'd not seen social media for over a week – a lifetime in teenage terms.

Sandra picked up her bag and rummaged through it for a moment before producing Hollie's missing iPhone. 'I had to get the screen replaced. It was smashed when you were...' she paused. The words appeared stuck in her throat, and tears welled in her eyes.

'It's all right, Mum. You can say it. *When I was kidnapped.*'

Sandra shook her head, clearly trying hard to fight away the tears. 'I just can't believe they put you through that.'

At that moment, DCI Phillips knocked on the door. 'I'm not interrupting, am I?'

'No. Not at all,' replied Hollie.

Phillips moved next to the bed, on the opposite side to Sandra. The back of her head had been recently bandaged. 'How are you feeling?' she asked in a warm voice.

'I'm doing ok. Thanks to you and DS Jones,' said Hollie.

Sandra Hawkins nodded enthusiastically. 'Yes, Chief Inspector. We really can't thank you both enough.'

Phillips smiled. 'It was a team effort. We were just doing what we get paid to do.'

Sandra nodded. 'It was a lot more than that, I'm sure.'

'How badly were you hurt?' asked Hollie.

'Just a few stitches and a couple of cracked ribs. Believe me, I've had worse,' Phillips chuckled.

Hollie smiled.

'So, what will happen to Spencer, now?' asked Sandra.

'Once she's recovered from her injuries, we'll have to wait and see. Technically, she's guilty of kidnapping and attempted murder. However, we'll need a mental health expert to decide whether or not she's fit to stand trial. The court may decide she needs psychiatric help rather than prison.'

'So, she'll get away with it, then?' said Sandra, her voice shrill.

Phillips shook her head. 'Far from it. She'll be treated in a secure hospital and remain there indefinitely.'

'And what about the others?' asked Hollie.

'Well, two of the gang are still at large. Hopefully, once Spencer's well enough to talk, she can help us identify them.'

'And what if she refuses?' asked Sandra.

'Rest assured, whatever happens, we'll keep looking for them, no matter how far away they've run.'

Hollie was almost afraid to ask her next question for fear of the answer. 'And Baker?'

Phillips took a deep breath. 'I'm afraid Marcus Baker died from his injuries an hour ago. He'd been shot in the stomach at close range, and there was little the surgeons could do to help him.'

Hollie dropped her head and stared at the white sheets covering her legs and waist. 'He saved my life, you know. She was going to kill me.' Tears rolled down her cheeks.

Phillips placed a reassuring hand on Hollie's shoulder and passed her a tissue. 'Try not to upset yourself.'

The room fell silent for a long moment before Phillips spoke again.

'Hollie. I hate to ask you more questions when you've already been through so much, but do you remember anything about the other members of the gang?'

Hollie wiped her eyes with the tissue. 'Just that the one they called Blue was a bit older than the rest. I heard Spencer saying he was old and stupid after he left the door open. He was quite kind to me and cooked me vegetarian meals.'

'Anything distinctive that you can remember? Distinguishing marks? Tattoos? His accent, maybe?' asked Phillips.

'He hardly ever said anything, but I think he was Irish or Scottish,' said Hollie.

'And the fourth guy? Anything that you can remember about him?' asked Phillips.

'Just that they called him White, and he was horrible. He

said I was a "spoilt little bitch", and he was going to feed me to the pigs.'

'Oh, my poor baby,' said Sandra as she stroked Hollie's head,

'Was there anything else you remember about him?' asked Phillips.

'No. Sorry,' said Hollie. 'He only spoke to me a few times. He gave me the creeps.'

'Did you ever hear the gang talk about who helped them snatch you from the club?'

Hollie shook her head.

'Or did they ever talk about heroin?'

'Heroin?' said Hollie. 'No. Why do you ask?'

'Well, we found a large stash in Spencer's car. I just wondered if you might have heard anything that might help explain how it got there?'

'Sorry. I don't remember anything like that,' said Hollie.

'Ok. Not to worry. Well, I think that's all I need to know for now.' Phillips gave her a warm smile.

'So how much money was taken from my dad in the end?' asked Hollie.

A look of surprise filled Phillips's face. 'Why do you want to know?'

'I just do,' said Hollie.

'Two million. We recovered Baker's and Spencer's shares from the boots of their cars. They had a million each.'

Hollie said nothing for a moment, then turned to her mother. 'Can you go downstairs to the coffee shop and get me a soy latte, please?'

Concern was etched into Sandra's furrowed brow. 'I really don't want to leave you again, baby.'

'I'm fine, Mum. And Chief Inspector Phillips will stay with me until you get back, won't you?'

Phillips appeared taken aback. 'Er, yeah, sure. Of course.'

Sandra produced a faint smile. 'Well, if that's all right with you, Inspector?'

'Not a problem.'

With that, Sandra left them alone.

Phillips took a seat next to Hollie's bed. 'Ok. So, now your mum's gone, why don't you tell me how you're *really* doing?'

Hollie began to tear up. 'I'm ok,' she said, and wiped her eyes again with the tissue. 'It's just all a bit surreal. One minute I feel happy that I'm free, then the next I just start crying for no reason.'

Phillips squeezed her hand. 'It's probably just shock, Hollie. You've been through a terrible ordeal.'

Hollie nodded. 'The consultant said I should start seeing my therapist again when I go home.'

'Sounds like a good idea to me,' said Phillips.

'Yeah. Maybe I should talk to them about my dad and what he's done?'

Phillips opened her mouth to speak, but appeared to think better of it.

Hollie continued. 'He's a bad man, you know. Baker told me he's responsible for the deaths of a lot of people, including British soldiers in Afghanistan. I think that's why they kidnapped me. To get back at him.'

'Baker said that?' asked Phillips.

'Yeah. He said that "Sir Richard" had got away with stuff because he has friends in high places. And Black said my dad had put people like them in great danger.'

Phillips nodded. 'I couldn't say whether that's true or not, but at the end of the day they *were* kidnappers. You shouldn't pay too much attention to them.'

Hollie nodded. She remained silent for a long moment, then turned to look directly at Phillips. 'Can I ask you something?'

'Sure.'

'Me and Mum were talking earlier, and she told me about you. About how you were in the news a couple of years ago for helping that radio presenter who was accused of murder.'

Phillips eyes narrowed. 'Oh yes?'

'Yeah, and she said the press wrote some pretty horrible things about you.'

Phillips folded her arms across her chest and sat back on the plastic chair. 'It's fair to say they did, yes.'

'Who was the worst?'

Phillips frowned. 'How do you mean – who was the worst?'

'Who wrote the worst stuff about you?'

'Ah, I see,' said Phillips, with a chuckle. 'That would have to be Don Townsend. He was brutal. He's an old-school journalist who only deals in sensational stories. He said some pretty hurtful things about me, that's for sure. He continuously questioned my integrity, and that really damaged my reputation. He's Manchester-based, but very well connected to the national papers. Thanks to him, I was given quite a hard time. It made my job very difficult for about a year afterwards. Why do you ask?'

Hollie shrugged her shoulders and smiled. 'Oh, nothing. Just wondering,' just as her mum returned with her soy latte.

Phillips stood slowly with a grimace. 'Well, I'll take that as my cue to leave.' She handed Hollie her business card. 'Take care of yourself. And if you ever need anything, or remember something that might help us track down Blue and White, give me a call, ok?'

'Ok,' said Hollie.

Phillips nodded. 'Look after her, Mrs Hawkins.'

'Oh, I will Chief Inspector. I will.'

And with that, Phillips left the room.

～

AT AROUND 10 P.M., Hollie finally managed to persuade her mother to go home. She had resisted at first, insisting she would sleep in the chair next to the bed, but Hollie convinced her it would be better if she went home to get Hollie some fresh clothes for the morning. Reluctantly she had agreed.

In the thirty minutes since she had gone, Hollie had found herself staring at the wall, running through the events of the last ten days, over and over, in her head. She wondered if White would ever be caught, and where in the world Blue was right now. Then her thoughts turned to Marcus Baker, the man who had taken the bullet meant for her. Having seen only his mask for nine days, his kind, handsome face would be forever etched in her memory. She wished that he, too, had got away to achieve his dream of doing something good with her father's dirty money.

At that moment, a nurse came in carrying a small paper cup with a single tablet in it, and a glass of water. 'This should help you sleep,' she said, and placed it on the top of the cabinet next to the bed.

Hollie, lost in her thoughts, didn't answer.

'Are you ok, love?' the nurse asked in a warm, motherly tone.

Hollie turned to look at her. 'Sorry. Yes. I'm fine. Just thinking.'

'Well, when you've finished thinking and you're ready to sleep, take that tablet, ok?'

Hollie nodded, and the nurse left.

After a long moment, Hollie pulled back the covers, got out of bed and walked over to the small wardrobe where her jeans had been hung. She reached into the pocket, found what she was looking for, and got back into bed. She then grabbed her iPhone, opened up the web browser and began typing:

'*Operation VOGUE*'.

48

NOVEMBER 11TH

IT WAS ALREADY 8.30 A.M. ON MONDAY MORNING AND, MUCH TO her chagrin, Phillips was at her desk, catching up on the mountain of paperwork that had backed up whilst she worked on the Hawkins case; expenses, time sheets and case-file updates, etc. There was a knock at the door. When she looked up, she saw Jones standing in the doorway, a newspaper under his arm and holding take-out coffees. He had a smile on his face as wide as the Manchester Ship Canal.

Phillips sat back in her chair and eyed him with suspicion. 'What are you looking so happy about this early on a Monday?'

Jones strolled in and passed a coffee to Phillips, then took a seat as Entwistle wandered in and dropped into the seat next to him. 'I've just got off the phone with Izzie at the hospital.'

'Oh, yeah?' Phillips sat to attention, her hands wrapped round the hot drink.

Jones's smile grew. 'Bov moved his legs yesterday.'

'Oh my God,' said Phillips, 'that's amazing.'

'Bloody brilliant news,' added Entwistle.

Jones nodded like an excited schoolboy. 'Yeah. Izzie say's the specialist reckons that, now the swelling has gone down on his brain and his spine, there's a good chance he can make a full recovery. He'll need physio, and stay in the hospital for a while yet, of course, but Izzie reckons he could be back to his old self in four to six months.'

Phillips breathed a sigh of relief and allowed herself to relax into the chair. 'That's such good news, Jonesy. God. I was so worried he'd never walk again.'

'Me too,' said Jones, as he took a sip from his drink.

'So, is he still in the spinal unit?' asked Entwistle.

'Yeah,' replied Jones, 'and Izzie thinks they'll keep him in there for the duration – to help get him back on his feet, so to speak.'

Phillips placed her coffee on the desk and dropped her head into her hands. The relief she felt was immense. Bovalino had been part of her team for so many years that the thought of losing him had terrified her. Now, thanks to the grace of God, he could be back with them by the middle of next year. She pulled her face away from her hands and noticed Jones staring at her, his face fixed in an inane grin. He appeared to have something else to say.

'Are you all right, Jonesy?' asked Phillips.

Jones nodded. 'Have you seen the news this morning?' he asked, clearly enjoying himself.

'No. I just got up and came straight into the office. Why?'

Jones picked up the folded newspaper from the floor next to his feet and tossed it over to Phillips. 'Check this out,' he said, with glee.

Phillips picked it up and read the headline aloud, "*TALIBAN DEATH SQUADS WERE ARMED BY MANCHESTER BUSINESSMAN – AN EXCLUSIVE BY DON TOWNSEND*". Bloody hell,' she said, and continued to narrate the article. "*Manchester multi-millionaire, Sir Richard Hawkins, is at the centre of a political storm today as it emerged that weapons and munitions manufactured by his company – Hawkins Industries PLC – were knowingly sold to*

Taliban fighters in Afghanistan.'" Phillips looked up at Jones and Entwistle, grinning. 'This is dynamite! *"It is alleged that Hawkins – who has long denied that weapons made in his Trafford plant were being used in war-torn countries against British troops – personally sanctioned the sale of millions of pounds-worth of arms to Taliban leaders. Information sent to us from a whistleblower within his organisation provides evidence that Hawkins used a network of middlemen in the Pakistan city of Peshawar to broker the deals, which netted him over fifty million pounds in the last ten years. It has emerged that hundreds of thousands of pounds-worth of Hawkins Industries munitions was discovered stockpiled in a Taliban compound in the aftermath of OPERATION VOGUE, undertaken by Allied Forces in 2008 – including members of the Parachute Regiment's 3rd Battalion. However, at the time, no action was taken to verify the claims.'"*

'Read the last paragraph, Guv,' said Jones.

Phillips dropped her eyes to the bottom of the page and once again read aloud. *"'Senior government officials have denied having any knowledge of Sir Richard's alleged connections to the Taliban, and have promised a root and branch investigation into all of Hawkins's business activities, which could result in criminal charges being brought against the multi-millionaire."*

'Today is the best day I've had in ages,' Jones said enthusiastically.

Phillips chuckled. 'Couldn't happen to a more deserving fella, could it?' She passed the paper back to Jones.

'So, who do you reckon the whistleblower is, Guv?' asked Entwistle.

Phillips reclined in her seat and folded her arms across her chest. 'Well, I wouldn't want to speculate without solid proof, Entwistle,' she said with a wry smile, '*but*, based on the conversation I had with Hollie Hawkins in the hospital the other night, it looks like the mighty Sir Richard Hawkins pissed off the wrong teenage girl.'

Jones shook his head. 'I've got two of my own. A rookie mistake.'

Phillips chuckled. 'Well, I have some good news too.'

Jones's and Entwistle's eyes widened.

Phillips continued. 'I've had an email from the CPS, and it looks like Gerry Donald will plead guilty to possession with intent to supply. Johnson has negotiated a reduced sentence, of course, but at least he'll do *some* time – maybe a year or two.'

'To be fair, that is good news,' said Jones. 'You know what Johnson's like. I fully expected her to get him off with a fine.'

'Me too, but the fact it was cut with fentanyl, which is so deadly, worked against him,' said Phillips.

'Well, as we're all sharing, I have an update of my own,' said Entwistle.

'Oh?' said Phillips.

Entwistle nodded. 'I heard back from the lab. It looks like the heroin recovered from Spencer's car is an exact match to that found in Cartwright's system.'

'So maybe she *was* murdered by the gang?' said Jones.

'Maybe,' said Phillips. 'Depending on Spencer's mental health, we may never know for sure, but we at least know where Cartwright got the drugs from. Who knows, it might even have been part of the deal to help the gang get in, and she did just take too much.'

'Or maybe Spencer *made sure* that what she took was deadly,' said Entwistle.

Phillips said nothing for a moment as she ran both scenarios over in her mind. If Spencer was deemed fit to stand trial, she would push her for the truth of what had really happened with Cartwright. But if she wasn't fit, then sadly, just as in so many cases before this one; they would never know the whole truth.

'Oh, and one more thing, Guv,' said Entwistle. 'Digital

forensics have come back to me on the CCTV footage from Baker's office the night Hollie was taken.'

'And?' said Phillips.

'It's fake. The timestamp was doctored. They say it was very well done, but the footage was from the month before. It looks like it was spliced into the system to appear as if it was filmed on the 31st October.'

'Clever bugger,' said Jones.

'Always one step ahead,' said Phillips, then clapped her hands together. 'Right. Well, I don't know about you two, but I know someone else who would appreciate an update on all this...'

'Mr Bovalino?' said Jones with a smile.

Phillips nodded enthusiastically. 'How about we go over to the hospital to see Bov and Izzie, and then afterwards we can head to The Briton's Protection for a few beers and some lunch on Chief Superintendent Fox? It's not far from the MRI.'

'Sounds like a plan to me,' said Jones.

'Yeah. It'd be great to see the big man. And they do a cracking pint in there,' said Entwistle.

Phillips stood.

'But before we go, Guv,' said Jones, 'I've been meaning to ask you something about your fight with Spencer,'

Phillips raised an eyebrow. 'Oh yeah?'

'Yeah. Where on earth did you learn to head-butt like that?'

Phillips produced a wide grin. 'Well, what can I say, Jonesy? You can take the girl out of Manchester, but you can never take *Manchester out of the girl.*'

ACKNOWLEDGMENTS

This book is dedicated to the memory of my cousin Thomas Joseph Patton, Lance Corporal, The Duke of Wellington's Regiment, my real-life action hero when I was growing up.

Deadly Vengeance would not have been possible without the constant encouragement and unwavering belief of my amazing wife, Kim. As ever, thank you for your patience, trust and faith in me.

My gorgeous boy, Vaughan. You constantly remind me that every day gives me a chance to be better than the day before.

A huge thanks to Mum for all your support, love and prayers.

Carole Lawford, ex-CPS Prosecutor, and Lambo, who helped me accurately reflect the complex world of British Law.

Joseph Mitcham, Kenny Hope and WO2 Dusty Rhodes, REME; my experts on all things British Military. Thank you for answering what must have seemed like abstract questions, day and night.

My coaches, Donna and Cheryl, from 'Now Is Your Time', who helped me navigate writing through the COVID-19 Lockdown.

My publishers, Brian and Garret, and my editor, Laurel, who inspire me to always improve.

And finally, thank you to my readers for reading *Deadly Vengeance*. If you could spend a moment to write an honest review on Amazon, no matter how short, I would be extremely grateful. They really do help readers discover my books.

Best wishes,

Owen

www.omjryan.com

ALSO BY OMJ RYAN

DEADLY SECRETS

(A crime thriller introducing DCI Jane Phillips)

DEADLY SILENCE

(Book 1 in the DCI Jane Phillips series)

DEADLY WATERS

(Book 2 in the DCI Jane Phillips series)

DEADLY VENGEANCE

(Book 3 in the DCI Jane Phillips series)

DEADLY BETRAYAL

(Book 4 in the DCI Jane Phillips series)

DEADLY OBSESSION

(Book 5 in the DCI Jane Phillips series)

DEADLY CALLER

(Book 6 in the DCI Jane Phillips series)

DEADLY NIGHT

(Book 7 in the DCI Jane Phillips series)

Published by Inkubator Books
www.inkubatorbooks.com

Printed in Great Britain
by Amazon